Karma

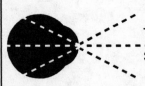

**This Large Print Book carries the
Seal of Approval of N.A.V.H.**

Karma

Carly Phillips

WHEELER PUBLISHING
A part of Gale, Cengage Learning

GALE
CENGAGE Learning·

Detroit • New York • San Francisco • New Haven, Conn • Waterville, Maine • London

LP
Fic
Phillips

Copyright © 2012 by Karen Drogin.
Wheeler Publishing, a part of Gale, Cengage Learning.

Wheeler Publishing Large Print Hardcover.
The text of this Large Print edition is unabridged.
Other aspects of the book may vary from the original edition.
Set in 16 pt. Plantin.

LIBRARY OF CONGRESS CATALOGING-IN-PUBLICATION DATA

Phillips, Carly.
  Karma / by Carly Phillips. — Large print ed.
    p. cm. — (Wheeler Publishing large print hardcover)
  ISBN 978-1-4104-5074-6 (hardcover) — ISBN 1-4104-5074-0 (hardcover)
  1. Large type books. 2. Police—Fiction. 3. Brothers and sisters—Fiction. 4. First loves—Fiction. 5. New York (State)--Fiction. I. Title.
  PS3616.H454K36 2012
  813'.6—dc23   2012021753

Published in 2012 by arrangement with The Berkley Publishing Group, a member of Penguin Group (USA) Inc.

Printed in the United States of America
1 2 3 4 5 6 7 16 15 14 13 12

Karma

ONE

Dare Barron heard the commotion in the police station earlier as his least favorite offender was brought in on a drunk and disorderly charge. Dare had been out on a nuisance call when the man had gone before a judge at the courthouse next door, but he was back now, in the cell downstairs.

Dare glanced at his watch, wondering how long before *she* came to bail her brother out. Every time McKnight got himself in trouble, his older sister, Liza, was never far behind to clean up his mess. McKnight was a rich bastard who thought his family money entitled him to special privileges.

And Liza . . . Dare didn't know what she thought. He only knew he looked forward to seeing her each and every time she walked through the precinct door.

A damned contrast to how he felt about her brother. Dare wished like hell he'd never heard of Brian McKnight, and those feelings dated back too many years to when a teenage McKnight had thrown a party. Dare, who at fifteen acted like he was much older, had gone, and his life had never been the same. Though Dare knew better than to think he could change the past, everything he'd done since then had been with his own atonement in mind.

But whoever coined the phrase "No sin goes unpunished" had never met Brian McKnight.

Or his sister, Liza.

Dare glanced up from his seat behind his desk to see her stride in like she owned the place. He wasn't above admitting he'd always had a thing for her, ever since he was a teenager. She was three years older and her parents had pulled her and Brian from public school, but the times she'd come to town with her friends, Liza had been hard to miss.

She still was. And Dare stared at her now without disguising his interest. She wore a basic black skirt and turquoise blue silk blouse. A simple outfit on anyone else. Liza McKnight was anything but simple. The skirt was long enough to be decent but short enough to call attention to seductively long legs, as did her black patent-leather mile-high heels accented by a delicate bow at the

8

back. All in all, a ladylike yet siren-sexy contradiction.

Her chestnut brown hair hung straight over her shoulders, her bangs not long enough to disguise her golden brown stare.

She reached his desk, propped both hands on the cold metal surface, and leaned in close. "I want to post bail for my brother."

Big surprise. Still, Dare shook his head, unable to conceal his disappointment. "Still enabling him, I see."

She frowned, but the expression only served to showcase her dimples and make her look even sexier. "I don't see how that's any of your business."

She was probably right.

He inhaled her warm, exotic scent. Vanilla, musky, and damned hot. "I'm sure everyone is working to release him as quickly as possible," Dare said, glad he had the desk to hide exactly what she did to him.

She straightened her posture but still managed to look calm and in control. "He was granted bail over half an hour ago. I can't imagine what the holdup is. Can you at least get the paperwork started on this end?"

Dare shook his head. "Sorry. I'm not the arresting officer. You'll have to take a seat and wait to talk to him."

There were three chairs in the waiting area

9

at the far end of the room. She settled into the one across from Dare's desk, crossing one delectably long leg over the other.

"So, what's he in for this time?" Dare asked, though he already knew. Conversation was conversation and Brian's record was what they had in common.

"Drunk and disorderly conduct," she stated without emotion.

Specifically, according to Officer Sam Marsden's report, her brother had left Joe's Bar drunk, walked out back to his car — which he shouldn't have been going anywhere near in his inebriated state — and paused to take a leak, singing at the top of his lungs the entire time.

"In other words, the usual," Dare said.

She closed her eyes for a brief second. Dark lashes fluttered over her soft skin, giving her a vulnerable look that made him want to pull her into his arms and comfort her.

"It wouldn't be the usual if Officer Marsden had just driven Brian home and let it go." Liza pinned him with a questioning look, the vulnerability gone as quickly as it had appeared, making him wonder if he'd imagined the emotion.

Dare shook his head, frustration gnawing at his gut. "So we should just let him break the law?"

"What? Are you guys so hard up for arrests that you can't find a real criminal to harass?"

He rolled his eyes. "Your brother is a real criminal." Dare spoke in a soft but realistic tone, almost feeling sorry for her.

She jumped up from her seat, suddenly a flurry of nervous energy, pacing in front of his desk. Her long legs ate up so much space she took two steps, turned, and started the process all over again.

From the corner of his eye, he caught sight of Sam walking out of the holding area. "There's the arresting officer." Dare nodded in his friend's direction. "He should know when your brother will be brought up." Dare softened his tone, not wanting to upset her any further.

He didn't know why he baited her in the first place except he hated her turning a blind eye to the truth about her sibling.

"Thank you." She actually smiled at him, her brown eyes sparkling with genuine gratitude.

Then she paused, drawing a deep calming breath and causing Dare's gaze to focus on the rise and fall of her breasts. Oblivious to his interest, she turned and zeroed in on Sam, heading over to deal with her brother's problems without looking back.

He let out an exhale and wiped his forehead with his sleeve, grateful the long day was almost over. The air-conditioning in the old building was on its last legs and the precinct was as sweltering inside as it was outside. Yet Liza had been completely cool.

Dare rubbed the back of his neck, where a steady pain had begun to throb. It drove him nuts that she made excuses for her screwed-up brother. Hell, he knew what it was like to have a troubled family member and not once had Dare made excuses for Ethan. Then again, that immovable attitude had kept him estranged from his brother when he could have been working toward reconciliation. Good thing he and eventually their middle sibling, Nash, had come around. The difference was, Ethan had changed and made an effort to fix the past. Brian McKnight showed no remorse and Liza didn't seem to care.

Dare groaned. It shouldn't bother him. Wasn't his problem. But she was a bright, educated woman. A talented architect. She had to know right from wrong and yet she consistently bailed out a man who, brother or not, she ought to have wiped her hands of a long time ago. Brian needed to be held accountable for his actions.

And Dare wanted Liza in his bed.

He jerked his head, wondering where *that* thought had come from. He'd never denied his attraction to her, at least not to himself. He'd always wanted her, even though he knew she was out of his league. But that hadn't been on his mind at the moment. Or maybe it had been. He'd been waiting for her arrival, his entire body on alert.

The scary truth was Dare almost looked forward to the times McKnight got hauled in, because it gave him a chance to see her. Scarier, he'd cut school all those years ago and gone to that damned party because it had been at her house and he'd had the chance to see the girl of his teenage dreams. But Liza hadn't been home that day and Dare's life had been forever altered by the events of that afternoon.

More than a decade had passed, one in which he'd seen major growth, both in his personal and professional lives and in his feelings for Liza. Before she'd been a teenage crush, someone he'd thought of and, yeah, jerked off to. But now? He'd grown up and each time he met up with her, she got to him on a level no other woman ever had.

He saw Liza as a woman who could bring him out of the darkness he hid inside him and into the light. He shook his head hard because wasn't that a nice dream. One that would never happen. Though he liked to think of Liza as an angel, that wasn't her at all. She enabled her brother, thereby condoning his behavior — *all* of his behavior, the past included, which made her no better than his brother. Or Dare, no matter how hard he tried to be a better man.

Yet that didn't stop Dare from wanting her, and damned if the yearning wasn't more than just physical. He was curious about who she was and what made her tick. Why last time she'd been at the station late at night she'd been wearing high black boots with killer heels covering legs encased in tight denim, her long hair cascading in sexy curls down her back. A far cry from the ladylike outfit she wore today. Of course he was equally attracted to her no matter what she had on.

Not that it mattered.

Because despite everything, she'd never once looked at him as more than a pain-in-the-ass cop she had to deal with whenever her brother found himself in trouble.

He glanced at his watch and exhaled in relief. He was officially off duty. Dare grabbed his keys and rose from his seat.

"Heading home?" Sam asked.

Marsden was a few years older than Dare and a darned good friend.

"Yeah. Shift's over," he said.

"Sure you don't want to wait?" Sam asked, eyeing him curiously.

"For what?" Dare asked.

Sam let out a whoop of laughter. "You really want to play dumb? Fine. Don't you want to wait until Ms. McKnight's brother is released? She's waiting for him in the outer hall."

Dare clenched his jaw, which didn't help his building headache. "And why would I want to do that?" Yeah, he was playing it dumb. Why the hell would he want to admit to his feelings and set himself up to be the butt of Sam's jokes.

"Because I see how you look at her, man. Only a blind fool could miss it." Sam leaned against the desk, eyeing Dare with way too much humor.

Okay, no need to admit it. Apparently Dare wore his feelings on his uniform. Fucking swell.

"Then I suppose you've also seen how she doesn't return the sentiment?"

"Jeez, you men are dumb!" This from Cara Hartley, another cop and good friend. The three tended to pull the same shifts and hang out together when they were off duty.

"Where'd you come from?" Dare asked.

Cara laughed, her dark ponytail flipping over her shoulder. "I'm stealthy. I walked over while you two were talking about Liza McKnight. But you're still both dumb."

Dare shook his head and stifled a groan. "I really don't want to know what you're thinking."

"Yeah you do." Cara deliberately bumped her hip against his. "You think she doesn't notice you. I'm here to tell you you're wrong."

He blinked in surprise.

Sam's grin was so wide Dare was surprised his face didn't split. Dare didn't need the two of them on his case about a woman.

"The thing is, every time you talk to Liza, you judge her for bailing out her brother. So tell me why she should think you're hot for her. Not to mention why should she want to bother with you."

Dare reached for the back of his neck once more, the muscle spasms getting worse. "Can we not talk about this?"

"Nope. It's on the table and it's staying there until I'm finished. Now let's say you happened to . . . I don't know . . . change your attitude toward her? Something tells

16

me she just might alter hers." Cara raised her eyebrows over her blue eyes.

Despite not wanting to give Cara a green light to get into his head, Dare mulled over her words.

"You thinking what I'm thinking?" Sam asked Dare. "That our girl here makes sense?"

Cara glanced at Sam with a pout on her lips. "I'm not your anything," she muttered. Cara being Cara hated any hint of condescension toward her as a woman. Touchy was her nickname.

"And I'm not thinking anything," Dare said. Nor was he conceding his feelings out loud.

"Just remember, I have a feeling you can turn this around. If you want to that is." Cara shrugged.

"Is that feeling your female intuition?" Sam asked. "Because Cara's is usually damn good," he reminded Dare.

Cara grinned, nodding her head in agreement. "Thanks for the compliment, Sam. Maybe I'll let that earlier rude comment slide. I might even let you buy me a drink at Joe's on Wednesday night." They usually hit Joe's for Ladies' Night since they were all off on Thursdays.

Dare laughed, but Sam was right. Cara's

gut instincts, on the job and off, were usually on target.

"Got a plan?" Sam asked Dare.

He rolled his eyes. "I'm going home, like I said."

"But —" Cara shook her head and groaned. "Never mind, do what you want. Nobody ever listens to me, even though I'm always right."

Sam grinned.

"As long as you're leaving, I'll walk out with you," Cara said to Dare. "I'm off duty too. You coming, Sam?"

He shook his head. "Not until McKnight's been released on bail. Catch you guys tomorrow."

Dare nodded Sam's way. "Night."

He headed out alongside Cara, who talked about the weekend Police and Firefighters' Festival where they would man the policemen's booth in order to raise money for the youth center where they all volunteered. Dare laughed at her jokes and admired her sense of humor, but being with Cara did nothing to make him forget about Liza, whom he just happened to pass as he left the precinct. She sat alone, waiting for her brother's release, alternately looking pissed and vulnerable, bringing up protective instincts Dare had never felt toward any other woman before.

Liza drummed her fingers against her purse as she waited for Brian to be brought up from the holding area. She wondered if the cell in the back of the police station had a plaque engraved with her brother's name on it. Heaven knew he'd been hauled in often enough. Just the thought was enough to give her a stomachache.

She shook her head and stifled a groan. "At least be honest with yourself," she muttered. It wasn't her brother's most recent arrest making her stomach churn.

It was *Dare Barron.* The cop who always seemed to be around when her brother was brought in. The sexy man who alternately looked at her like she was the hottest thing this side of a hot fudge sundae or the dumbest enabler on the planet.

Like she wasn't aware of what she was doing? She was. She just had no choice. Brian was family. He was her brother. Besides, she owed him.

However, she didn't have to explain herself to Dare, even if he did have "big bad cop" written all over him. His dark brown hair with flecks of gold and those gorgeous brown eyes were enough to melt her on the spot. But that didn't mean she had to answer to anyone but herself. That's how it had been for longer than she cared to remember. But now, as an adult, she wouldn't trade her independence for anyone ever again.

She rose to her feet, annoyed Brian hadn't been brought up yet. She couldn't imagine what the holdup was. The attorney she kept on retainer had shown up and done his job, and Brian's arraignment had been blessedly brief. So where was he?

Finally she heard her name called by a gruff male voice. She turned, hoping to see her brother. Instead, she saw Dare on his way out the door with a pretty female police officer by his side. Liza knew the woman's name was Cara Hartley. She was a year younger than Liza's twenty-nine, while Dare was three years younger, making him twenty-six. From the way Cara and Dare were laughing together, they were close.

An unwanted ribbon of jealousy unwound in Liza's stomach, and she ruthlessly forced it aside. Whether Cara and Dare were friends or something more, it didn't matter. Liza had her hands full with her delinquent brother. The last thing she needed in her life was an attraction to one of Serendipity's finest.

Her brother's arrival reinforced that truth

and she rose to meet him. He must have sobered since she'd seen him in court because he appeared more withdrawn and down instead of chipper and happy to see her. Since she'd paid his bail and signed all the appropriate papers, they headed out the door together. Liza's stomach growled, reminding her she'd been at the courthouse and the police station for the better part of the day.

She waited until they were settled in the car before turning to her brother. "Hungry?" she asked.

He nodded. "But I need a shower more. I can't go anywhere looking like this."

Now he was worried?

His white-collared shirt was wrinkled and dirty and he looked like he'd been on a twenty-four-hour bender. Which wasn't true. Liza had seen him at work earlier this morning, at McKnight Architecture, the firm her grandfather had founded and where Brian also worked. Brian was an accountant, and as one of the bookkeepers, his job had few direct responsibilities. He had a supervisor to oversee his performance, something her father had made sure of during his tenure.

"You can take me home, and while I shower, you can go pick up something for dinner," Brian said.

It wasn't a suggestion, Liza noted.

She gripped her fingertips tighter around the steering wheel. "How about I drop you off home and I head out to get dinner myself, like a human being? You can fend for yourself. I bailed you out, Brian. Isn't that enough?"

He reached over and squeezed her arm. "You know I appreciate you, Liza Lou." The nickname was a throwback to their childhood when he'd first seen *How the Grinch Stole Christmas.*

Liza used to wear her hair up in a high ponytail, reminding him of Cindy Lou Who. She'd liked the nickname then. Now all it served to do was remind her of the brother she'd lost. She wasn't even sure when he'd taken that wrong turn. It just seemed that from the time he'd reached adolescence, trouble found Brian. Or maybe it was Brian who found trouble.

She clenched her jaw tight before speaking. "If you appreciate me, how about you take a good look in the mirror." She reached over and flipped down the visor, revealing a covered mirror that she also opened for him. "Who are you and what have you done to my brother?" she asked softly.

He shook his head and closed up the visor. "You know the cops in this town are hard-asses," he muttered. "They have it in for me."

She raised an eyebrow. "Why weren't you at the office this afternoon?" she asked, ignoring his stupid comment.

"I had a business lunch."

"At Joe's Bar?" she asked sarcastically.

"Nothing wrong with buying a client a drink."

"What client would that be?" And since when did his job as a bookkeeper require him to schmooze with any client?

Brian let out an annoyed sound. "I don't have to answer to you," he said, folding his arms across his chest and looking out the window.

She ignored him once more. Nothing positive could come from engaging him in an argument. Besides, they were almost home.

In the distance, she saw the house on the hill, the main landmark in the town of Serendipity, looming in the distance, proud and majestic against a cloudless sky. There was a time Liza had visited the house often, back when she'd been friends with Faith Harrington, who'd grown up there. Faith's parents had lived there until last year when her father had gone to jail for securities and investment fraud, and Ethan Barron had purchased the house on the SEC auction block.

Dare Barron's brother.

How could she stop thinking about the man when he cropped up in her mind every time she turned around?

Liza shook her head and forced her thoughts elsewhere. Anywhere. Like back to the landmark she'd just driven past and its previous occupants.

Liza had attended school with Faith, at least until Brian had started acting out and had gotten himself tossed out of public school. Livid that the institution to which they paid their taxes had treated their son so badly, Liza's parents had sent *both* kids to private school in a neighboring town. They'd ripped Liza away from her friends and her life, not that either of her parents had cared about that. Brian was always their main concern.

Liza managed to keep in touch with Faith and her other friends for a while, until she made friends at her new school, most from the neighboring town where the private school was located. And though she would still hang out in Serendipity from time to time and run into her old girlfriends, things had never been the same. Eventually she'd

24

drifted and lost touch.

People tended not to stick in Liza's life and she'd learned from a young age not to count on anyone. The one time she'd let down her guard, she'd been rewarded with Timothy Barker, a charming college senior to her sophomore, and she'd lived to regret the impulse.

She shook her head, hating that all those old memories came back to her now. It was the house on the hill, she thought. The mansion wasn't just a town landmark, it was a marker of many things to many people. To Liza, it had brought back the past, a place she didn't intend to revisit.

As long as Liza remained in the present, she'd be fine.

She snapped her attention to tomorrow's calendar. Coincidentally, her first meeting was with Faith Harrington. The new Mrs. Barron was the head of the Beautification Committee's fund-raiser and Liza had signed onto the committee.

Realizing she'd reached her destination, Liza turned onto the long driveway of her parents' house where Brian still lived. It wasn't as grand as the old Harrington mansion, but the house was huge and on the "right" side of town. Although her parents had moved to Palm Beach, Florida, full-time, they'd kept the house in Serendipity, allowing Brian to stay on. Whether he paid them rent or not, Liza didn't know nor did she want to. They were all equally at fault when it came to enabling him.

She knew it. Understood Dare was right in his assessment of the situation, but damn it, what else could she do? Leave him in jail to rot?

No. Not when she'd inadvertently contributed to the fatal day that still haunted them both. And then there was the fact that Brian had been there to save her from her own poor judgment and colossal mistake. Brian might be a loser, but he'd been there the one time Liza needed him, and without him who knows what her ex might have done to her.

But that didn't mean she had to take care of him or be around him any more than was absolutely necessary. At this point he could get help or not, but she wasn't going to be his caretaker.

"We're here." She cut the engine and glanced over, realizing he'd passed out in his seat.

Well, that explained the silence and why she'd been able to go off on all sorts of tangents in her own mind.

Liza jolted him by pushing against his

26

arm. "Brian!"

"What?" he barked grumpily.

"You're home. Go inside and clean up," she said, more gently than he deserved. "And don't forget to eat."

"You're the best, Liza Lou." He leaned over and kissed her cheek.

She winced and tried not to gag at the smell of alcohol, sweat, and jail that surrounded him. "Night," she managed.

He opened her car door and stepped out, stumbling once before he righted himself and made his way to the front door.

Liza waited until he was safely inside before driving away. She was exhausted and looking forward to changing into sweats and going to sleep early. First, she'd microwave herself leftovers, eat, and then fall into bed. No late night for her. Tomorrow was a busy day with back-to-back meetings, beginning with an important 9:00 A.M. with Faith.

Liza had an agenda for joining the Beautification Committee. In past years, the committee had raised a fortune at their fundraisers but had spent the money on the parts of town that were already well cared for. This year, Liza hoped to convince them to steer some of the immense funds raised toward a more worthwhile cause, the youth center downtown.

The center was a place for kids to hang out, take art and music classes run by volunteers, and play basketball and other sports games in a safe environment. The center was close to Liza's heart because it represented a future to kids who might have none. And she couldn't help but wonder if just maybe had it been around when Brian was younger and acting out, things might have been different for him.

Who am I kidding? she thought with a shake of her head. Nothing short of discipline would have shaped up her brother and there'd been nobody to give it to him.

But the center had volunteer counselors and teachers who didn't mind taking a tough stand with the kids. Unfortunately, it was also always short of funds. The Police and Firefighters' Festival that was scheduled for this coming weekend raised money for the center, but it was never enough. And that was because the wealthier residents, like Liza's parents, couldn't be bothered with a place that helped the less fortunate.

By working with the committee, Liza also hoped to up her credibility within her hometown. McKnight Architecture flourished thanks to out-of-town referrals and business. Their work spoke for them, but here where she'd grown up, Brian's reputation had tarnished her own.

So for the last two years, Liza had attended beautification meetings and ignored the more uppity members who'd tried to freeze her out, slowly making younger acquaintances and giving her views. Then at last month's meeting, they'd surprisingly announced that Faith Harrington would be the new fund-raising chair.

Surprising because Faith hadn't been a committee member before. And because Faith, like Liza, had committee members with immense bias against her. In Faith's case, thanks to her father's criminal behavior. Still, Faith's husband had money, and rumor had it that Ethan had gifted the mansion to his wife as a wedding present, making Faith the current owner of *the* premier landmark in town and cementing her role as the fund-raising chair.

Liza couldn't be more pleased. She'd liked Faith when they were kids and it seemed they had a similar uphill battle against the snobs in Serendipity. She hoped to get Faith on board with her idea to use the money raised at the annual fund-raiser, a black-tie event of the elite and the wealthy, for the youth center.

Liza believed she had a shot. Unless, of course, Dare told his sister-in-law about her brother's latest arrest, and Faith decided working with Liza and implementing her ideas was a liability.

Liza groaned. One way or another, she'd know soon enough.

Two

Liza walked into Cuppa Café, the coffee shop on Main Street in town, and looked for Faith. Although she hadn't seen the other woman recently, Liza recognized the pretty blonde sitting at a back table immediately. She wore a simple pair of jeans and a pink flowing top, making her appear delicate. Liza knew better. She had read the interview Faith gave to Elisabetta Gardelli for the *News Journal* magazine last fall. There was nothing soft about Faith Harrington. The woman was incredibly tough and resilient. She'd had to be in order to survive her father and ex-husband's betrayal.

"Faith?" Liza asked, walking up to her.

"Liza!" Faith rose from her seat and suddenly the years seemed to disappear as she hugged the woman she hadn't seen since they were children.

"How are you?" they both asked at the

same time.

Laughing, Liza settled into a chair and Faith returned to hers.

"You first," Liza said. "You're married!" She glanced down and the sparkler on Faith's left hand caught her attention. "Gorgeous," Liza said of the diamond ring and matching wedding band.

"Thanks!" Faith smiled, a wide, happy grin. "Wait, let's get coffee before we catch up."

Liza nodded. They headed up to the counter, and a few minutes later they returned to their seats with their cups of coffee. "Now tell me all about you."

Faith nodded. "There's not much to tell. I'm running a new interior design business and helping Ethan raise his half sister, Tess. I'm busy. And you?"

"Half sister?" Liza asked, not ready to delve into her own personal stuff just yet. She wanted to hear more about Faith and now Tess, who just happened to be Dare's half sister too.

"There's some gossip that hasn't gotten around?" Faith asked, laughing.

Liza grinned. "I suppose it depends on what circles you run in. I'm so busy working I don't have time to socialize much." And when she did it wasn't in Serendipity.

32

Faith braced her hands around her cup. "Tess and her sister, Kelly, arrived last summer. Nobody knew about Tess, and she's been a handful, but she's come a long way since then." Faith spoke with obvious pride.

"And Ethan? How did you end up with him?"

Her eyes lit up at the mention of her husband. "Ethan and I met up again when I came back to town. Right before Tess showed up. We sort of . . . I wouldn't say picked up where we left off because we didn't have a past relationship. But we did have this connection . . ." A pink blush stained Faith's cheeks.

There was a story there, Liza knew. If the rosy glow on Faith's face was an indication of that connection, Liza hoped she'd hear all about it one day. She might not believe in happily ever after for herself, but if it worked for others, what the hell.

"Well, I'm happy for you. I really am."

"Thanks." Faith smiled. "Now about you?"

Liza nodded, knowing she'd have to divulge some things. The easy things. "Not much to tell. I went to New York University and lived in the city for four years, got my degree, and came home to join the family business."

"That's a good thing, yes?"

Liza thought about it and nodded. "Actually it is. My parents retired to Florida, which leaves me to run the place as I see fit. I love restoring old buildings, finding ways to keep their history while modernizing them at the same time."

"Well, good." Faith glanced down. "No ring, so you're not married?"

Liza shook her head back and forth quickly. "No, not me." To get married would mean she'd have to trust a man to get close to her again, to potentially break her heart, her spirit, and maybe even something more.

Not ever again.

"I'm more of an affair kind of girl," she said, knowing how that sounded and not giving a damn.

Faith raised an eyebrow but said nothing.

Liza kept quiet too. She'd long since stopped apologizing for who she was and what she wanted. If it was fear of making another major mistake in judgment driving her, so what? She certainly didn't *act* like she was afraid nor would she admit it out loud. Which meant she was able to enjoy her life and brief relationships with men, have fun, and stay safe. Nobody got close and she liked it that way.

"Hey, whatever floats your boat," Faith

said lightly. But those golden eyes were too perceptive, making Liza squirm. "You know, I was married before Ethan," Faith said, taking Liza off guard. "The guy was a self-centered jerk who used me for my father's connections and cheated on me, probably from day one."

Faith's sudden admission cemented Liza's certainty that Faith saw much more than she said aloud.

"I'm sorry," Liza said, not mentioning she'd read Faith's history in the magazine article.

Faith smiled. "I'm not. It made me stronger and I found Ethan."

Liza admired the other woman's attitude.

"Listen to us, talking so easily, like no time has passed," Liza said, grateful her old friend hadn't changed.

"I'm not surprised. I was looking forward to meeting you today. I'm glad the committee got us back in touch again."

"Me too. Speaking of the committee, how'd you wrangle the fund-raising chair? Not that I'm complaining. I'd much rather work with an old friend than an old biddy any day."

Liza grinned and Faith burst out laughing.

"Caroline Bretton, the president of the

Beautification Committee, is a client and an old friend of my mother's. The committee was dying to have the fund-raiser at the mansion and they knew better than to think Ethan would open his house to the upper crust of Serendipity just because they asked." Faith wrinkled her nose, her disdain for those particular people evident.

Knowing the Barron brothers' past, growing up on the *wrong* side of town among other things, Liza could understand that. "So what made you want to talk him into it? Never mind take on such a huge responsibility?"

Faith sighed. "You know, I'm not sure. I do know Caroline was good to me when I first opened my business. She was one of my first clients, taking a blind leap of faith. No pun intended." She chuckled at her own joke. "And she stood by my mother when, frankly, she didn't deserve the friendship." Faith shrugged. "I guess I thought it was the right thing to do."

"And Ethan? How does he feel about opening his house for such a huge gala?" Liza asked.

Faith cringed. "He hates it. But he's doing it for me." And suddenly the warm, dreamy look entered her eyes once more.

Watching her, goose bumps rose over Liza's skin, making her not just envious but even a little sad at the thought that she'd never have that kind of connection with a man. She'd never have someone who'd do anything just because she'd asked. But that was a choice she'd made, and in as much as it kept her free and safe, Liza was content.

"So, ready to get down to business?" Faith asked, oblivious to Liza's thoughts.

"You bet. I don't have enough clout with the committee to land any kind of chairmanship, but I really wanted to help with the fund-raiser." Liza spread her hands out in front of her. "I'm yours, so put me to work."

"Well, I can't tell you how grateful I am." Faith pulled a notepad from her large purse and Liza did the same. Obviously they had organization in common too.

Liza knew she'd have to broach her main idea sooner rather than later, and since she and Faith were getting along so well, she decided not to waste any time. "I have a question about the proceeds. Has there been any talk about which projects to fund this year?"

Faith clicked her pen open. "There's been talk of putting up a new gazebo in the town square," Faith said, sounding like she disapproved. "Why?"

"Well, I had a thought. I know for a fact nobody would take anything I said seriously —"

"Why not? When Caroline Bretton told me we'd be working together, she said you've been on this committee for the last couple of years. Why wouldn't they listen to you?" Faith asked.

Liza dropped her stare to the table. And here it came. The thing she hated talking about. "The McKnight name doesn't exactly inspire confidence unless it's in architectural design. At least not in Serendipity."

"Because of Brian?" Faith asked softly.

Liza met her gaze. "You've heard, huh?"

Faith sighed. "Well, of course I remember the party all those years ago and Stuart Rossman's death." She spoke low, with sympathy and no rancor.

At the mention of the teenager's senseless passing at a party thrown by her brother, nausea rose in Liza's throat. "Yeah. And my brother hasn't changed or sobered much since." If anything, he'd gotten worse and a part of Liza blamed herself. "Brian's been pretty much in and out of jail on one minor charge or another."

"I'm sorry."

Liza shrugged, pulling her armor around her emotions like she always did when it

38

came to Brian. "Thanks, but it is what it is. Anyway, that's exactly why nobody on the committee would listen to my ideas. You know what most of those old women are like. They barely tolerate me."

Faith sighed. "Considering they ostracized my mother and the only reason I hold this position is because they need my house? Yeah, I know. I believe it's called guilt by association."

Liza couldn't help but smile. "Good thing misery loves company then." She shook her head and laughed. "Gotta love those clichés. They've been around so long for good reason."

Faith inclined her head. "So, what's your idea?"

Liza warmed her hands against her coffee cup. "Instead of using the money to beautify the already-perfect parts of town, which really makes this a committee in name only, I thought we could donate the proceeds to the youth center downtown." She went on to explain why the center was important to her, but Faith's eyes had already lit up and she was nodding in agreement.

"You've sold me without the explanation! My best friend, Kate Andrews, is a teacher who volunteers there after school and during the summers. My brother-in-law Dare works with the kids, and Tess spent some time there last summer. The center is important to my family too."

Faith's eyes sparkled as much as excitement pulsed inside Liza. Ignoring the mention of Dare, which wasn't easy considering her body's eager response to his name, Liza met Faith's gaze. "You're really on board!"

The other woman nodded. "Doesn't mean the rest of the committee will be, but that will be our first order of business. Lobbying the members we know we can sway."

Liza's adrenaline spiked and she was unable to contain her enthusiasm. "You're amazing! We're amazing. We can do this. I know we can."

"You bet we can. It's time to change up the way this town does business and make a difference."

"Here, here," Liza said.

They touched their coffee cups together in a toast. "Let me do some prep work and see who I can get on board with the idea before we broach it at the next meeting. I'll call you and we'll get together soon to talk actual gala details, okay?"

Liza nodded. "Sounds great."

Faith grinned.

Their cause was worthy, making Liza proud. And for the first time in years, Liza felt a kinship toward someone again and she looked forward to the renewal of their friendship, something she hadn't had in her Serendipity life for way too long.

"Change your grip!" Dare called to fourteen-year-old Charlie Skeets, "Skeeter" for short.

The fourteen-year-old choked up higher on the baseball bat and got into position, waiting for the next pitch.

Dare coached a youth league, and this was the end of practice at the field near the lake on the edge of town. All he had left was Charlie's at bat, a pep talk, and then Dare was out of here for the night.

Ten minutes later, he'd given each kid a summary of their strengths and weaknesses. When he finished, the kids scattered, some walking home together, a few lucky others picked up by their parents.

Dare put his spare equipment into the large duffel he kept in his trunk, hefted the bag over his shoulder, and headed for his car, a black metallic Ford Edge. He tossed the bag into the back and wiped his dusty hands together before slamming the trunk, then walked over to the water fountain and rinsed off his hands.

No sooner had he finished and turned to

leave than he collided with a jogger on the sidewalk. He'd raised his hands to block contact and he realized he now braced his palms against a very feminine chest. Soft, round, full breasts molded to his hand.

His body registered that fact and reacted accordingly.

"Sorry," he muttered, taking a deliberate step back.

"Me too. I wasn't watching where I was going," a familiar female voice said.

Startled, Dare glanced up to see Liza pulling the iPod buds out of her ears. "Liza."

"You," she said at the same time.

He met her gaze and she blinked, focusing her coffee brown eyes on him. Touching her had nearly knocked him on his ass and her gorgeous eyes almost completed the job. Then there were the damp handprints he'd left on her chest, which he couldn't stop noticing.

He had to divert his focus or he'd be in big trouble.

"I do have a name other than *you*," he reminded her in a teasing voice.

"Officer Barron." She ducked her head after she spoke.

This shy female was distinctly different from the take-charge woman he was used to seeing at the police station, softer and more approachable.

Dare found himself drawn to her even more. "I meant, I have a first name." And he wanted to hear her say it.

She lifted her gaze. "Dare." Her expression was wary but with a hint of a smile on her lips, she teased him with a glimpse of those sexy dimples in her cheeks.

"Better." He allowed himself to take in her running gear, a pair of black shorts with white piping, a black tank that did little to hide her breasts, and a worn pair of sneakers.

"Do you always jog in the evening?" The sun was setting and he'd prefer she didn't run here at night.

"No. I usually run in the morning near my house, but I had an early meeting today so I put it off till later."

He nodded, feeling better about her jog. "Well, then, lucky me. Are you okay? From our collision I mean?"

She nodded. "I'm fine. I should have been watching where I was going, but I was distracted." A blush stained her cheeks, making him wonder what she'd been thinking about.

"So was I." He was even more distracted now.

Silence descended and she shifted from

43

foot to foot.

"Well, I should get going," she murmured.

He paused and before he could think about it, he said, "I was just going to get a slice of pizza. Want to join me?"

Her eyes flickered in surprise.

She couldn't be any more shocked than he was, since he was scheduled to have dinner at his brother's house in an hour. But he wasn't ready to let her go.

"Umm . . ." She seemed to struggle with the decision and he knew he'd bail on the family if it meant the chance to go out with her.

"I can't tonight. I have to work. I need to put the final touches on a presentation I have in the morning."

He nodded, understanding but still disappointed. "No problem."

He wondered if he should take it as an outright rejection, then realized she hadn't said *I can't.* She'd said *I can't tonight.*

"Maybe another time then."

Her eyes widened, as if she couldn't believe he'd push the issue.

"Maybe," she said softly.

His heart jump-started inside his chest and his thoughts immediately turned to what Cara had said about turning things around. He'd always judged Liza harshly, but now he'd treated her to the real Dare and she'd softened.

"Can I walk you anywhere?" he asked, reluctant to let her leave.

She shook her head. "My car's parked by my office," she said, pointing down the tree-lined street.

"Be careful."

"Always," she said and treated him to a full-fledged genuine smile.

As he watched her jog toward her office, he realized something had shifted between them. And suddenly it didn't matter who her brother was or what he'd done, Dare needed to get to know Liza better.

Liza reached her car. The BMW Z4 Roadster convertible was her baby. With its all-white outside with black interior, she loved the vehicle. She opened the car and grabbed the bottle of water she'd stowed in the back, guzzling it down, not caring if it gave her a cramp later. Her mouth was dry and her heart was racing — and the solid jog she'd been on before bumping into Dare Barron had nothing to do with it.

He did.

The man, in his gray Champion sweats that molded to his firm thighs and groin and the white T-shirt stained with dirt and sweat, had her drooling. She'd smacked right into him and he'd cupped her breasts, leaving them damp, her nipples hard and aching.

And then he'd asked her to dinner. As if the last time she'd seen him they hadn't been adversaries arguing over the necessity of arresting her brother.

She wiped the sweat from the back of her neck and leaned over in an attempt to catch her breath. Because she knew she'd never regain her equilibrium ever again.

Dinner at the mansion. Dare would give anything to eat alone and have time to think. Instead, he had to deal with the weekly family dinner, all the while pretending he wasn't preoccupied with thoughts of Liza McKnight.

He ought to be glad she'd turned down his dinner invitation. This get-together wasn't optional for anyone named Barron. And the only way he'd get through it was to force Liza to the back of his mind. He'd think about her and how he'd move forward later. Now he stared up at the mansion, reminding himself why he was here.

What had started as a strained weekly event to give his half sister, Tess, a sense of normalcy had morphed into something all three brothers enjoyed. Of course it helped that the two Barron wives, Faith and Kelly, insisted nothing short of death would be an acceptable excuse, but over time they'd all come to like the sense of family these dinners gave them. One they'd lacked for too long.

By now Dare ought to be used to the monster mansion Ethan owned, but the sheer size never ceased to amaze him. They'd grown up on the other side of town in a small house with three bedrooms and two and a half bathrooms, which was tiny in comparison to most homes in the area. Back then they'd been a family of five with their share of problems, including three rambunctious boys. Ethan, the oldest, caused his share of trouble and had had his own room. Dare shared his bedroom with Nash.

Everything had been normal until one night after Ethan turned eighteen and was arrested. Their parents went to bail Ethan out and were killed by a drunk driver on the way to the police station.

Had Ethan stuck around to raise his siblings?

Hell, no, he'd taken off for parts unknown, not coming home until ten years later. *Almost one year ago,* Dare thought. Time they'd spent first fighting, then forced to get along when Tess ended up on Ethan's doorstep, the product of an affair nobody knew their father had had. She'd been a juvenile delinquent, dropped off by her half sister, Kelly Moss. She and Tess had the same mother.

A clusterfuck of a mess that somehow had brought them all together as a family. Including his middle brother Nash, who was now married to Kelly.

Shaking his head, Dare rang the doorbell, not surprised when the delinquent herself answered the door. Except Tess now bore no resemblance to that messed-up kid. Gone was the black hair with a purple stripe, eyebrow ring, and all-black clothing topped with an ever-present army jacket and combat boots she'd even worn in ninety-degree heat. Instead, she dressed in a pair of leggings and a concert T-shirt. Bare feet peeked out, toes revealing royal blue nail polish. And her hair was a light brown, her blue eyes pronounced in her tiny face.

"You gonna stare at me all night or are you coming in?" Tess asked, breaking into his thoughts.

Okay, so the sarcasm occasionally remained, Dare thought with a grin, but the Tess standing at the door was a normal teenage member of the Barron family.

Dare pulled her in for a hug. She squirmed but accepted the gesture. "You're the last one here. Let's go eat."

"I need to wash up first." He headed to the downstairs bathroom, cleaned up the best he could, and met Tess again outside the door. Apparently she'd decided to wait so she could drag him into the dining room.

Just like she said, he was the last one in and, as usual, the most underdressed. But the family was used to him in his uniform or his sweats or even a pair of old jeans.

"You're next to me." Tess pointed to their side of the table.

Ethan sat at the head, Faith by his side, then Nash and Kelly on one long side, Dare and Tess across from the newly married couple. Their wedding had been a Christmas event, family only, in the mansion, just like Ethan and Faith's had been in October.

Dare was the lone bachelor.

"Sorry I'm late," he said instead of dwelling on that subject.

"No problem, we just sat down because Rosalita said dinner was ready and Miss Impatient here insisted she needed bread or she'd pass out." Faith shot a fond look at Tess.

"You indulge the brat," Nash said under

his breath, but the grin on his face gave his true meaning away.

"I heard that," Tess said through a mouthful of buttered roll.

"You were supposed to." Nash winked at her.

The rest of the family rolled their eyes and laughed.

Nash and Tess had had the rockiest time coming to terms, but Tess now idolized all three of her brothers equally. Nash and Tess just liked to give each other the hardest time. Like real siblings, something Dare had desperately missed when he'd gone to live across town in the Garcias' foster home without Nash.

"So, what'd I miss?" Dare asked.

Rosalita, Ethan's housekeeper, who he liked to say came with the house, began serving dinner. To Faith and now the rest of them, Rosalita was like family, as she'd worked for Faith's parents when they'd lived here, and she'd practically raised Faith. Now she was helping out with Tess.

"Faith was just telling us about her new job," Kelly said.

"She's on the Beautification Committee of Serendipity," Ethan added, sounding proud of his wife.

"And I'm recruiting volunteers," Faith

said, her stare never wavering from Kelly's.

Kelly ducked her head and concentrated on her food. "I'm a full-time paralegal and a newlywed. I don't have time," she said, without meeting Faith's gaze.

"I'm sure your husband slash boss would give you time off to help your favorite sister-in-law." Faith grinned.

To their credit, both Ethan and Nash, the respective husbands, didn't say a word.

"I'll help!" Tess said.

"And I'll take you up on that. Thank you. At least someone in this family wants to help the *youth center*," Faith said.

No doubt as she'd expected, everyone paid attention at that.

Dare was especially interested. "What does the youth center have to do with the Beautification Committee's fund-raiser?" he asked.

All he knew of the committee was that they held a yearly formal gala where the upper crust of Serendipity turned out in tuxedos and fancy dresses, and the cops had to play traffic directors wherever they decided to hold the affair.

Ethan began a slow, steady cough.

Faith patted his back. "Are you okay, honey?"

"He's fine. He just knows how pissed

everyone's gonna be when they find out," Tess said, the glee in her voice unmistakable.

Uh-oh. "What is she talking about?" Dare asked. The youth center was his place.

He volunteered, knew the kids by name, and they knew him.

All the cops and firefighters broke their butts to raise money for the center, but it was never enough to really support the programs they needed.

"Faith's having the gala here!" Tess jumped up from her seat in excitement. "And she said I could come. We all have to be there and she's gonna buy me a new dress and everything."

"Now she likes dresses," Nash muttered to Kelly.

Dare shook his head. "Why is the gala here? And what does that have to do with the youth center?" He felt like he was lost in a tornado, not knowing which end was up.

Which was normal in this family, but still.

"Caroline Bretton asked me to chair the fund-raising committee. You know she gave me my first real decorating job —"

Ethan cleared his throat.

"Sorry." Leaning over, she kissed his cheek. "She gave me my second real decorating job." This mansion had been her first, when Ethan had hired her. "I felt like I owed her."

"Even though she was only offering you the position because it's so much work nobody else wanted it and because she had an agenda. She wanted to hold it here and she knew I'd never go for it," Ethan reminded his wife.

She nodded. "All true. She also knew you'd never say no to me."

He leaned over and kissed her on the lips.

"Eew. No PDA! I told you two to go to your room when you want to . . . you know!" Tess said.

Again nobody paid her much attention. Everyone was used to her by now.

"So, since the event is here, I expect you all to attend. And thanks to my brilliant new assistant, we are going to push for this year's proceeds to be donated to the youth center." Faith picked up the thread of conversation without missing a beat. "Considering I'm lending the use of our home, I think they'll come to see things my way."

Or else was the implied threat, though Faith didn't say as much specifically.

"Is she good or is she good?" Ethan asked, admiration filling his tone.

"She's something, all right," Nash muttered. "I hate black-tie affairs."

Dare agreed.

Kelly wrapped her arm around her husband. "Suck it up, Nash. It's for a good cause."

He groaned and she leaned over and whispered something in his ear. Something that made Dare's normally uptight brother flush.

Even Dare squirmed. "Now you two get a room."

Faith tapped her glass with her fork. "The date is the Saturday night of Labor Day weekend, so mark your calendars. Is everyone excited?"

"As much as I'd be for a root canal," Dare replied.

"How will you get everything organized in a little over a month?" Kelly asked.

"The committee knows the date a year in advance, so the caterer, the music, and decor person are all booked. All I have to do is choose specifics such as the menu, the events of the evening, and coordinate accordingly." She cleared her throat. "Of course, another pair of hands would help."

"Okay, okay, you made your point. Yell if you need me," Kelly finally said, obviously resigned.

Faith grinned. "I knew you'd give in

eventually. I'll give my assistant your number. Her name is Liza McKnight."

THREE

"So, Kelly, you can expect to hear from Liza soon," Faith said, continuing her conversation about the fund-raiser. "She can't wait to get involved in planning the gala."

Dare heard Liza's name, swallowed wrong, and began coughing, his eyes tearing uncontrollably.

Ethan, starting to rise from his seat, eyed him warily.

"I'm fine," Dare choked out before his brother could begin the Heimlich and break one of his ribs. Dare reached for the water, and a few minutes later he was breathing better.

"Are you sure you're okay?" Nash asked.

Dare nodded. "Something got caught in my throat."

"Are you upset that I'm working with Liza?" Faith asked. "Because she's Brian's sister?"

Upset was hardly the word Dare would

use. He'd just been shocked to hear her name after seeing her not thirty minutes before.

As for Faith, Dare understood why she'd worry he'd be upset. The whole family had become aware of Dare's deepest secret. That he'd been at Brian's party the night Stuart Rossman died. Such a stupid, tragic incident. One that could have been avoided or at least handled so much better than it had been, both at the party and then afterward.

Especially afterward.

Pain, regret, and suppressed anger gnawed at Dare then and still did today. Nobody had truly paid for Stuart Rossman's death. Because Brian's parents — Liza's parents — were friends with the district attorney, Brian had only been charged with misdemeanor assault, assured youthful offender treatment, and spent no time in jail.

No one else had been charged with a crime.

It had been so easy to cover things up. *Too easy,* Dare thought. And once the wall of silence had gone up around the incident, nobody spoke of it again. But Dare suffered with the nightmare that had been his reality.

With no one to turn to and afraid to even admit the truth out loud, fifteen-year-old

Dare buried the incident deep inside him, wrapping himself in the persona of the happy kid nobody could tie to the tragedy. But he lived with the knowledge that he'd run. No matter that he'd only been a kid himself at the time, he knew better.

Dare hadn't forgiven himself yet. He didn't know if he ever would.

"Hey, you okay?" Nash asked, concerned.

Dare nodded, then glanced at Faith. "Sorry. Of course I'm not upset you're working with Liza. She's not her brother."

He might have equated her with him before, but five minutes in her company outside the police station and he knew she was different. Not innocent exactly but more open and honest in her emotions. And despite all sound judgment, she pulled at something deep inside him.

Suddenly that formal gala didn't seem like something to dread after all.

"I'm glad," Faith said. "She seems so excited about the fund-raiser and I'd hate to cause upheaval here." She glanced around the table and everyone knew what she meant.

They'd all come so far; nobody wanted to lose the family they'd managed to create. The rest of the meal passed in relative quiet, if one could consider any meal where Tess was instigating trouble quiet.

A couple of hours later, Dare had thanked Faith and Ethan for dinner and said his good-byes.

"Wait up," Nash said, meeting him by the front door before he could leave. "What's with your reaction to Faith working with Liza McKnight?"

"I choked," Dare reminded his brother.

Nash smirked. "Tell that to someone who can't read you like a book."

Dare frowned, but his brother was right. Nobody read him like his middle sibling. Nash knew Dare. Hell, there'd been only one thing Dare had ever kept from Nash, and Dare had paid for the secret in spades. They'd gotten past the lie and Dare didn't want to go back to the days when his middle brother had shut him out completely.

"So? You and Liza?" Nash pushed.

Dare closed his eyes, and a vision of Liza as he'd last seen her in tight spandex and wet handprints on her breasts flashed through his mind.

"She's . . . interesting." Dare met his brother's gaze.

Nash cocked an eyebrow. "In other words, you're hooked." He grinned, arms folded across his chest. "How do you know her?"

"How do you think? She's always at the

station bailing her brother out of jail." No reason to give Nash any more to needle him with. His brother was worse than Sam and Cara when it came to giving him a hard time.

"Does she know you've got a thing for her?" Nash asked.

Why bother denying the truth? Dare merely shook his head. "She thinks I'm a judgmental asshole." At least she had. After their recent run-in, Dare had no idea what she thought of him.

Nash burst out laughing, catching Dare by surprise.

"What's so damned funny?" he asked.

"You're the most mellow of the three of us. Most people like you best. So why in the hell would Liza think that?" Nash's blue eyes, so like their mother's, glittered with amusement.

But tonight's encounter was still fresh in his mind, the feelings so new he had no desire to share them with his brother. "Because every time she shows up at the station, all I can think about is what a waste it is that someone so smart and beautiful continually enables her piece-of-shit brother."

Nash's lips quirked in a grin. "So, she's beautiful, huh?"

"I'm leaving." Dare reached for the door handle.

"I'll call you tomorrow." Nash turned and headed back toward the family room, laughing the entire way.

Liza stared at the flyer on her desk. Her assistant had left the blue paper for her this afternoon, along with the mail. The Police and Firefighters' Festival was always the first weekend in August, a fun fairlike atmosphere held at the park next door to the youth center.

Most years, Liza donated to the cause but didn't attend. No matter how much she admired the work they did, thanks to her brother, she'd never felt comfortable around the cops of Serendipity. Instead, she'd usually head out of town on the weekend of the fair, and her friends in Manhattan expected her this weekend.

The girls from her college days at NYU were her closest girl friends and they'd remained a tight group, she thought with a smile. But here at home, Liza had few friends. Most had gone to out-of-state schools and moved away. Others eventually distanced themselves when Brian's behavior began to impact Liza's social status among their peer group. Which was why, when she wanted to let loose and have fun, she dressed in her edgier clothes and hit the New York club scene with her college friends.

It was easier to be herself in a big city where she wasn't judged so harshly. She'd move there if not for the business and, of course, Brian. She just didn't fit in with the wealthier people in Serendipity who had money or with the regular working people who were wary of her. She was somewhat of an oddity, Liza thought, which was why she'd felt so comfortable with Faith the other morning. They had more in common than Liza had with anyone else.

Except now, she looked at the flyer and thought of Dare Barron and his dinner invitation. He hadn't looked at her like she was the strange woman with the trouble-making, alcoholic brother. At least not last night.

So instead of reaching for her checkbook and then dumping the flyer in the trash, she was actually reconsidering her weekend in New York.

She glanced up to see Jeff Montana, an architect she'd recently hired, waiting to talk to her. "Hi, Jeff. Come on in."

He stepped inside and grabbed a seat in front of her desk. Jeff had moved to Serendipity from the Midwest. He'd been looking for a job in Manhattan, planning to commute by train since it was too expensive to live in the city. He'd been unsuccessful in his job hunt there, but Liza had been all too happy to snap up someone with his talent. He fit in here at the office and she liked him a lot.

"What can I do for you?" she asked.

"I just wanted to talk about the Mystic Building Project." A project they were considering taking on in Connecticut.

She nodded. "Of course."

"Are you going to the fair this weekend?" He pointed to the flyer still in her hand.

She frowned at the reminder. "I'm not sure. Are you?"

He shrugged. "Same. I don't know too many folks here, so I thought it would be a way to meet people. On the other hand, I don't know too many people around here." He treated her to an endearing smile.

"Have you been to Joe's at all?" The main bar in town was also a good place to mingle.

Jeff shook his head. "Same reason," he admitted, looking away.

His shyness was sweet. With his jet black hair and easy charm, he'd likely be snapped up by some single woman in Serendipity as soon as word got out about him.

He just needed to meet people. "Since we're both on the fence about going, do you want to meet there? I'd be happy to introduce you around."

And he could be her buffer. She wanted to see Dare, but she still wasn't sure he'd want to see her. He'd asked her to dinner, but his demeanor was so at odds with the man she dealt with at the station, she couldn't imagine why. He'd looked as shocked as she'd felt by the invitation.

"You'd do that for me?" Jeff asked.

She nodded.

She almost felt bad he didn't know he'd be doing her a favor in return, but no way would she discuss something as personal as her own discomfort in her hometown with someone from work. Or with anyone at all.

Was it any wonder she was so alone?

She forced a more genuine smile at him. "It'll be fun. Do you want to meet at . . . one o'clock?"

Late enough to give people a chance to congregate, not too late to miss people who decided to leave early. Liza might not have a lot of close friends in Serendipity, but she did have people she enjoyed being with. People she could introduce to Jeff.

"Sounds great!" Jeff said, obviously looking forward to the day.

Liza nodded. "Good. Now, about the Mystic project . . ."

They spent the next hour discussing the viability of taking on the restoration and the historical significance of the building involved along with the costs. By the time Jeff went back to his own office, Liza was closer to accepting the project and giving Jeff the lead on the design.

She was about to head out for lunch when her phone buzzed, a signal it was an interoffice call. "Hello?"

"Liza, it's Peter from accounting."

"Yes, Peter, what can I do for you?" she asked, resigned to waiting a little longer to eat.

"I'm looking at submitted receipts and there are expenses here I'm not comfortable authorizing," the other man said.

So what else was new? The man called too often with too many questions about routine expenses, things he should be able to sort through on his own. Peter was about ten years older than Liza and he'd been with the firm for the last five, but he always checked and double-checked before making a decision.

"What kinds of expenses?" she asked patiently.

"Lunches at Joe's Bar. Your brother has

submitted a number of them for reimbursement, but the totals are too high for business lunches."

In other words, there were probably alcoholic drinks on the bill, raising the total.

"I take it Brian's not there for you to be talking so freely?" Liza asked.

"That's correct."

Liza sighed. "Don't sign off on them. I'll talk to him. And thanks for being diligent." It would be all too easy for him to approve and then Liza would find out too late that her brother was wasting company money. Though after his business lunch excuse for his last bender, she was alert to the problem.

"No problem," Peter said. "I'm glad you're happy with my work performance."

Another thing with Peter Dalton. He had a need for her to excessively praise him and it just wasn't her work style.

Liza said good-bye and hung up, uncomfortable as always after dealing with the man. But she couldn't deny he was good at his job and he kept Brian from taking advantage of his position there.

She wished she had the fortitude to do the same thing.

Wednesday night at Joe's had become a ritual for Dare and his friends. With Thursdays off and one day a weekend it was the one weeknight they could kick back and enjoy. Once his brothers had put aside old grudges, even they occasionally began to show up. And Dare had to admit that for the first time in a long time, life was good.

He ordered a round and joined everyone at their usual table, passing longneck bottles to his friends. Cara and Sam were there along with Alexa Collins, who'd grown up in Serendipity and returned after medical school to work with her father in his medical practice.

"Did you all get your assignments for the fair?" Alexa asked.

"Cop car," Cara said, meaning she'd be giving kids the chance to sit in the back, the front, and run the siren while she talked about being a cop.

"Not too bad," Dare said. "I've got the DARE assignment."

They all rolled their eyes at the irony of the name, but it was his favorite way of interacting with the kids. Teaching them about the Drug Abuse Resistance Education was Dare's main way of dealing with the mistakes of his past. He'd been the one to push to get DARE into the middle and high school. It was the old way of thinking to believe that telling fifth-grade kids about the hazards of drug use would keep them from caving to peer pressure when they were in ninth grade.

"And you?" Cara asked Sam, pulling on a long sip of beer.

"Dunking booth," he said with a frown.

Dare let out a loud laugh and Alexa joined him.

"Can't wait to test my pitching arm," Cara said, swinging her arm around for good emphasis.

"If you dunk me, you'll pay," Sam warned, his eyes glittering dangerously.

Instead of backing down, Cara merely rubbed her hands together in anticipation. "I can't wait to see you try to make me."

Alexa rolled her eyes.

Dare agreed with the assessment. "Sometimes you two act more like brother and sister than friends." He took a sip of his cold beer, enjoying the brew and the relaxed atmosphere. "What about you?" he asked Alexa.

"Dad's taking the day off, so I'm on call. Which means I'll be around to take a throw or two of my own," she reminded Sam with an evil grin.

"Not worried. You throw like a girl."

"Hey!" she said, clearly offended.

"Isn't that your sister-in-law?" Cara asked,

interrupting and pointing to the front of the bar.

Dare turned. Sure enough, Faith stood in the front of Joe's, Kelly by her side. "It's both of my sisters-in-law, actually." He craned his head, but he didn't see either of his brothers come in behind them. Dare hadn't spoken to them this afternoon, so he had no idea what their plans were for the night.

"So how's it feel to be the lone bachelor in the family?" Sam asked.

"I'm happy for Ethan and Nash, but my life's just fine the way it is. I need to get a bigger place, though." Dare was living over Joe's, having taken over Kelly's sublease.

The apartment over the bar had become the family road stop. Faith had rented over Joe's before she married Ethan and moved into the mansion, then Kelly had taken over her sublease until she'd married Nash. Now it was Dare's turn to take over the small apartment until he found something more permanent.

Cara leaned back in her seat. "Did you ever consider buying? I know we're young and all, but I know you've been saving and it's a buyers' market. There's a condominium complex I'm looking at in Easton. It would take about ten minutes to drive to and from work and it's within the twenty-mile radius the department insists on. Want to check it out?"

Dare didn't have to think twice. "Definitely."

She nodded. "Okay, we'll figure out something after work one day this week or next."

"Well, well, if it isn't all of my favorite police officers," Faith said, walking up to the table.

Dare glanced up at his sister-in-law. "Hi, Faith. Kelly." He smiled at the women. Since his friends knew his family and visa versa, no introductions were necessary. "What are you two doing here solo?"

Faith shrugged. "I thought we'd get together and discuss committee work, but I forgot it was Ladies' Night. It's so noisy I don't think we'll be getting much work done here."

"What kind of committee?" Alexa asked.

"I'm the chairman of the Beautification Committee fund-raiser this year."

"Congratulations," Cara said, more to be polite than because she cared at all. "What are you planning to do with the money this year? Plant more flowers in the center of town?" she asked, deadpan.

The center of town was overflowing with colorful beds and a bird fountain. It didn't need another thing to complete its look.

Faith merely shook her head and grinned, obviously not insulted by Cara's comment. Besides, Dare knew she was in complete agreement with the sentiment.

"Actually, we're going to push for the money to go to a cause near and dear to all of your hearts. The youth center."

"Get out!" Cara's smile broadened. "I'd like to see the look on the rest of the committee members' faces when you broach the idea. And for the thought alone, next round's on me." Cara finished her beer and rose to her feet. "What do you all want?"

"I'll take a diet soda this time," Alexa said.

"Just a club soda for me," Faith said, turning to her sister-in-law. "Kelly?"

"Same as Cara, and thanks."

Another thing Dare had come to appreciate about his brothers' wives: no false pretenses for them. Especially not for Faith, who'd returned to town to regain a sense of self, not what her upbringing dictated.

He stretched in his seat and suddenly Faith's earlier words registered in his brain. "You said you're meeting your assistants?" he asked Faith. "As in plural?"

"So Nash was right," Faith said, her knowing stare on Dare. "You *are* interested in Liza!" His sister-in-law practically shouted

71

her thoughts.

Dare shook his head and groaned. "Faith?" he asked through gritted teeth.

"Yes?"

"Shut up. And I mean that in the nicest possible way."

She patted him on the cheek. "You're cute when you're embarrassed." She glanced over his shoulder. "Oh, those people are getting up! Be a sweetheart and pull that table together with this one before someone else grabs it."

Before Dare could reply, Sam did as she asked and soon his small group of three had become one of five, just as Cara returned with Joe, carrying drinks for the expanded table.

"I thought you said this was a business meeting," Dare said to Faith.

"But I also said it was too noisy to work tonight." Faith shrugged and shot him a smile, leaving his stomach in knots as he waited for Liza to show.

Liza normally didn't hang out at Joe's. Too many people and too much of a chance of running into her drunk brother, but Faith had insisted they meet there tonight. Although the other woman mentioned getting together to discuss the fund-raiser, the sign

72

outside the bar said LADIES' NIGHT and the crowd she waded through was so thick that Liza figured little work would get done tonight.

She searched the bar area first but didn't see Faith, though it was hard to tell at a glance. Then she worked her way around the room, checking individual tables. She caught sight of Faith's blond hair and made her way over only to discover Faith wasn't alone, nor was she just with her sister-in-law, Kelly.

No, Faith was sitting with Brian's arresting officer, Sam Marsden, a cute woman Liza didn't recognize, and the pretty cop who was even more attractive out of uniform and with her brown hair let down . . . and Dare.

He also wasn't in uniform, and with a hint of scruff on his face, he was even better looking. He wore a faded gray T-shirt with the police department logo and the acronym SPD emblazoned on the upper left side of his chest. His gold-flecked dark brown hair was messy and casual, and oh boy, he had a tattoo that curled around his left bicep. She hadn't noticed it the other night. His shirt had to have covered the marking because no way would she have missed it otherwise.

The only thing that stopped her from

drooling was the fact that he'd seen her and those gorgeous eyes locked with hers.

"Liza!" She vaguely heard Faith's voice over the noisy crowd.

All she could focus on was Dare.

His hot gaze slid over her, making her acutely aware of her body's reaction to his stare. Thinking she'd be meeting two women at a casual bar, she hadn't given a thought to her clothes. She'd run home after work and changed into the first things she'd found on top of the laundry basket of clean clothes she'd yet to put away. Never mind that he'd seen her in damp running gear — suddenly her skinny jeans and cropped top that exposed a hint of her stomach felt way too snug and revealing.

Drawing a deep breath, she forced her gaze away from his, walked to the table, and smiled at Faith. "Hi."

Faith nodded. "So glad you could make it on short notice. This is my sister-in-law, Kelly, and she'll be working with us on the fund-raiser."

Liza glanced at the woman she knew by name, though they'd never been formally introduced. Unlike Faith, who possessed an uptown look no matter how much she dressed down, Kelly was more like the pretty girl next door with her straight brown hair and blond highlights.

She greeted Liza with a warm smile. "Hi."

"Nice to meet you," Liza said in return.

"Do we have a place where we can talk about the gala?" Liza asked without looking at the rest of the table, though she knew they all stared at her.

Faith shook her head. "Can you believe I forgot it was Ladies' Night here? Silly me," she said, tapping the side of her head with her palm.

"Yeah, silly you," Dare said in an odd tone of voice.

"Well, since it is like a zoo, there's no way I can concentrate on little details," Faith said. "I think we should just enjoy the night here and meet up another time to do fund-raiser business."

"I'm all for enjoying girls' night," Kelly said, raising her beer bottle. "That okay with you?" she asked Liza.

As if she had a choice now? Liza nodded. "That's fine." She'd drink and be merry with the cop who made her think of nothing but sex whenever he was around.

"Can I get anyone another drink? I was going to get up and go to the ladies' room anyway," Kelly said.

Everyone murmured no-thank-yous, since they'd just had their drinks refilled.

"Liza?" Kelly asked her.

Still feeling the heat of Dare's stare, Liza managed a nod. "I'll have a glass of white wine. And thank you."

"No problem. Next round's on you." Kelly grinned and rose from her seat, winding her way through people more easily than Liza had.

"So, Liza, are you going to sit down and join us?" Dare asked, forcing her to look directly at him again. He leaned back in his chair, muscular arms folded across his chest, a pleased smile on his lips.

"Where are my manners?" Faith asked, laughing. "Yes, Liza, please sit." She patted the empty chair beside her that Kelly had just left behind.

Which just happened to be next to Dare. "I couldn't take Kelly's seat."

"Sure you can. I'll just head over to the back room and take one of Joe's spares," Sam assured her.

Amazed that the cop who'd arrested Brian was being so nice to her, Liza smiled. "Thank you." Out of options, she walked over and lowered herself into the seat only to find herself squeezed between Faith and Dare.

Faith she could handle, Liza thought, suppressing a nervous laugh. Dare, on the other hand, was way too close, his body heat radiating off him in enticing waves. He smelled like Ralph Lauren's Polo. She'd sniffed the woodsy fragrance in Neiman Marcus with her teenage girlfriends, and Liza had been a sucker for the masculine scent ever since. Now she had a man to associate with the heady cologne and her body throbbed in response.

"That's better," Faith said, oblivious to Liza's runaway hormones. "Now just in case not everyone knows names, Liza, this is Dr. Alexa Collins." Faith pointed to the auburn-haired woman. "And these are Officers Sam Marsden, Cara Hartley, and Dare Barron. Who also happens to be my brother-in-law. Everyone meet Liza."

"Nice to meet you all," she said politely.

"Likewise," Cara said, watching Liza intently over the rim of her drink.

"Happy to have another woman among these Neanderthals," Alexa added with a welcoming smile.

Thankfully neither Sam nor Dare mentioned how they knew her. And nobody mentioned Brian.

"Now that that's over with, what were we talking about?" Faith asked.

The topic turned from one subject to another and Dare leaned in close to Liza,

77

but he didn't say a word, as if waiting for her to talk first.

"We really have to stop meeting like this," she blurted out.

Dare, his head close to hers, merely grinned. "Really? Why is that? I kind of like seeing you outside of the station." His warm breath fanned her ear, and Liza's stomach churned with unsettling emotion.

"Dare, did you hear Tess has been asking for a puppy?" Kelly asked, obviously unaware she was interrupting a moment.

"I'm glad it's their problem," Dare said, and soon they'd launched into a discussion of a rambunctious destructive puppy in the huge mansion.

Liza didn't know how Dare held on to the thread of conversation. For her, time passed in a haze because he sat so close his hard thigh kept brushing hers. If she shifted away, somehow he'd move and end up touching her again.

Not that he seemed affected by her closeness in the least. He carried on conversation with his friends and family, never losing his train of thought, never uncomfortable or at a loss for words.

They all seemed happy enough to have Liza there, but she wasn't really a part of their world and she envied their easy banter and closeness. And though she appreciated the fact that they'd included her, she knew she'd never really belong.

She never had.

Since she'd already bought everyone a round of drinks and fund-raising discussion wasn't going to happen, Liza reached for her purse on the floor and rose.

"Where are you going?" Faith asked, sounding upset she was ready to leave.

"I need to get home. I have work," Liza lied.

Dare immediately stood. "I'll walk you out."

She shook her head. "You don't need to do that. Stay with your friends."

He grasped her elbow. "I know I don't need to. I want to."

All the breath left her body in a rush of air.

Good-byes were said. Plans were made to meet up next week for the fund-raiser, but if they'd chosen a day, Liza wouldn't remember it.

At that moment, Dare's hand on her arm as he escorted her outside was the only thing that mattered.

FOUR

Liza rushed through the crowd, her exit faster than her entrance had been. Dare was right behind her, his hand on her arm, but she didn't stop. She needed the open space and fresh air where she could think more clearly without his body heat so close it suffocated her. And not in a bad way.

No sooner had they reached the sidewalk, the noise and buzz from inside the bar receding, than she turned to face him. "I don't understand you." She looked into his handsome face.

His expression told her he was clearly confused. "What? That I wanted to walk you out?"

She shook her head. "Since when do you want anything to do with me at all? Before I nearly ran you over yesterday by the park, every conversation we've ever had bordered on contentious and mean." She braced her hands on her hips, knowing the little bit of

80

alcohol she'd had — which she usually stayed away from because of both her own past and her brother's tendency to overindulge — was responsible for her bold outburst now.

He frowned, obviously not pleased with her at all. "You are so wrong I don't know where to begin," he muttered and did the last thing she'd expected. He extended his hand. "Come with me."

"Where?" she asked warily.

He again thrust his hand toward her. "Trust me?"

"I don't trust anyone." Now why had she said that? She bit the inside of her cheek at the spontaneous admission.

He groaned. "Fine. Surprises are out then. We're going for ice cream and then we're going to talk."

Startled, she blinked. He wanted something as simple and easy as ice cream? "Really?"

"Yeah. Now will you go with me?" he asked, sounding as if he really wanted her company.

She knew she wanted his and that scared her. Spending time talking led to a closeness she normally avoided, especially with men.

But she wanted to try and figure out why

he got to her so badly. Maybe she'd get answers. At the very least she'd get fed and she was starving.

So she placed her palm in his.

He stared at their connected hands and shook his head in disbelief.

She knew the feeling, but she couldn't bring herself to walk away.

"You could've told me ice cream was the key," he muttered as he wrapped his fingers around her hand and led them down the street toward the shop that had been in town longer than she could remember.

They reached the store and bells jingled as they walked inside. "Know what you want?" Dare asked.

She didn't hesitate. "Mint chocolate chip in a sugar cone."

"I like a woman who knows her mind." He winked at her and a flood of warmth washed over her.

He turned to the high school kid who worked behind the counter. "One mint chocolate chip in a sugar cone and one vanilla. Same kind of cone."

"That's it? Plain vanilla?" Liza asked.

He shrugged. "What can I say? I'm a simple guy."

If only that were true, she thought. He might be easier to resist.

He took their cones from the teenager. "Can you hold mine a second?"

Liza nodded and grabbed the desserts.

Dare paid and she decided not to argue about it, and when he was finished, she handed him back his cone. "Thank you," she said.

"You're welcome." His grin was hot enough to melt the ice cream in her hand.

They walked back outside. "Do you want to sit here?" He pointed to a wooden bench on the sidewalk outside.

"Sure." A hot summer night in Serendipity — they were lucky the bench hadn't been taken.

For a few minutes, they ate in silence. Liza savored the cool mint in her mouth and snuck glimpses of Dare as he licked and ate the ice cream, unable to control thoughts of him using that mouth and that tongue on her.

She stifled a groan and looked away.

He finished his cone much faster than she had and suddenly he turned toward her, stretching his arm on the bench behind her, his knees touching her thighs. "I never meant for you to think I don't like you."

His words took her by surprise. He obviously didn't believe in easing into a conversation.

Liza swallowed hard. "I never said —"

"You called our past conversations contentious and mean. And you were right." He glanced down as if embarrassed by the admission. "But when you said you didn't think I'd want to spend time with you? You're wrong about that."

His voice dropped a deep, husky octave and her stomach twisted with pleasure she shouldn't be feeling. "I understand why we wouldn't get along. What I don't get is why . . ." She trailed off, unwilling to say what she was feeling.

"You don't get why we're drawn to each other?" Dare asked, voicing her very thoughts.

She frowned. "That's creepy. You shouldn't read people's minds," she said, laughing.

He laughed too. "Normally I don't. I just happen to know exactly what you're feeling. I don't get this thing between us either. I just know it exists." He reached out and twisted the end of her hair between his thumb and forefinger before meeting her gaze. "And until just now, I thought it was one-sided."

She shook her head, wishing she could deny the truth of his words. "It's not," she whispered. It was very mutual.

But, oh, how she wished it wasn't. Liza kept people at a distance for a reason. Those closest tended to disappoint her or hurt her. Her parents, her brother, and the man who'd taught her how dangerous it was to let people in. Since then, relationships didn't exist in her life. She didn't have boyfriends and she didn't do long term.

She did occasionally have sex. No woman could live without sex. Well, Liza couldn't. Her life was barren enough with her college pals in the city and nobody here she trusted not to turn her away if Brian got embarrassing enough. Sometimes she needed companionship. Human contact. She hated the term *friends with benefits,* but she had a guy who fit that description who lived in New York City. If it happened, it happened, and neither of them had any expectations beyond that. It helped that Steve had been a friend first and she trusted him as much as she did her girl pals, and that was good enough for her.

But Dare Barron was different.

He stared at her now with those seductive eyes and the pull was strong. Attraction she understood. Attraction was easy, but there was more to this thing between them. She thought about him more often than she should, but that wasn't all. He slipped past her defenses without even trying. He made her *feel* and very few people in her life managed that feat.

Take tonight. In the short time she'd been at Joe's Bar, she'd fought a host of feelings that had begun to suffocate her so badly she'd needed to escape. She'd felt alone and out of place, but like simple attraction, those were things she understood. The longing to be a part of the obviously close relationship Dare had with his sisters-in-law and his friends?

That yearning didn't make sense and it frightened her. Because if she wanted, she became vulnerable. Something she wouldn't let herself be ever again.

"Watch it," Dare said, intruding on her thoughts.

"What?"

He reached out with his finger, catching the green ice cream dripping over her cone.

She'd been so lost in thought she'd forgotten all about her dessert. "Thanks."

"You're welcome." He grinned and licked the minty flavor off his finger.

She knew he didn't intend the gesture to be sexy, yet she couldn't tear her gaze from his mouth. A day's growth of beard shadowed his face, and his lips were just full and firm enough to tease her with possibilities.

Arousal suddenly burned inside her.

"You need to stop," Dare said.

She barely recognized his deep, husky voice, but that didn't prevent her from asking, "Stop what?"

"Stop looking at me like you want to devour me like you did to that ice cream or . . ." The glint in his eyes told her what would happen next.

The tone in his voice should have scared her away. Instead, it tempted her beyond reason.

"Or . . . ?" she asked, deliberately tempting him.

"This." He slipped his hand behind her head. He cupped the back of her neck in his firm hand and captured her mouth in a kiss.

Her eyelids closed and sensation took over. His lips were cool from the ice cream and of course he tasted like mint. Unable to help herself, she darted her tongue out for a more thorough taste. "Mmm." She heard the sound, shocked it had come from her.

He tightened his grip around the back of her neck and with a groan, parted his lips and their tongues tangled. No longer cool, his mouth burned with heat. So did her body as she savored the sensations flowing through her, growing in intensity as his tongue swirled back and forth inside her with lazy, seductive strokes.

When was the last time she'd experienced such a powerful kiss? One that took her over and rocked her soul?

Never, she realized, and the thought should have sent her running. Instead, she let out another soft sigh and he responded, swirling his tongue from side to side, learning her, tasting her, making her feel as if he couldn't get enough. Heaven knew she couldn't.

But when the sound of voices penetrated her foggy mind, she remembered where they were. Apparently so did he because he broke the kiss, but he didn't immediately pull away. Instead, he rested his forehead against hers.

The intimate gesture made her breath catch in her throat.

"That answer your question?" he asked, sounding out of breath.

That kiss had scrambled her brains but not so much that she didn't remember she'd asked him what would happen if she didn't stop staring.

She shook her head and managed a laugh. "Excellent answer, Officer."

He sat up straighter and grinned.

Cocky male, she thought, enjoying him far

too much. She glanced down and realized her cone had begun to melt, the sticky ice cream now all over her hand. "I need to throw this out and go inside to wash up."

He nodded. "I'll wait here."

"Okay, I'll be right back."

Liza headed inside and Dare used the time to get himself under control. No way could he stand until he'd talked himself down. Literally.

Ten minutes later, he'd escorted Liza to her car, a sporty convertible that suited her. He intended to go right on upstairs to his apartment until he realized Faith would be wondering what happened.

Better to see her now than to have her come looking for him later. He reached the table and discovered his brothers had joined their wives and the alcohol still flowed. He groaned, wondering if he'd get out of here at a decent hour.

"Dare!" Faith jumped up from her seat and came up beside him. She hooked her arm through his and led him a few steps away from the table.

Ethan shot him an *I pity you* look and Dare wondered how he could get retribution.

"So? How'd it go? Did you two connect?" she asked.

"Do you really think I'd tell you my

personal business?" he asked his sister-in-law.

"Of course I do," she said, not the least bit offended. "And I'll tell you why. I have Liza's ear. We're not just working on the fund-raiser together, we go way back. Which means I know her. I have insight you're going to need. So instead of waiting until you have to come begging me for information, you share with me and I'll do the same." She batted her eyelashes at him in a very unpracticed move.

Faith, for all her teasing now, wasn't manipulative nor was she nosy. The woman cared about everyone in her life — those she let in anyway. Now that Dare was one of those people, no way would he get off telling her to mind her own business.

"We came to an understanding," he told Faith. They'd agreed they had chemistry and then kissed to prove it, Dare thought.

Faith raised her eyebrows. "What does *that* mean?" she asked.

"It means that's all the information you're getting tonight," Ethan said, coming up to his wife and rescuing his brother. "When and if Dare needs help with his love life, he knows where to find you." Ethan slipped a finger into a belt loop on the back of Faith's jeans. "Come here and bother me instead of Dare."

Faith opened her mouth, no doubt to object. Ethan pulled her closer and whispered in her ear. "Okay, then. Home it is," she said, a flush rising on her cheeks.

Dare shook his head and bit his tongue before he used Tess's line about getting a room because it sounded like that was what they had in mind anyway.

"I'm going upstairs," he said. "Night, all."

"Dare, wait. I just wanted to say one serious thing. Did you notice how Liza sat at the table with us but never really joined in?" Faith asked.

He shook his head. He'd been too busy trying to hold a conversation with his friends when all he wanted to do was get Liza alone.

"She holds herself back from people, something I know all about from personal experience."

"Your father betrayed you, Faith. You had good reason."

"Liza hasn't had it any easier. I haven't seen her in years and I can still tell she doesn't trust people easily."

Dare frowned. She'd said as much to him, but he figured she just didn't want to make it easy on him. He wanted to know the reasons Liza was so wary of people. Of him.

But even if Faith knew the answers, Dare would rather Liza tell him herself. Because doing so would mean she trusted him.

When Dare realized he desired that trust even more than he wanted *her,* he knew that when it came to this woman, he was in deep trouble.

The rest of the week flew by and Saturday arrived, bright, sunny, and hot. A perfect day for an outdoor event. When Liza had decided to attend the youth center fundraiser, she never thought she'd do so having kissed Dare Barron. She hadn't heard from or spoken to him since, not that she'd expected to. But she couldn't have imagined the potency of that kiss and wondered if he'd felt it too.

Was he interested? Or maybe he kissed every woman who gave him an opening. Or maybe he'd decided that she wasn't worth the effort, what with her ties to her troublesome brother. Liza didn't know what Dare thought or felt but she'd been torturing herself with the possibilities for the rest of the week.

She exhaled hard, feeling ridiculous. It wasn't like she'd never kissed a guy, then had to face him afterward. Seeing Dare again would be a piece of cake. She bit the inside of her cheek, picked up her bag, and headed out the door, calling herself a liar the entire drive to the youth center.

Luckily, Jeff was waiting for her when she paid her entry fee and walked onto the grassy lawn behind the center, the buffer she'd been so eager to have.

She waved and met up with him. "You're prompt."

"I aim to please," he said with a grin. "Can I get you a soda or anything to eat?"

She shook her head. Her stomach was already churning with a combination of excitement and nerves. Not that she'd let him get her anything anyway. "No, thank you, but if you're hungry, we can stop by any of the food stands."

"I'm good, thanks." He tipped his head to the side, indicating they should start milling around.

Liza walked beside him, uncomfortable when he placed a hand on the small of her back like they were *together* together. Not ready to say something in case she was over-reacting, Liza strode along the grass, passing carnival-like booths run by many police officers she knew too well, fire-fighters she knew by sight or name, and kids obviously recruited to help. As they walked, Liza was surprised at how many people she saw that she knew and was even more pleased at how many friendly hellos she received.

They met up with Bianca Raye, Liza's assistant. "Hey there!" the perky red head said, greeting them with a smile.

"Hi, Bianca!"

Jeff smiled at her.

"Fancy meeting you two here," Bianca said. Jeff's hand lingered on Liza's back and the confusion on Bianca's face echoed the feelings inside Liza. She took the opportunity to step closer to the other woman and away from Jeff's too-familiar touch.

"I offered to meet up with Jeff and introduce him to people, since he's new in town," Liza explained as much to Bianca as to reinforce her reasons to Jeff.

Before Bianca responded, a teenager with a big sign reading ZEPPOLI 50 CENTS hanging from his neck walked by.

"Oooh, fried dough!" Bianca exclaimed, obviously distracted. "I'm meeting friends, but I got here early. I'd love to hang with you guys until they get here. Can you wait until I grab something to eat first?"

Liza nodded, grateful to have another woman with her.

"Thanks!" Bianca darted off to the *zeppoli* stand behind them.

Jeff didn't say anything but his silence and

lack of a smile spoke for him.

"Umm, Jeff, is everything okay?" Liza asked.

He tipped his head to the side, looking a combination of confused and embarrassed. "This isn't a date, is it?"

Liza opened her mouth, then closed it again, searching for the right words. "Date?" was the best she could do.

"When you asked me to meet you here . . . never mind," he said, shaking his head.

Liza was mortified, both for herself and for him. "No, it's not a date," she said softly. "I only meant it as an offer to introduce you around, ease your transition to town. I'm so sorry if you thought otherwise."

His face flushed red. "It's the hick in me, I guess," he said sheepishly.

"No!" she said, meaning it.

"Okay, I'm back!" Bianca returned, interrupting the embarrassing moment. "Bought extra." She waved the *zeppoli* in front of Liza and Jeff.

He accepted the offer, taking one. Liza decided she'd just earned the treat.

"Guess who I ran into over by the fried-dough stand?" Bianca asked. "Peter from accounting," she said before they could offer a guess. "And he was alone. Even at a social event like this one, he's such a loner.

Sad." She shook her head and bit into her doughy treat.

"Did you ask him to join us?" Liza asked.

Bianca nodded. "He said he's more of an observer than a joiner, but thank you anyway. Whatever that means," she said with an eye roll. "He's an odd duck."

"But good with numbers and that's what matters to me."

Bianca nodded. "I can't believe how hot it is today," she said, changing the subject.

"But it's not raining, so that's a good day off in my book," Jeff said, finally speaking and obviously eager to move on from their misunderstanding.

Liza took his cue and tried to forget about it too. It wasn't easy. She'd never meant to lead him on. As nice as he was, Liza wouldn't date someone from the office. She wasn't interested in dating period.

Oddly, that didn't stop her interest in a certain police officer she hadn't run into yet today. On the heels of that thought came a surge of disappointment and she couldn't help wondering if Dare had thought about her at all, if he'd looked for her today the way she was looking for him.

"Liza? Are you coming?" Bianca asked.

She shook her head hard. "Sorry. Am I coming where?" She'd been too lost in her own thoughts and had stopped paying attention to Bianca and Jeff.

"The dunking booth. It's a chance to nail the cops!" Bianca waggled her eyebrows, laughing.

Taking in the other woman's miniskirt and cropped tank top, so different from her office attire, Liza figured there was a good chance the cops would be eager to let Bianca have a shot at them. As long as it wasn't *her* cop, Liza thought, and immediately stifled the thought.

"I wouldn't miss this." Liza followed them to the far end of the area where the dunking booth had been set up.

Jeff kept his distance from Liza, focusing more on Bianca, allowing her to chat away like they were old friends. And though Liza was relieved, she was still uncomfortable. The last thing she wanted was any awkward office moments.

The walk to the dunking booth took a while since Bianca was stopped often. They passed Peter Dalton, and though Liza waved, he merely watched them, nodding as they passed. Bianca was right. The man was an odd duck.

The rest of the people they stopped to talk to were Bianca's friends, most of them younger than Liza's twenty-nine. Bianca herself was only twenty-three, coming to work for Liza straight out of college. She'd been with Liza for a little over a year and despite her chatty demeanor, she handled her phone calls professionally and kept Liza's work and appointments well organized.

Bianca introduced both Liza and Jeff to her friends. They all seemed to like him, especially the women, who were obviously thrilled to meet a new guy in town. His discomfort from earlier seemingly forgotten, Liza was again struck by how easygoing the man was. The Midwest must breed their males to be friendly because Jeff had no trouble fitting in. Liza watched from the sidelines. Once again she felt on the fringe of a group instead of a part of it and she was grateful when they started walking again.

At the dunking booth, a large crowd had gathered, making it impossible to see the tank.

"I wonder who's in the booth." Bianca craned her head to try and see over and around the people.

"It's Sam Marsden," a woman standing in front of them offered.

Brian's most recent arresting officer. Despite what she spouted in defense of her brother, Liza didn't fault the police for taking Brian in when he deserved it. But she still wouldn't mind watching Officer Marsden receive a good soaking, she thought with a grin.

"Throw, throw, throw, throw!" The chant came from the crowd, obviously eager to watch the confrontation.

"Let's get closer." Bianca plowed forward, barreling through the crush of people.

Jeff followed.

Normally Liza wouldn't push her way through, but she didn't want to be left behind, and besides, she was curious to see who had it in for Officer Marsden.

As soon as Liza reached the front and had an unobstructed view, she wished she hadn't asked herself the question. She wished she'd remained on the fringe of the crowd and she definitely wished even harder that she'd followed her yearly impulse to avoid this event altogether.

Because her brother, Brian, stood in front of the dunking booth, a ball in his hand, his best friend, Rob, by his side. Like Mutt and Jeff, the two were rarely separated. If one got in trouble, the other usually followed. Brian's eyes were red-rimmed and bloodshot, his shirt wrinkled as if he'd slept in it last night.

"Oh, no," Liza muttered. Nothing about

this scene could end well.

Jeff turned to her, understanding and sympathy in his eyes. Bianca didn't say anything. And really, what more could she add?

"Throw, throw, throw, throw!" The crowd's chants grew more boisterous, egging him on.

Liza debated dragging Brian away or letting the whole incident play out. Based on the balls littering the ground around the booth, Brian had thrown and missed before, but he wasn't doing anything more than glaring at the cop in the tank.

With a little luck, Brian would finish his turn and walk away without causing trouble, and if that were the case, all Liza's interference would do was create a scene.

One she didn't want to be a part of.

She turned, just about to walk away when Brian called out, "You're going down, cop."

Liza shook her head, her gut and past dealings with her brother screaming a warning.

She had to do something now.

FIVE

Dare hated the dunking booth and avoided getting that assignment like the plague. Sam, on the other hand, didn't seem to mind, as he'd been in and out of the tank for the better part of the day. Dare had finished the morning shift for the DARE program and another officer had the afternoon. He was free for the day.

"Isn't that your girl?" Cara asked as she walked up to him.

Dare knew who she meant without bothering to look over. He'd been aware of Liza's presence for the last thirty minutes, but he'd been tied up talking to kids and their parents. Now he could finally give her the attention she deserved, but he didn't need Cara as his audience.

So he ignored her.

"You see what I see?" she asked, none too delicately nudging him in the ribs.

If she meant the tall guy with dark hair

who stood way too close for Dare's liking, yeah, he saw.

Dare merely grunted in reply. As far as he was concerned, that question didn't deserve an answer. Besides, he planned to break up whatever was going on over there as soon as he ditched his nosy friend.

"Officer Barron!" a young girl called out to him. "I have a question."

Cara chuckled. "At least the young ones fall at your feet."

"Don't you have something better to do?" he muttered.

Cara laughed. "Go talk to your little fan. But when you're finished, get your ass in gear and find Liza before that new guy weasels his way in."

Cara patted him on the back and walked off, leaving Dare with his stomach twisting with jealousy. Unfortunately, he had no choice but to deal with the precocious child he remembered from his last DARE session.

He turned to the ten-year-old girl, whose mother had joined her and together they kept him talking for a good ten minutes. Dare knew he answered their questions, but he couldn't remember the details of their discussion. He was too focused on Liza and the guy who'd put his hand on her back and led her away.

When he was finally alone, Dare drew a deep breath and headed in the direction he'd seen Liza last. Luckily she'd gone toward the dunking booth. If Dare couldn't find her, he at least planned to get a few good shots in and sink Sam.

He arrived to find a huge crowd and lots of cheering going on. Rarely did this booth draw such a huge crowd, no matter which officer held the honors of sitting in the dunk tank. An uneasy feeling settled in Dare's gut as he pushed his way through the many people blocking his view.

"Throw, throw, throw, throw!" The words circled around the crowd.

Dare finally stepped into the open. He glanced from Sam in the booth to the current player and muttered a curse. The last thing this family-oriented fair needed was Brian McKnight causing trouble and making a scene. And though Sam was in the tank, kids from the youth center were running the booth and they weren't equipped to handle this.

Dare had to distract McKnight and give someone else a shot at Sam before things got out of hand. He took a step forward but someone beat him to it.

Liza called out her brother's name, the

distraught look on her face pushing all sorts of emotional buttons Dare hadn't known he possessed.

Brian turned her way, his glassy gaze focusing on his sister. "Liza Lou! What are you doing here?" he slurred.

"I think you've been at this long enough. Let's go get a soda or something."

"It's still my turn," Brian said, winding his arm and tossing the ball at the target that would release Sam into the tank. Brian's pitch missed by a mile. They'd be lucky if he didn't hit someone with his wild throws.

Dare was torn between stepping in and possibly embarrassing Liza with his presence and letting things play out. A glance at the booth told him Sam sat in a relaxed pose, arms folded across his chest, obviously unconcerned about a possible dunking, since McKnight's aim was way off.

And unlike when the high school kids tossed balls at him, Sam didn't yell back any taunts or reply to the smart-ass remarks with good humor. He knew better than to engage a drunk.

"Brian, please," Liza said once more.

Dare saw the pointing and heard the murmurs of people around him. They were talking about the McKnights and the scene they were making.

Brian wasn't listening to his sister, his sole focus on Sam. "I wouldn't look so cocky if I were you," the drunk man called to Sam. "You're going down, Officer Asshole!"

Liza visibly winced at his language, knowing as Dare did that they were surrounded by kids and their parents, some of whom started to drag their children away. Others chose to stay and watch the spectacle.

Someone had to take control. "McKnight!" Dare stepped forward. "Why don't you move it along and give one of the kids a chance?"

Hearing his voice, Liza turned and met his gaze. Where he'd been hoping she'd be happy to see him, now pure mortification settled over her pretty features and her cheeks burned a bright shade of red.

"Brian, let's go!" she said, her jaw clenched in anger.

"Listen to your sister," Dare suggested.

Brian shook his head. "I paid for this last ball and I'm going to take my shot." He stumbled but righted himself before he fell.

Dare needed to get that ball away from McKnight before his next throw hurt someone badly. "Hand it over," Dare ordered, using the tone he would use for "Drop your weapon."

"No damned cop's going to tell me I don't have the right to get what I paid for," Brian spat. Brian wound his arm, ready to pitch.

Dare bolted forward, intending to grab him, but Liza was closer. She reached for Brian at the same time her brother pitched his arm forward, his fist and the ball cracking against her head with a solid thud.

The sound echoed in Dare's ear as she fell to the ground. He immediately dropped to his knees at Liza's prone body.

Another cop grabbed Brian, who seemed unaware that he'd clocked his sister.

"Okay, everyone, show's over," Cara said.

Dare wasn't aware of anything around him except the injured woman on the ground. Heart in his throat, he bent his head close to hers. "Liza?"

She didn't respond.

"Baby, you with me?" He stroked his hand down her cheek, unable to believe the fear that had settled deep in his gut.

Memories of another time Brian had taken someone out with his fist came flying at him, the image of Stuart Rossman hitting the ground, the sound of his head cracking against the floor reverberating in his head.

"Let me through." The guy Dare had seen Liza with earlier stepped forward.

"She needs space," Cara said, immediately

blocking the man from getting near Liza.

"She came here with me," the man said.

"But I'm taking over from here." Dare spoke low, his tone dark even to his own ears.

"Jeff, let's go. You can check on her later," a redhead said to him.

"But —"

"No buts," Cara said in cop mode.

Dare owed her one.

"We're leaving," the other woman with Jeff promised.

Liza's sudden moan of pain caught Dare's attention. She was conscious. "Liza?" Dare asked.

He glanced at her pale face as her eyes opened. "Brian. I need to get to Brian."

"He's being taken care of," Dare said, keeping his voice level and calm. If he expressed even half of the anger he was feeling toward her sibling, she wouldn't want anything to do with him. And right now he desperately wanted to be with her and make sure she was okay.

"I need to see him." Liza lifted her head but winced and stopped the sudden movement.

Dare settled cross-legged beside her and gently moved her head into his lap. "The paramedics are on their way," he assured her, hoping he was right.

"So is Alexa," Cara said. "She okay?" Cara gestured to Liza.

"I think so," Dare said. But he wasn't. He was grateful Liza couldn't stand because Dare would lay odds his own legs wouldn't be steady just yet.

"I'm fine," Liza murmured. She wasn't moving her head, but at least she was talking and coherent.

"How's the pain?" he asked.

"Better." But her unshed tears proved that claim was a lie.

"You know if you wanted my attention all you had to do was ask. Getting hit by a flying fist is a little extreme." He forced out the joke with a grin and was rewarded by a small smile. Followed by another wince.

"What happened?" Alexa knelt down, her doctor bag in her hand.

"She was hit by someone about to throw a ball at the tank," Dare said.

Liza ran her tongue over her lips. "It was an accident," she said.

Dare clenched his jaw at her explanation but said nothing to contradict her. He kept his mouth shut while Alexa checked Liza's pupil dilation, asked her questions, took her blood pressure, and generally made sure she was okay.

"Can you sit up?" the doctor asked.

Liza attempted a nod but clearly regretted it. Instead, she allowed Alexa to gently lift her into a sitting position.

"Give yourself a minute," the doctor suggested.

Though Liza still looked pale, she seemed more composed and Dare's heart rate began to return to normal.

"I thought maybe she'd want some water?" Cara handed Dare a fresh, cold bottle.

"Thanks," Dare said.

"Any nausea?" Alexa asked.

"No."

"Good. Drink slowly," Alexa warned Liza. "I'd like you to go to the hospital and get checked out. Have a CAT scan done."

Christopher DeMarco, a paramedic Dare knew from school stood waiting to help.

"No," Liza said immediately.

"Okay," Dare spoke at the same time, contradicting her.

"I don't need a hospital. I didn't black out. I'm sure I'll have a nasty bump and it'll hurt like hell, but I'm fine. Really."

Everything inside Dare rebelled at the thought of letting her just go home like nothing had happened. He couldn't stop thinking about Stuart Rossman, remembering how Dare had done nothing to help him, and Stuart had died.

"If you refuse, you'll have to sign a paper saying you declined," Christopher said, looking none too pleased.

Alexa frowned, obviously not happy either.

Dare wasn't about to accept her no. "What about that actress who refused treatment and died a few hours later?" he asked, pressing the issue.

"Natasha Richardson?" Alexa asked.

"That's her. All the newspapers said she claimed to be fine after she fell. She was joking around, but by the time she went to the hospital it was too late."

Liza blinked into the sun and immediately looked down.

Alexa placed a hand on Liza's shoulder. "Natasha Richardson died of an epidural hematoma due to a blunt impact to the head. In layman's terms, you were hit by a hard fist and a harder ball." The doctor paused for emphasis. "You need to get checked out."

Liza sighed. "You're taking his side because you're friends," she muttered. "Unfair ganging up on me."

"She's taking my side because I'm right," Dare said.

"Fine, I'll go."

Dare hadn't realized how tense he was

until she agreed and his muscles went slack with relief. "I'm riding with her," he blurted out.

Liza didn't reply, telling him the pain and stress were clearly wearing on her or else she'd probably argue.

Not that he'd let her fight him or win. He already knew her brother would be driven home to sleep off his stupor and Liza's parents no longer lived in town. She kept to herself like Faith had said, so she had no one to take care of her now or afterward, when the pain really kicked in.

She'd go to the hospital, have those tests, and then he'd bring her home and take care of her himself.

Liza didn't know what was worse: her brother humiliating himself in front of the entire town, her unsuccessful and equally embarrassing attempt to stop him, or the fact that Dare had witnessed the entire thing. Though she had no desire to go to the hospital, between the insistent cop and the paramedic, she'd felt cornered. And something in Dare's voice and expression told her that her getting checked out was important to him. She couldn't put her finger on why but she sensed it was so much more than making sure her thick skull would survive another day.

Once she'd agreed, Liza lost control of the situation and found herself taken by ambulance to University Hospital. Though Dare had said he'd go with her, he'd ended up driving his car and following behind so he'd be able to take her home later, another thing she'd been given no choice over.

He'd met up with her in the ER and then they'd taken her for tests and now she waited alone in a small cubicle for someone to tell her when she could go home.

"Is that scowl because you're in pain?" a familiar female voice asked.

Liza glanced into Dr. Alexa Collins's concerned green eyes.

"No, the scowl was over something else," Liza said.

"And the pain?" the doctor asked. "Can you describe it?"

"As long as I don't nod my head, move too much, blink, or do much of anything else, it's not too bad." Liza laughed at her own joke and her head pounded harder. "Obviously it's pretty bad," she admitted.

The other woman nodded. "When you're sitting still, on a scale of one to ten, one being the least amount of pain, how is it?"

"Four," Liza said.

"And if you move?"

"Eight."

Dr. Collins nodded. "The good news is the tests showed there's nothing life-threatening to worry about. The bad news is it's a mild concussion. I can prescribe some painkillers and send you home, but you'll either be in too much pain to walk around and take care of yourself or too woozy from the meds. Do you have someone who can help you out?"

No, Liza was alone. Always had been. "I'm sure I'll be okay. I'm pretty low maintenance."

The pretty doctor cocked a skeptical eyebrow. "Let's see you get up and walk yourself to the bathroom before I discharge you." The doctor braced her hands on her hips, not offering her help to rise.

Knowing she didn't have handrails on her bed at home, Liza tried to push herself into a sitting position first. The pain blasted through her head and she ended up flat on her back, staring at the ceiling waiting for the agony to subside.

"Do you have family I can call?" the doctor asked more gently.

"Not local."

"Friends?" the doctor persisted.

Rachel and Tawny, her college friends, were in Manhattan. If she called, they'd come in a heartbeat to help her, but Liza hated asking them to disrupt their lives for her.

"She has me."

Alexa turned to stare at Dare.

Liza hated feeling helpless and at anyone's mercy. And she refused to meet Dare's gaze as she automatically argued with his offer. "I'm sure you have more important things to do," she told him.

"Actually, I don't." He eased his hands into his jeans' pockets, looking all too sexy and sure of himself. "I'm off the whole weekend."

"All right, then." Alexa turned back to Liza, a grin on her face. "Since you're in good hands, I can release you."

Liza didn't fight this time. She couldn't. She obviously needed help, he was offering it, and she ought to be a lot more grateful. She just didn't understand *why* he was being so sweet to her. Before their kiss, they'd barely tolerated one another.

They weren't friends.

They didn't have a relationship. Liza didn't *do* relationships. Her first and only serious pick of a man had been so far off base, she wasn't willing to try again. Besides, even those closest to her, like Brian and her parents, consistently hurt her. Why add anyone else to her almost nonexistent inner circle?

So what did Dare see that made him want to help her? Why didn't he view today as a prime example of an *I told you so* situation where her brother was concerned? She didn't know, but apparently she'd have the weekend to find out.

"I'll go write up the prescriptions and your release papers. A nurse will be back in to go over everything with you," the doctor said.

"Thanks, Alexa," Dare said.

"It's my job." She smiled at him. "But if you need anything later on, don't bother with my service. Just call me at home. You have my number."

And *that* had nothing to do with her job, Liza thought.

"Will do." Dare waited until the doctor disappeared behind the drawn curtain and turned to Liza.

Walking over, he lowered the side rail and settled onto the mattress beside her. "How are you doing?" he asked, his voice gruff.

That tone triggered memories of his reaction in the minutes after Brian nailed her and she'd fallen to the ground.

"You called me 'baby,' " she said, remembering. "After I got hit, I mean." She knew it was an inane comment, but she couldn't believe it then or now.

"Yeah, I guess I did." Dare paused. "Does that bother you?"

No, actually she'd liked the familiarity. "It's just that *baby* implies we have a connection or something."

Then again so did his stepping up and offering to take care of her.

"Are you saying we don't?" he asked.

He lifted her hand, threading his fingers through hers. Heat exploded across her skin, making his question purely rhetorical.

"Come on. Let me help get you home. Right now you need to sleep a hell of a lot more than you need to analyze us."

She couldn't argue with that point either. So she exhaled and placed her hand inside of his.

Liza gave Dare the address to her house right before leaning her head back and falling asleep, leaving him with nothing but time to think about Liza and the puzzle she presented him with. He might not know her well, but there were two things he'd figured out about her already. Intimacy scared her and she didn't like needing anybody for anything.

A challenge.

He liked that in a woman.

Too many females in his past were too easy and tended to fall into one of three categories: they liked being with a cop, they liked being in a relationship, or they liked easy sex. And though Dare enjoyed sex as much as the next guy, he was tired of coming home alone to the small apartment he called home. Not that he'd admit as much to his brothers or their nosy wives.

Living over Joe's was better than living with either of his brothers, but Dare was coming to realize he wanted more out of his life. He wasn't sure what jarred these feelings loose. Maybe Ethan and Nash's settling down had Dare more antsy. Or maybe it was the simple fact of living in a one-bedroom above a bar that left him feeling so unsettled.

He pulled into the small driveway of Liza's home. With her asleep, he took in the small house, an off-white clapboard with black shutters and white trim. The grass had been recently mowed, the shrubbery was obviously new, and she clearly loved flowers. Pink, white, and red impatiens blossomed around the foundation of the house. Dare wasn't a gardener, but he had spent a day under duress with Ethan, Faith, and Tess, choosing new flowers for their backyard. Tess said she wouldn't go unless Dare did and she'd turned those pleading eyes on him, begging him to come along. So he recognized impatiens when he saw them.

He cut the engine and walked around to Liza's side of the car. She predictably balked at him carrying her and Dare had dealt with enough women to know when to give in and when to fight the good fight. He was here and that's what mattered. He plucked her keys from her hand and helped her walk to the front door.

She disabled her alarm, which he was glad to see she used, and they stepped inside. She'd already begun to sag against him.

"Which way to the bedroom?" he asked.

"Up the stairs and to the left." Because the house was a small split-level, there were no more than four steps up.

"Ready?" he asked when they reached the banister.

"Yep." She took one step, then another, her smaller body leaning heavily against his.

She trusted him. Either that or she'd given into her body's inability to handle any more today. She curled into him, her soft curves and warm flesh tempting him beyond reason, which made him all sorts of a jerk considering the pain she was in. Still, it wasn't easy walking her into her bedroom.

A feminine scent immediately surrounded him. He gritted his teeth and eased her over to the bed and gently lowered her to the mattress. No sooner had she sat down than she immediately let herself crash into the fluffy decorative pillows set up against the headboard.

What now?

Stepping back, he glanced around him. Her personal space surprised him. She hadn't chosen the more ruffled feminine type of furnishings nor had she gone for heavy floral. Instead, the bedding was a light taupe and cream with an occasional lavender accent. Very unique. Very Liza, he decided, and smiled, the thought bringing his focus back to where she lay among the pillows. Her short skirt had hiked up her legs, revealing an expanse of thigh along with a teasing glimpse of pink lace underwear.

Dare stifled a groan. "Do you want to change into something more comfortable?" he asked. Something he could look at and not get hard would be preferable.

"Can't move." She burrowed farther into the pillows.

An afghan blanket was folded at the end of the bed. He opened it up and covered

119

her bare skin. "This way you won't be cold," he said.

She didn't answer. She'd already passed out.

"Great." He stood by the bed for a few more minutes watching her sleep, wanting to be certain she was breathing easily and not in too much pain.

Her breathing came deep and even now, so he walked out, leaving her door open so he'd hear her if she woke up.

He wasn't sure what to do with himself, so he headed for the kitchen to see if he could find something to eat. The kitchen was bright, the sunlight pouring in from windows on all sides. Unfortunately, the refrigerator was nearly empty inside except for a container of soy milk, some yogurt, and three boxes of Oreos.

He counted again. Yep, three boxes of Oreos. A woman after his own heart.

His cell phone rang and before he could analyze that thought further, he answered it. "Barron."

"It's Nash," his brother said. "I heard there was some excitement over at the fair."

"You wouldn't believe it," Dare muttered. He glanced around but was already sure from the silence that Liza was still upstairs. "The asshole hit his sister in the head with his fist and the ball."

"How'd she make out at the hospital?" Nash asked.

Dare explained the situation and the fact that he was at Liza's house now. "Want company?" Nash asked.

"Not so sure that's a good idea," Dare said, uncomfortable having guests over while Liza was passed out. Especially since he was barely an invited guest himself.

Dare heard Kelly in the background and then Nash spoke again. "Kelly said to ask you if you're capable of making Liza something to eat when she wakes up."

Dare rolled his eyes. But the truth was even if Liza had had food, Dare wasn't much of a cook. "Her fridge is pretty empty."

"Then help's on the way," Kelly said, obviously having grabbed the phone from her husband. "And don't worry. If she wakes up and it seems like you can have time alone with her, we're gone."

Before Dare could respond, Kelly hung up. And despite his reservations, Dare had to admit he was grateful to have family to help out.

Unlike Liza.

He shook his head, bothered more than he should be by the fact that she was injured and nobody close to her knew. Didn't anyone care? Her parents? Friends?

Alone and lonely were two different things, and Dare couldn't help wondering if Liza was both. Regardless of who did or didn't line up for her, Dare knew enough to realize the first thing she'd ask him once she woke up was about her brother. With that in mind, Dare called Sam to find out the status on Brian, who, as expected, had been driven home and left there to sober up.

The memory of the man hitting his sister was as fresh in Dare's mind as the party Brian had thrown back in high school. His parents had been away and there was a mix of kids from both private and public schools. Brian had gotten into an argument with Stuart Rossman and punched him. Already intoxicated, Stuart had gone down hard and cracked his head on the pavement. The kids who'd witnessed the event, Dare included, had either run or helped Brian cover up the reality of what happened. Dare still hated himself for leaving and not calling 911. Simmering anger at Brian lived in Dare. Liza deserved so much more than she received in the way of family, he thought in disgust.

Not wanting to think anymore, Dare wandered from the kitchen to the den and settled into Liza's comfortable couch, remote in hand. Then he turned on the television, finding a Mets baseball game to watch while he waited for Nash and Kelly to arrive or for Liza to wake up, whichever happened first.

Six

Liza woke up surrounded by her throw pillows, her neck at an awkward angle. Her head pounded and her mouth felt bone dry. She didn't have to wonder why either. The scene at the fair came back to her in vivid detail and she let out a groan.

How would she ever show her face in town again? And what was she going to do about her brother? Knowing she couldn't think clearly about anything right now, she decided there were more important things she needed to do.

Like determine how she was feeling. She pushed herself to a sitting position, not an easy maneuver. Her head hurt as badly now as it had after Brian had hit her. While she waited to get her equilibrium, she noticed water on her nightstand. She reached for it, succeeding only in knocking over the tall glass.

Tears of frustration filled her eyes and she

lay back against the pillows.

"Liza?"

Dare's voice startled her through the pain. Though she remembered being hit, until now she'd forgotten he'd taken her home.

And she definitely hadn't remembered he'd be staying.

"Are you okay?" he asked, sounding closer.

"No." Embarrassment meant nothing to her at the moment and she answered him honestly.

"That's probably because the meds have worn off. You slept for almost four hours. Is the pain bad?" he asked.

"Yes." One-word answers were the most she could manage.

"Okay, first things first. Let me clean up this water and then I'll bring you something to eat. Your last painkiller was a shot and Alexa said it's not a good idea to take the pills on an empty stomach."

She heard the sounds of him getting a towel from her bathroom and cleaning the nightstand beside her. "I'll be right back, okay?"

"Okay."

Some time later, his weight dipped the bed as he sat down beside her. "I wasn't sure what your stomach could handle as far as food," he said.

She forced her eyes open and found him looking down at her, concern in those gorgeous brown eyes. "Hey," he said, smiling at her.

"Hi."

"So . . . food. I made you some toast and jelly. That always works on an upset stomach and Alexa said you might be nauseous from the concussion. I also brought you some soda. Coke or ginger ale?" he asked, pointing to two separate cans on her nightstand.

"This is so embarrassing," she finally said, completely unused to anyone being there for her. "And you're a prince to do this for me."

He glanced away, obviously embarrassed. At least she wasn't the only one unsettled by this situation.

"Come on," he said, ignoring the compliment. "Let's get you into a sitting position."

He held out his arm for her to brace herself against and she used the leverage to lift herself up slowly. It wasn't easy and her head pounded like a son of a bitch, but she finally managed.

"Now give yourself a minute," he instructed.

How he knew her head reverberated like a bass drum, she had no idea. Thankfully, a few minutes later, the pain eased.

"Here." He placed a plate in front of her on the bed.

She glanced at the toast and jelly and realized she was starving. "I didn't have any of this in the house," she said before taking a bite.

"Kelly and Nash stopped by and dropped off food," he said, relaxing while she devoured the small meal.

More people who'd do anything for him. More people she now owed. "That was really nice of them."

He raised an eyebrow. "Family and friends are supposed to help each other," he said gently.

What could she say to that? They'd done it for him, not her, so she remained silent.

"Here. Take the pill. It should help the pain in about twenty minutes."

She smiled gratefully and did as he asked.

After he cleaned up the plate with the food and brought the dishes to the kitchen, he returned. "I think you'd be more comfortable if you changed clothes, don't you?"

She glanced down. Her legs were covered by a blanket but she knew her skirt had ridden up completely. Her shirt was wrinkled and now that he'd mentioned comfort, she realized her bra pushed at certain body parts, irritating her like crazy.

She'd love to change clothes. "In the top drawer in the dresser you'll find some things," she murmured.

He looked in the drawer and walked back to her with the only sleepwear she owned, a Victoria's Secret set of matching boxers and a tank top dangling from his fingertips.

She blushed at the sight of her small clothes in his much larger hand. "I hate feeling confined when I sleep," she murmured, sure her cheeks were flaming.

"No worries. I sleep stark naked," he said with a wink that was obviously meant to put her at ease and make her laugh.

But his words had the opposite effect, since all she could think about now was that gorgeous, tanned body lying beside her in bed. The current in the air was suddenly charged and electric.

"Do you need help changing?" he asked, that gruff voice back.

She swallowed hard. "I think I can manage. If you just . . ." With her fingers, she indicated he should turn around.

Like a gentleman, he faced the door and she slowly maneuvered her old clothes off and her pajama clothes on, aware of the few seconds she bared her breasts and exposed her pink lace bikinis.

"You had some phone calls," he said as she changed.

She'd appreciate the effort at normal conversation if his voice didn't sound strangled and tight. He was as aware of the fact that she was changing as he was.

"I was going to let it go to the answering machine, but I didn't want the ringing to wake you," he continued.

"You can turn back now," she said, finally dressed. Or as dressed as Victoria's Secret would allow.

He faced her again and walked closer to the bed.

"Who called?" she asked.

"Your brother . . . and your parents."

Her stomach cramped and she folded her arms across her chest. "What did they want?"

Dare set his jaw, wishing he could avoid this particular conversation. His brief talk with her family members had given him a glimpse into her life that was truly painful.

"Brian wasn't sober, so I wouldn't worry about what he had to say." There'd been a lot of whining and talk of how she should have let him take his turn against the cop. No mention of an apology nor did he ask how she was feeling. In fact, Dare wondered if he'd even remembered what had happened.

"Where is he?" she asked, unable to meet his gaze.

"I know that someone from the department drove him home and confiscated his car keys, so he's home. He'll have to come down to the station to get them when he's sober."

"And my parents? I'm guessing someone called and told them what happened?"

In Dare's mind, this was a tougher revelation. "Yes. They'd heard about Brian's scene."

"And that he hit me?" she asked, her eyes wide in her pale face.

He nodded.

"And? Don't hold back on me. Wait, I'll make it easy on you and tell you what they said. How could I let Brian make such a public scene? Why didn't I stop him? Is he okay, or should they come home and be with him?" She stared at him, her expression hard. "Well? Which one was it?"

He swallowed over the lump in his throat. "A combination of all three. After they got past the fact that a strange man had answered your phone and how would that look to their friends here. I explained that I was a local cop as well as a friend who was just

130

here looking out for you until you could take care of yourself."

Liza blew out a long stream of air. "You shouldn't have wasted your breath. They don't care about me."

Though he wished he could argue, his quick talk with her parents merely confirmed what she thought. Which really made him sick. They hadn't asked about Liza or her condition. Their only concern was for Brian or, more accurately, Brian's behavior and how it reflected on them.

"You really stepped into a lot more than you bargained for by helping me."

"Why? Because your family is as dysfunctional as mine?" He shook his head, amazed that she really couldn't see it. "You do know the infamous Barron family history, right?"

"I know your parents died in a car accident," she said softly. "But I'd switched schools by then and Brian started getting into real trouble . . . so not really."

"Are you sure you want to hear it? It's a long story."

She smiled. "I have nowhere else to be and you volunteered to hang out here, so you might as well make yourself comfortable," she said, laughing.

The sound settled inside him. He preferred this lighter, warm version of Liza. "Is

131

the pill kicking in?" he asked.

"Mmm-hmm." She patted the space beside her. "So come tell me a story."

He grinned and accepted the invitation, easing back into bed. To his surprise, she curled into the crook of his arm, resting her head on his chest. Man, that pill vanquished her inhibitions, he thought, his every breath filled with the scent of her shampoo. He was hard and aching. He wanted her badly.

Good thing he knew just how to take the edge off that particular problem. "My family was a mess even before I knew they were," he admitted. Yeah, that took the edge off his desire, all right.

Until he felt her easy breathing against his chest.

"Keep going," she murmured. "It takes my mind off the pain."

"Well, it turns out my dad was having an affair with his assistant. I didn't know. I'm not sure my brothers knew. We just knew it wasn't always happy around the house. Ethan stayed out more and more and got into trouble. One night when I was fifteen, he was arrested for joy riding. My parents went to bail him out and they were killed by a drunk driver."

She sucked in a breath. "I'm so sorry."

"It's been a long time," he assured her. Yet

the pain accompanying those words never went away. "Ethan was eighteen. Nash and I thought he'd take care of us, but . . ." Dare shook his head, still unable to believe what happened next. "He took off without a word."

"God."

He found comfort in her presence and began to run his hand up and down her arm, her bare skin soft to the touch. "We ended up in the foster care system. Nash went to the Rossmans."

"I don't think I really knew this," she murmured.

"You'd have been away at school by then."

"Stuart Rossman's parents?"

"That's them."

"You didn't go with him?"

He shook his head. "It's a long story." And one he wouldn't get into now, since ultimately it involved the night her brother threw the party and the punch that killed the couple's son. He had no desire to get into a discussion over her brother or that part of his past. "It wasn't the right place for me, so I ended up with the Garcias on the other side of town."

She struggled to sit up but Dare held her in place. He didn't want her looking into his eyes and seeing his pain, his guilt, or anything else. "You need to rest, so keep still and relax," he said.

Liza immediately snuggled back into him. "Was it bad?" she asked.

"It was livable. A lot of kids, which made it easy for me to fly under the radar. And Nash used to bring me his old clothes and extra food at school." And though he was grateful, he still felt so damned guilty accepting anything from the couple at all.

"What happened when Ethan came home last year?" she asked, perceptively jumping ahead to the real family drama.

"Nothing good. Nash and I wanted nothing to do with him and I doubt we would ever have made peace if it weren't for Tess." As always, he couldn't help but smile when he thought of his half sister. "She was the result of the affair we didn't know my father had."

"Ouch."

"Yeah. Kelly is her half sister too. They share the same mother and she's another story all on her own. But she abandoned Tess, and when Kelly couldn't deal with her anymore she dropped her off on Ethan's doorstep for the summer. And that's what forced us to come to terms with the past and with each other."

"And you're all living happily ever after?"

she asked.

"Nothing so fairy tale–like, but yeah, we've become a solid unit."

"You're so lucky," she whispered.

Dare was uncomfortable, his arm falling asleep. He readjusted his position on the bed, helping Liza settle into the pillows beside him. Then he propped himself up on his other arm and met her heavy-lidded gaze.

"You need sleep." The pain pill had obviously kicked in.

"Soon but not yet." Her brown eyes studied him earnestly. "I like talking to you."

Dare smiled. "I do too." In fact, he couldn't remember the last time he'd bared his soul to anyone about his childhood, but he couldn't regret having done it with Liza. "Your turn, though."

He knew the medication had lowered her inhibitions, but that didn't mean he minded getting whatever information she wanted to give.

She yawned and he thought that would be the end of their sharing.

"My parents should never have had kids."

He was wrong and he couldn't be more pleased she was opening up to him.

"But they had me and then they had Brian. I don't know why, but I was always in the way. Brian was the golden child, the boy who made Dad proud just by being born. But even with that, my parents couldn't really be bothered with us. They were rarely there. Even when they were present, they weren't there."

Her eyes had glazed over with the memories and Dare hesitated to interrupt. Her voice was slurred a bit and he knew she didn't have much more talking left in her.

"So Brian started acting out early on. He ran with a rough crowd, my parents never knew where he was and he'd always come home drunk or high."

She frowned, which wrinkled her nose, and it was all Dare could do not to lean over and kiss her right then and there.

"And then there was that party . . ." She shook her head.

That she didn't groan in pain told him the pills were definitely working. And knowing where she was headed next, Dare almost wished he could take one of those pills too.

"I was supposed to be home that night keeping an eye on him because my parents had grounded him and taken his car keys. But I'd just started going out with this older guy and he kept begging me to go out with him that night." She exhaled hard. "I agreed. I figured since Brian couldn't take the car, I could leave for a couple of hours and come back home after."

Dare didn't ask what happened next. He already knew.

"What I didn't know was that Brian had told Jesse — that's the guy I was seeing — that as long as he brought him a keg of beer, he wouldn't tell my parents I ditched babysitting."

"So that's where the alcohol came from."

"I felt so guilty," she said, her voice cracking.

"Hey, you did a normal teenage thing. You weren't the one who bought alcohol for minors."

"But I brought Jesse into Brian's orbit and I bailed on my responsibility. If it weren't for me, Stuart Rossman would still be alive."

Apparently Dare wasn't the only one who suffered with major guilt from that one night. He wondered if the only one who didn't was the man who threw the deadly punch.

"Baby, there's a lot of blame to go around," he assured her.

"You called me baby again." Her eyes lit up at the endearment that slipped so easily off his tongue. "I like it," she admitted.

He liked *her*. Reminding himself she was injured and in pain, he curled his fingers into fists, preventing him from reaching for her. In time, he promised himself.

Right now she needed something different. "I don't think you're in any way close to being responsible," he assured her.

"Too bad my parents didn't agree with you," she said in a small voice. The sparkle disappeared from her eyes. "Brian was my responsibility and I failed him. He never would be as bad as he is now if that night hadn't happened."

She sounded like she was repeating words that had been ingrained in her over the years. Words that were untrue and absolved the wrong person of guilt and Dare's anger at Brian returned.

"I'm so sorry," she said.

"Is that why you keep bailing him out?" Dare asked.

"It's part of it," she said over another yawn.

One more question, he thought, and then he'd shut up and let her sleep. "What's the other part?" he asked.

Sleepy brown eyes met his. "Brian was there for me when I needed him. When nobody else would have bothered," she murmured, her eyes closing, her words trailing off.

"Liza?" he asked softly.

No answer.

Well, he wouldn't be learning anymore about her tonight, but he'd already discovered so much about who she was and what made her tick.

What a number her parents had done on her, Dare thought, and blew out a frustrated breath.

No wonder she kept bailing Brian out and making excuses for his behavior. It was all she'd been taught, all she knew how to do.

All these years Liza had been shouldering the blame for her brother's actions and in her mind, she was making up for failing him way back when. Dare fought to control the anger surging inside him at the damage her parents had done. Ironically, with their choices, they'd hurt both their children, including the golden boy they so wanted to protect.

Dare watched Liza sleep, emotions rioting inside him he couldn't name or understand. Soft feelings for a woman he was coming to know and the need to shield her from any more pain. And not just because he was a cop and to serve and protect was his motto.

Liza woke up entangled with a hard male body wrapped around hers and awareness hit her immediately. Her back was to Dare, her head beneath his chin, his arms holding her tight and one leg was wrapped around hers. She ought to be mortified, but she liked the feeling too much to ruin it. Instead, she breathed in deeply, taking a minute to savor the heady sensation of heat and awareness surrounding her.

Her head still hurt but not with the same deathly intensity as it had yesterday, for which she was grateful. The last thing she remembered was their deep talk about family. He'd revealed painful memories and she'd admitted to embarrassing truths. In her mind that made them even and again she refused to be embarrassed.

The problem was she'd opened up to him in a way she'd never done before. Something about Dare Barron inspired trust and the thought was beyond frightening. She knew she ought to give in to the impulse demanding she slam up walls between them, but he'd stepped up to take care of her and in her eyes that was huge. She couldn't hurt him by freezing him out, and besides, that wasn't what she wanted.

She wanted him. As long as she remembered that his presence in her life was temporary, she could enjoy the short time they had.

She lay in silence and listened to his deep,

even breathing. Every place his body touched felt hot and sensitive and the longer she remained cocooned in his arms, the more aroused she became.

Suddenly she became aware of a change in his breathing pattern and a few seconds after that she felt his erection swell and harden against her back.

He was awake.

"Good morning," she murmured.

"No need to ask how you knew." His deep chuckle reverberated throughout her already-tingling body and he started to pull away but Liza grabbed his arms.

"Going somewhere?" she asked, wanting to keep him right where he was.

"Feeling better?" he countered.

She couldn't help but smile, not that he could see. "Depends on your definition of better. I'm alive, and even though my head hurts, it's not as bad as yesterday."

She pushed herself forward, separating them only so she could roll over and look into his eyes. "Thank you for staying with me," she said, truly meaning it.

"My pleasure. I didn't mean to fall asleep in here."

"It's fine." She'd actually slept better with him here. She was normally a light sleeper, hearing everything all around her, and though the pain pills probably accounted for her deep sleep, a part of her recognized his presence soothed her. Which scared her. She didn't want to like anything about having him here beyond appreciating his care and enjoying his company. She couldn't let herself depend on anyone.

"It definitely wasn't a hardship," he said. "Well, until a few minutes ago, anyway."

Despite herself, she grinned, knowing he was teasing her about waking up with his erection snuggled against her back, a hot sensation that still caused a delicious tingling between her thighs.

She took in his disheveled morning look, the messy hair, the razor stubble, and the intensity in those chocolate brown eyes. A girl could melt in that gaze. There was no harm in admitting that truth in her mind, if nowhere else.

"Didn't I warn you not to look at me like that?" he asked.

She licked her dry lips, words eluding her.

He reached out and ran his thumb over her bottom lip, the simple touch sending currents of electricity to strategic body parts. She couldn't pretend to be immune to him even if she wanted to.

She didn't.

"What if I can't?" she asked on a whisper.

Something about this man caused her to ignore every warning bell in her head.

"Baby, you already know the answer to that."

She supposed she did. "Dare?" she asked softly.

He eased in closer to her. "Yeah?"

She swallowed hard. They were so close. In her bed. She was in her barely there tank and shorts. He, she realized, was still in a T-shirt and jeans.

Waiting for her to speak.

"Kiss me," she said, opting for the simple request.

He groaned and eased himself over her, careful not to jostle her head. The big bad cop could be so gentle when he wanted to be, she thought, as his lips closed over hers.

His kiss was feather light and soft, starting at one side of her mouth, kissing her, licking at her lips, tasting her slowly, reverently as if she would shatter. If he kept up this sensual assault, she just might. The light nibbles with his teeth, the soft sweeps of his tongue, and the oh-so-tender caress of his thumb over her cheek were devastating to her senses.

He clearly didn't want to overwhelm her, was taking his time, being careful, and that care did more to break down her defenses than anything else might have. When he slid his tongue over the seam of her lips, her entire body trembled with desire, and then finally he slid his tongue past her lips to take possession.

And possess her he did. His tongue gliding over every part of her, each sweep taking her deeper and deeper into a web of longing that took her beyond thought, beyond reason. He kissed like he did everything else, with confidence and determination, sweeping her along with him.

She shook beneath him, needing him in every sense of the word. Needing to touch him, she slid her hands beneath his shirt, placing her palms over his heated flesh, feeling his taut muscles against her hand. He was hard and firm, just as she'd imagined. And all the while, he slid his lips back and forth over hers, letting her know with each kiss, each touch, how much he wanted her.

Clearly as much as she wanted him. Caution and rational thought fled as she scraped her nails over his flesh, moving upward to graze his nipples. He shuddered, letting out a low groan before breaking away, flipping over onto his back, one arm over his eyes.

They'd gotten carried away and she was grateful he'd been thinking when she obviously hadn't. She backed off too, and as she caught her breath, she became aware of the steady pounding in her head.

She heard a moan and realized the sound came from her.

He rolled to face her once more. "Are you okay?"

She didn't know what to say and remained silent.

"How is your head?" he asked, his breathing ragged.

Hers was too. "Hurts," she admitted.

"Which is exactly why I stopped. If we'd done anything more, you'd be hating me." He lifted himself up and leaned over for a long, gentle kiss.

One she couldn't and didn't want to resist. Fun and temporary, she reminded herself. The fun part would come when she was feeling better. The temporary wasn't something she wanted to dwell on. It merely had to linger in the back of her mind.

"Trust me, this isn't over, only delayed," he said, breaking the kiss.

"Promise?" She didn't know what had gotten into her.

He brought out a cheeky, playful side she hadn't known she possessed. Even in pain, she had to admit it felt good to just smile with someone.

"Oh, yeah." His sizzling stare promised

her more to come when she was better. "Now I'm getting up to bring you a quick bite to eat and your medicine."

"I'd like to try and get away with Advil only today."

"Only if you swear to take the heavy stuff if the ibuprofen doesn't work."

She raised her hand in the air. "Promise."

Before he could stand, her phone rang and he glanced over at the nightstand. "Do you want me to get it?"

"If you don't mind."

He picked up the receiver. "Hello?" he asked, and as he listened to the caller, his features darkened. "She's not up to taking calls."

"Who is it?" she asked him.

He held up a hand. "Look, Montana, if she wanted to talk, she'd have picked up the phone. She's doing better but still in a lot of pain."

Liza winced, remembering yesterday's awkward incident.

"Yeah, I'll tell her you called," Dare muttered. He hung up the phone and glanced at Liza. "I suppose you got that?"

She shut her eyes and sighed. "I asked him to meet me at the fair because he's new in town. I thought I'd introduce him to some people." She bit her lower lip. "When we got there, I realized he thought it was a date."

Dare's dark glare almost had Liza retreating to the edge of the bed. There was something almost proprietary in that look, but she refused to let herself read too much into it. Because if she did, and Dare was getting possessive over her, she'd have to end things sooner rather than later.

And she hadn't gotten nearly enough of him to walk away just yet.

SEVEN

By Sunday night, Liza was well enough for Dare to leave, and by Monday morning she was able to go to work. She didn't make it to the office on time, but she blamed being late on a lack of sleep more than her head injury. She didn't like the reason. Since Dare left after dinner on Sunday, she'd been restless and found herself tossing and turning until well after midnight.

She arrived at the office at 10:00 A.M. Monday to find that her employees were all waiting and worried about her. It warmed her to know they cared and she had to admit they all seemed genuinely concerned. She hadn't returned any phone calls over the weekend, which probably contributed to their worry. Luckily Jeff was out at a job site, which let Liza put off any awkwardness until another time.

After reassuring everyone that she was fine, Liza holed up in her office, where the first thing she did was make a list of people she needed to contact and thank.

Dare being at the top. It still overwhelmed her, how he'd stayed by her side. Sure they had chemistry, but nobody stepped up the way he had for eventual sex. No, Dare was a good man and for some reason that scared her even more than her abusive ex-boyfriend, Tim. Good men would eventually come to expect more and she didn't have it to give. Then again, he didn't seem to be pushing or asking for much of anything.

Live in the moment, she ordered herself. That's what she did best.

So she'd have to find a way to thank Dare, and then she added Nash and Kelly to the list. A few minutes later, she'd received a phone call from Faith, who insisted she come to the house for dinner tonight — because, after all, why should she have to worry about cooking and food after working a full day? Unable to say no, Liza wrote down Faith and Ethan Barron as well. Dare's family really pulled together for him and again she couldn't help wondering why they'd put themselves out for her.

Family and friends are supposed to help each other, Dare had said. But they were his family. His friends. She was merely an

149

injured outsider.

"Admit it, you're not used to people caring, period." She shut her eyes against the pain that thought caused, but it was the truth.

It was also the reason she hadn't returned her parents' phone call. They didn't care how she was holding up — they only wanted to make sure she took care of Brian. If they cared so much, she often wondered why they hadn't just stayed in town and handled him themselves, but the answer was obvious. He might be their favorite, but that didn't mean they still weren't the same two selfish people they'd always been. Why take responsibility when they had Liza to do it for them?

She rubbed her hands over her forehead, wondering if the pounding in her temples was due more to stress than the injury she'd sustained to the back of her head.

A knock sounded on her door. "Come in," she called, grateful for the distraction from her thoughts.

The door opened and Liza caught sight of a big spray of flowers, carried in by Bianca. "Someone has a delivery," she said with a smile, and placed the pretty arrangement down on Liza's desk. "Who are they from?"

Liza hadn't a clue. "Let's find out." She

looked at the flowers and surrounding tissue paper, searching for a small envelope or clue to who'd sent it. "No card. How odd."

"Maybe whoever sent them just assumes you'll know who they're from?" Bianca said, wriggling her eyebrows for emphasis. "Like a certain police officer who was extremely possessive over you the other day."

Liza shivered at Bianca's choice of words. She'd had enough of possessive men to last her a lifetime. "What do you mean he was possessive?"

"You don't remember Jeff trying to get near you after you were hurt? Officer Barron wasn't letting anyone close. Especially another man." Bianca let out what sounded like a dreamy sigh. "I wish a hot guy would get all alpha over me like that."

Liza shook her head, immediately regretting the motion. "I don't remember much of what happened right after," she said.

But she did recall Dare's dark look when Jeff had called her home the other day. She'd thought his actions were protective, not possessive. Still, she'd never thought Tim's jealousy over her college friends, women and men both, would have led where it had. No, she didn't think Dare was anything like Tim, but the reminder put her on edge.

Since she didn't intend to go down memory lane with Bianca, she deflected with a joke. "Trust me, you wouldn't have wanted the hit in the head that inspired Dare to come to my rescue."

"Good point," Bianca said, her eyes narrowing with worry. "Are you sure you're up to being back?"

"I'm fine," Liza assured her.

"Good. So are you going to call Officer Barron and thank him?" Bianca asked, settling into the chair across from the desk and staring at Liza.

"I will when I'm alone," she said pointedly. Yet she was unable to suppress a grin at Bianca's eagerness to watch her call Dare.

"Fine." Bianca raised her hands in defeat. "Don't let me live vicariously through you. I'll just have to find my romance in a good book or something."

She let out an exaggerated sigh and Liza rolled her eyes. "This from the woman who has a date almost every weekend?"

Bianca grinned, then rose and let herself out.

Alone at last, Liza placed her hand on the phone, knowing she should call Dare yet feeling awkward anyway.

Before she could gather her courage, another knock sounded at the door. "Come in," she called out again.

This time her visitor wasn't as welcome. "Brian."

"I'm so sorry," he said. "I didn't even know I hit you until Mom and Dad called me the next day. I can't believe someone would rat me out to them."

Liza set her jaw, which didn't help the pounding in her head. "Is any of that supposed to make me feel better?"

He ran a shaking hand through his hair. "I'll stop drinking, I promise."

Moisture filled her eyes but she held back tears. "Don't make promises you can't keep, Bri. But if you want to do something for me —"

"Anything," he said, sounding sincere. His hazel eyes bore into hers.

"Get help."

"Except that."

Pain exploded inside her head. "For heaven's sake, why not? You can't stop drinking without support and therapy!"

"No damned outsider can begin to understand!" he said, the pain and distress on his face all too real.

"Maybe not, but there are other people just like you who can. I have the name of group counselors. Treatment centers. Any way you want to do this, I'm here for you," she pleaded, already reaching into her desk drawer where she kept the ever-growing stack of information for her brother.

Her heart pounded in her chest as she prayed he'd listen.

"I don't need help," he said through gritted teeth. "I can do this alone."

His words both disappointed and angered her. "Because you've done such a bang-up job so far?" she shouted at him, immediately wincing from the pain.

Brian ducked his head, not meeting her gaze. "I haven't really tried yet. Just give me another chance, Liza Lou."

Liza didn't answer and Brian walked out, his shoulders slumped in defeat. She released her hands that she'd clenched into tight fists and slumped back in her seat.

What a mess his life had become and somehow he was dragging her down with him. Knowing she'd just exhausted whatever reserves she'd had, Liza headed home to take a painkiller and crawl into bed. Hopefully she'd be better in time to join Faith and her husband for dinner.

"Stop pacing, Liza said she's coming. She'll be here. In the meantime you're making me dizzy," Ethan muttered.

Dare paused in his lap around his brother's family room. "Her assistant said she left work early. She didn't even make it till lunch." Which concerned him.

"And that's why inviting her for dinner was a good idea. So she doesn't have to worry about making it herself," Faith said. "Ethan's right. You need to relax."

"Otherwise you'll scare her off by moving in permanently to take care of her," Ethan said wryly.

Dare gave him the finger.

But when Liza was twenty minutes late and didn't answer her cell or home phone, neither Ethan or Faith argued when Dare drove over to her house to check on her.

Her car was in the driveway and his gut told him she was home, but when he rang the doorbell, nobody answered. He called her from his cell and when she still didn't pick up, he began banging on the door.

Finally, Liza answered. "Dare!" She looked surprised but not unhappy to see him and stepped back, motioning for him to enter.

"Are you okay?"

"I am. Really."

He scanned his gaze over her from head to toe, and though she looked like she'd just woken up, she seemed okay.

"Did Faith send you because I was late

for dinner?"

He wasn't about to admit he'd been pacing for the last forty minutes. "She was worried."

Liza nodded. "Well, I was just about to call her. I came home from work and took half a pain pill and fell asleep. I set the alarm, but I swear I must've hit snooze and I don't remember." She blushed. "I'm never late and I feel awful that they waited for me."

He waved away her concern. "Don't worry about it. Faith's the most understanding person I know. It's Tess and her stomach you have to worry about," he said, only partially joking.

"I just need a few minutes to pull myself together."

She was wearing her clothes from work, which were now wrinkled. Obviously she'd come home and crawled right back into bed. Too much too soon, something he'd already figured out.

"Look, I'll just be a few minutes and I'll meet you back over at Faith's, okay?"

He shook his head, knowing he wasn't about to walk away. "I don't mind waiting and driving you over. No sense getting behind the wheel if your head is still bothering you and you've taken pain meds."

She paused, obviously unsure, whether it was of him, of *them,* he couldn't be sure. Dare only knew that despite whatever reservations she had or barriers she wanted to erect, he intended to get past them.

Whatever it took.

"I'll bring you home whenever you're ready," he promised. "Even if it's in the middle of a killer dessert." He raised his eyebrows and waited for her to reply.

Her sudden smile took him by surprise and lit up her face. "Well, if you put it like that, then you must really not mind."

Did she really trust him so little? "I wouldn't have offered if I did."

While waiting in her family room, he made a quick call to Faith to let her know they'd be there soon. A few minutes later, Liza walked back into the room, wearing a pair of jeans and a loose T-shirt. She'd washed her face, which was now makeup free, and had pulled her hair into a loose ponytail. The casual look worked for her. In fact, he'd never seen any woman so effortlessly sexy in his entire life.

"Ready?" he asked.

"Just let me grab a bottle of wine. I can't drink, but at least I won't walk in empty-handed."

He smiled at her thoughtfulness, knowing

Faith and Ethan expected nothing more than her company, but she didn't understand that yet.

They drove to the house on the hill in comfortable silence. He'd just pulled into the driveway when Liza turned to him. "Before we go in, I meant to thank you earlier."

"Didn't we go over this before I left last night? No thanks are necessary. I wanted to be there for you." He'd wanted to spend the weekend with her.

He shut off the engine and turned to find confusion in her expression.

"I meant thank you for the flowers."

"I didn't send flowers." Though now he wished he had.

"Oh!" Her eyes opened wide, a flush staining her cheeks. "I just thought . . ."

"You received flowers today?"

She nodded.

"Was there a card?"

"No and I just assumed . . ." She glanced down and stared at her hands. "No wonder they say when you assume you make an ass out of you and me," she muttered.

Dare fought back the tide of jealousy rising inside him. "I honestly wish I'd thought of it, but they weren't from me. You have no idea who sent them?"

158

She spread her hands in front of her. "Not a clue. I guess I could call Millie's tomorrow," she said of the floral shop in town.

"Good idea. Could it have been your brother?" he asked, hoping for family and not competition.

"Not a chance." She raised her head, her eyes dull as she answered. "We had it out today, and believe me, flowers for me are the last thing on his mind."

"I'm sorry." Reaching over, he placed his hand over hers. No wonder she'd left work early and needed something heavy for the pain. He had no desire to force her to revisit her argument with her brother. "How about we go inside?" he suggested.

"Sounds good." She opened her door before he could get around to help her. "I didn't realize you'd be here tonight," she said as they walked up the path leading to the front door. She paused before they headed up the steps, turning to face him. "But I'm glad you are."

His reservations eased and he rang the bell. "Prepare yourself," he said, looking at her from the corner of his eye.

"What do you mean?"

The front door swung open and his half sister stood on the other side. Arms crossed over her chest, foot tapping in annoyance,

Tess stared from Dare to Liza and back again. "It's about time. I'm *hungry,* and because we're having real company, nobody let me eat first."

Liza raised an eyebrow at the hellion he called his sister. "You must be Tess. I'm Liza. I've heard a lot about you," she said.

"Yeah? What'd you hear?" Tess asked. "Anything good?"

"How about it's nice to meet you too?" Dare asked. He placed a hand behind Liza's back and led her inside.

"It is nice to meet her," Tess muttered. "It's hard to be polite when my stomach's growling."

Liza laughed. A real laugh, the sound actually light and carefree. "I know that feeling. I wasn't feeling well and fell asleep. I missed lunch and almost slept through dinner, so I'm probably as hungry as you."

Dare frowned at her admission. The woman was probably more hungry. Tess was a bottomless pit, but she was constantly snacking. "You need to eat if you're going to keep up your strength."

"Dare? Liza?" Faith walked into the hallway and straight over to Liza, pulling her into a hug. "I've been so worried about you!"

At the other woman's sincerity and

warmth, Liza nearly broke into tears. "Thank you. I'm okay, really." She drew a deep breath, pulling herself together. "I've had a really good caretaker."

"If you're talking about my brother, that's pretty hard to believe," an unfamiliar male voice said.

Liza stepped back and looked up at the man who had to be Faith's husband, the oldest Barron brother. Like Dare, Ethan had brown eyes and even darker hair. She vaguely remembered him from when they were younger as a bad boy on a motorcycle.

"You must be Ethan." Liza stepped forward. "Thanks for having me to dinner," she said with a smile.

"Any friend of Faith and Dare's . . ." he said, extending his welcome.

"Ahem. Can we eat now?" Tess asked, her annoyance clear.

"We're still working on her manners," Dare explained.

Faith nodded. "No matter how hard we try, she insists on acting like the Neanderthal of the family. Let's go into the dining room." Prodding the girl in the back, Faith edged her forward.

Rosalita, who Faith reminded Liza had been around since Faith was a little girl, served a delicious chicken dinner. Liza was starving and truly appreciated the good food.

"Thank you so much for having me," Liza said to Faith. "You're right. I wouldn't have been up to making anything for myself."

"I had a concussion last year, so I completely get it." Faith offered her an understanding smile.

"Really? What happened?" Liza asked.

Tess cleared her throat loudly. "So, you're Dare's new girlfriend?"

Liza nearly choked on her water.

Beside her, Dare let out a groan. "I am so going to kill you," he muttered to his sister.

"Tess! Cut that out," Ethan scolded the teen.

"Sorry. That's Tess's way of changing the subject," Faith explained. "She doesn't want to talk about how I got my concussion," Faith explained.

Tess met Liza's surprised gaze and grinned shamelessly. With her blue eyes and lighter brown hair, she resembled Nash more than her other brothers. But her impish grin was pure Dare.

"So you're not his girlfriend?" the teenager asked.

"I'll answer that if you tell me how Faith ended up with a concussion." Liza raised her eyebrows, determined to hold her own with the teen.

"Touché," Dare said, and beneath the table he reached over and squeezed her leg in silent support. Of course his grip on her thigh had the effect of sending a pure bolt of desire sizzling throughout her body and she found herself reaching for her water glass once more.

Tess, meanwhile, looked at Liza with something like admiration in her baby blues, but she still had a determined expression on her face that made Liza wary.

"Okay, no girlfriend talk. So . . . I heard your brother has a mean throwing arm," the teenager said next.

"Tess!" Every adult with the last name of Barron yelled at the teenager at the same time.

Liza shifted uncomfortably in her seat.

In the silence that followed, Liza realized Dare was staring at his sister with distinct anger in his gaze. Liza didn't want to be the cause of problems and was about to nudge Dare to let it go when Tess spoke.

"Sorry," she said, looking at Liza. "I was just kidding."

"Some things aren't funny," Dare told her.

"That's okay, Tess. I'm just not used to big joking families." Liza didn't know what possessed her to admit such a thing, but though Tess had a smart mouth, she didn't seem to mean any harm.

And a part of Liza wanted Dare's sister to like her, she realized, the thought taking her by surprise.

"Okay, then," Faith said. "Let's talk about something else."

Tess nodded, picked up her fork and began to eat once more. Liza followed her cue. Thankfully, the rest of the meal passed with easy conversational talk about things like scheduling a meeting in the next few weeks to go over the fund-raiser details, Tess's art and school, and other innocuous things. All earlier tension gone, the easy banter returned, and an hour later Liza realized she'd just experienced the real Barron family.

The night showed Liza that her instincts about Tess were right. She hadn't gone after Liza to be mean. Tess tested everyone in her orbit. Over and over again. She held nothing back, not in teasing her siblings or showing surprising moments of openness and vulnerability, and in return the Barrons gave back to Tess in equal measure.

The overwhelming emotion at the table was love and acceptance. It was obvious this family had become a unit, no matter how hard the road getting there had been. For anyone else, the night might have been normal, but Liza's experience with family was anything but. She'd never been on the receiving end of love or acceptance, and Liza grew increasingly uncomfortable despite the fact that they all tried to include her in the conversation. She was grateful Nash and Kelly weren't there or she would have been even more overwhelmed.

She hadn't realized she'd completely spaced out on what was going on around her until Dare placed a hand on her shoulder.

"Ready to go?" he asked quietly, so no one else could hear.

Liza blinked, startled.

"Unless you want dessert, but you look exhausted and I'd guess your head hurts?" he asked softly. His understanding gaze told her he knew she'd had enough.

Her head had begun to throb and her anxiety level had kicked up a notch. His suggestion came just in time and she nodded.

"I'm going to take Liza home," Dare said to Ethan and Faith.

"Thank you so much for dinner," Liza said. "It's just been a long day."

"It's been a long weekend, I imagine." Ethan's wry tone expressed a combination of seriousness while still mocking his brother.

Liza couldn't help but grin.

Dare pulled out her chair and Liza stood. They said their good-byes, and as Liza passed by Tess the teenager slipped her one of the precious chocolate-chip cookies she'd taken from the kitchen while Rosalita had her back turned.

As acceptance went, Liza was officially blown away.

Dare walked Liza up to her front door. She'd been deliberately quiet on the drive back home, and as if sensing her need, he'd left her alone with her thoughts. Liza had used the time to compose herself and think about how her insular existence had changed in such a short time. Her brother had gone over the edge and Dare Barron had insinuated himself into her life.

She didn't mind his presence. Far from it. She liked him too much, even if his family could be overwhelming. And though she hadn't been good company and she'd been asleep more often than awake, he seemed to want to spend more time with her too.

The sun had dipped below the horizon and the lights outside her house had gone on while the summer heat pulsed around them.

It seemed the right time for questions to be answered. "So how did you know I needed to leave?" She'd been wondering since he'd declared it was time for them to go.

His eyes twinkled with amusement as he shrugged his broad shoulders. "A hunch."

"It was more than that. It's like you *know* me." As well as she knew herself. He'd picked the exact moment her flight instinct was kicking in.

He exhaled a long, hard breath. "It's more like I can read you."

She let herself process the statement and it made her squirm. Not that he'd be able to read her but that he'd want to try. Thanks to the humidity she'd broken into an uncomfortable sweat, which didn't help the discomfort in her head. She searched her purse and found her key.

"Do you want me to come in?" he asked before she could invite him.

She didn't hesitate and merely nodded, hoping she knew what she was getting herself into with this man.

She locked up after him and leaned against the door, palms braced behind her.

"Now where were we?" he asked. "Ah, yes.

I said I'd read you. And realized you were uncomfortable with my family. Not that I blame you. They can be overwhelming on a good day and Tess wasn't exactly on her best behavior."

"I like her, though." Liza couldn't help but grin. "And it's not that I don't like your family. I do. A lot. I definitely appreciate how nice they've been to me."

"I know. But you withdrew into yourself at dinner. You'd stopped talking, you weren't listening to anything anybody said." He raised his hand before she could argue. "You were polite and friendly, but I could tell you weren't comfortable."

"Am I that obvious?" she asked, embarrassed.

"Only to me, I hope." His intimate smile heated her from the inside.

She bit the inside of her cheek. "You're right. I was uncomfortable," she admitted. "I'm not used to close friends and family."

He nodded, his understanding gaze meeting hers. "I know that too and I wanted to give you the space you needed. And I'll make sure you aren't put in those situations often."

She raised an eyebrow, surprised by his words. Enough that her breath caught in her throat. Her flight instinct was screaming at her again, but she understood she was facing a crucial moment. He'd given her an opening, one where she could find out what exactly he wanted from her and whether it was something she was willing to give.

Before she lost her nerve.

Liza ran her tongue over her lips. "Umm, just why would I be in that situation again?"

"I'd think that was obvious. He grinned and stepped closer. "Because I hope you'll be seeing a lot more of me." He said *hope,* but he spoke with the certainty of a man comfortable in his own skin. Comfortable with himself and with her.

He was irresistible, Liza thought, which meant one thing. She was in deep trouble.

EIGHT

Dare took a step closer to Liza, crowding her against her front door, wanting to be sure they had a clear understanding. "Did you hear me? I want to see a lot more of you."

She ran her tongue over her lips. On any other woman he'd take it as a tease. With Liza, he knew it was an honest statement of nerves. "I want that too," she said.

He smiled and brushed her hair off her shoulder, pleased to see her tremble. "Good."

"But Dare?"

"Hmm?" He leaned in and inhaled her fragrant scent. His body hardened immediately.

"I don't do relationships."

He stiffened but didn't back away. He wasn't about to let her innate fears rule what he knew could be damned good. "Let's clarify that." He placed a kiss on her jawline. "You want to see me too?" He followed that question with a lick of his tongue.

"Mmm hmm." Her words came out like a moan.

"Well, I don't share. So if you're seeing me, you won't be seeing anyone else. Agreed?" He braced one hand on the door behind her and nuzzled her neck. Damn, she tasted sweet.

She exhaled a trembling breath. "As long as when you're with me, you're following the same rule."

He swallowed a pleased laugh. "That's fair. So, is there anyone you need to end things with before we . . ."

She ran a finger down the razor stubble on his cheek. "No, anyone I've seen is in the city and to be honest, it's just an occasional thing that has no strings, no expectations."

"What about that work guy?" He hated asking but he had to know.

"Just a work guy. I don't date co-workers and I'm not interested in him anyway." She paused. "What about you? Any women who might come after me with a butcher knife? Boil a bunny in my kitchen?"

He tipped his head back and laughed. "Hell, no. I don't do those kinds of games. I already told you I'm a relationship guy.

When I'm with a woman, I'm with her."

Needing to taste her, he followed a trail of kisses up her neck until he was at her ear and bit down on her lobe. Her knees shook and her response to him eased any lingering jealousy.

"You're kind of a rare breed, huh?" she asked him.

He hoped she'd find that a good thing. "I'm just me." He kissed her sweet lips, licking lightly with his tongue. "And we're just us. And just so you know?" He deliberately paused a beat. "That's what I call a relationship," he murmured before sealing his mouth over hers.

The kiss started hot, letting him know she was equally invested — in sleeping with him at least. But he wasn't interested in a quick fuck and he certainly didn't plan on doing anything with her while she was injured. He'd already gotten what he wanted tonight, an acknowledgment that she knew he was in this and she wasn't pushing him away. So he slowed things down, trying to calm his body, and instead planned to do something he hadn't concentrated on in a while.

Enjoying a kiss.

He stepped back and grabbed her hand, leading her into the family room and over to the couch, where he pulled her onto his lap and picked up where he left off. Threading his fingers through her hair, he returned to her luscious mouth, kissing her slowly and thoroughly. She curled into him and they made out like they were teenagers. There was no other word for the greedy kisses they exchanged. He slid his tongue inside her mouth and he groaned at how good she tasted, how aroused she made him with just one kiss. Her fingers gripped his shoulders and little sighs of delight escaped from the back of her throat and made him rethink his plan to just kiss her senseless and leave her to get some sleep. Obviously her head wasn't hurting all that badly after all.

He threaded his fingers through her hair and nibbled at her lips. "Mmm. I taste chocolate chips."

She laughed. "That's Tess's fault."

"Yeah, I saw her slip you a cookie. She likes you." He looked into her flushed face and glazed eyes. "So do I."

"I suppose you want me to say it?" she asked, blushing.

"I can handle it if you don't." But he wouldn't be happy.

She smiled and nearly blew him away. "I like you too. But don't let it go to your head. And don't think just because you seduced me into accepting your version of a relationship that I've changed my mind."

He forced an easy grin. "Wouldn't think of it. As long as we're on the same page."

She nodded. "For as long as we're together."

"Works for me." He wasn't going anywhere for a long while, he thought, and brushed another kiss over her lips. "Now let's get you tucked into bed. You're still recuperating." It wasn't what he wanted, but he had to make the suggestion.

Her frown gave him hope and his cock jumped inside his pants at the possibility.

"Do you think you're leaving me worked up like this?" she asked, deliberately squirming in his lap.

He blew out a relieved breath. "I hope not. But being a gentleman, I had to make sure you're feeling up to anything more."

He wanted to stay, Liza thought, and everything inside of her eased. She wanted the same thing. Because let's face it, he made her heart race faster and just being with him put a smile on her face. She could even learn to deal with the intimacy of being around his family every once in a while. He kissed that good. He took care of her that well. Not to mention he made her feel a whole host of other things she wasn't about to look into too deeply.

"I'm up to it," she assured him.

He grinned. "So am I."

"I see that. Or should I say I feel that." She laughed and wriggled in his lap.

"Okay, you. Up. Unless you want me to take you here on the couch."

To her surprise, the thought had its appeal.

"Didn't I tell you not to look at me that way unless you were prepared for the consequences?" he asked gruffly.

She hadn't realized she telegraphed her desire on her face and swallowed hard. "I don't believe you finished the thought last time. At least not in words." It had led to their first kiss, though, and her body flushed with heat at the memory and pulsed at the hope of going further tonight.

"That's it." Somehow he stood with her in his arms. "Bedroom?" he asked in a dark, desire-laden voice.

This was her last chance to say no. "What are you waiting for?" she asked him instead.

With a low growl, he headed for her room, and next thing she knew he laid her down on the bed. She took in the predatory gleam in his eyes and everything inside her went to liquid mush. Moisture slickened between her legs, dampening her panties. Her breasts felt full, her nipples hardened. And her stomach clenched with unfulfilled need.

All that from one look.

"I wish you didn't have to worry about being gentle," she admitted, wanting him with everything she was.

"Slow and easy's good for the first time," he assured her. "There'll be other times for hard and fast."

True to his word, he began to undress her at a leisurely pace, unbuttoning her jeans and pulling them down over her legs. He paused to run his lips over her bare skin, licking a delicious trail from her stomach down her calves, past the sensitive flesh behind her knees, to her toes, only to travel up again. With painful slowness that let her feel his lips over her skin, he finally returned by the same path, lingering on the inside of her thighs but skipping the parts hidden by her skimpy underwear.

She trembled beneath the sensual assault until his tongue dipped into her belly button, then worked its way down to the top of her panties and her stomach clenched in building need. He continued to torment her, his tongue trailing along her panty line until her clit throbbed painfully and the pulsing between her legs wouldn't be denied.

He ran one finger down the center of her sex.

Her hips arched upward against his hand and she let out a moan. "I wouldn't have taken you for a tease."

"It's not teasing, it's foreplay." His voice sounded richly decadent and she swallowed a sigh at the sexy rumble.

Dare merely chuckled and returned to his task. He hooked his fingers into the sides of her panties and pulled them down and off, revealing her to his heated gaze.

"Nice," he murmured, his eyes darkening.

She knew what he saw, having been to her favorite spa last week. She wasn't bare, but she was cleanly waxed, and he clearly approved, she observed, as he lowered his head and set about tasting her.

His warm mouth touched her damp heat and set her entire body on fire. He'd promised slow and steady and damn him, the man kept his promise. Long strokes of his tongue along her almost bare outer lips were merely a prelude and she raised her hips, pushing herself into his mouth, silently begging for what he wasn't yet ready to give.

His low chuckle sent hot air circling over her sex. "You want more, baby?"

She loved when he called her that. "Yes," she said on a hiss. "More. Please, more."

"Since you asked so nicely." Without warning, he parted her opening with his fingers and thrust his tongue deep inside.

She cried out, shocked that he'd elicited such a guttural sound. Liza liked sex, but this? Wow, the man had talent. He alternated between unexpected nips that at once stung and heightened her pleasure followed by soothing, loving sweeps that had her squirming beneath him, shifting then arching her hips as he drove her higher and higher still.

Could she come from this? She never had before.

Without warning, she had her answer, the building waves reaching a crescendo and crashing over her, taking her out of her body and mind. The incredible sensation went on and on and Dare didn't let it end quickly either. He stayed right where he was, nuzzling at her until the peak receded and she came back to earth, her body still shaking, her mind a puddle of mush.

"Good?" he asked.

A lazy grin edged her lips. "Amazing," she admitted, surprised she could speak. "Yet I feel strangely empty." As if to make her point, her hips rotated in needy circles, her body begging to be filled.

Before she could react in embarrassment for being so brutally honest, he pushed himself up and met her gaze, his brown eyes nearly black and full of need. "Then we definitely need to rectify that."

He didn't ask her if she was prepared. Instead, he pulled a single condom from his jeans' pocket. Though she might wonder later that he kept one on hand, as if the need arose often, right now she was simply grateful to avoid any lengthy discussions of their sexual past, and besides, she never had sex without protection.

She'd had enough taking. She needed to give as he'd given to her. She wanted to participate, to touch him. She held out her hand, silently asking him to place the wrapper in her palm.

Dare raised an eyebrow and complied.

She wasn't usually bold, but he made it easy, and the next thing Liza knew, she was opening the packet while Dare quickly stripped off his clothes and rejoined her, sliding beside her on the mattress.

His body heat wrapped around her as he brought his mouth down on hers. She moaned and opened for him, amazed at how right it felt to be with him this way. She still held the condom in one hand but used the other to work her way down his body, feeling the differences between his skin and the taut muscles beneath.

When her fingers reached his rigid flesh, she encircled his impressive erection, and he groaned low and deep, releasing another surge of moisture between her thighs.

"We'd better get on with it or it's going to be over too damned fast," he muttered.

Liza bit the inside of her cheek. "What happened to slow and steady?" she asked laughing, pleased she could work him into the same frenzy he caused in her.

He grasped her other wrist in his hand. "Put it on now."

"Yes, sir." She sat up and got the first real look at him naked. It was all she could do not to whistle in appreciation. He was tanned, hard, and strong. *A damned good-looking man,* she thought.

And while he was here, in her bed, he was all hers. On that notion, she sheathed him with the condom, rolling the latex slowly over his rigid shaft. His entire body shook and he seemed to grow harder and thicker beneath her touch.

She wanted him just as much and the thought made her smile.

"What's the grin for?" Dare asked, his entire body on edge as she finished her task.

She blinked once before she finally answered. "I do this to you," she said, sounding completely in awe.

"Yeah, you do." And it floored him too, the depth of his yearning. He wanted nothing more than to flip her onto her back and take her as hard and demanding as his body desired.

Unfortunately, he still had to worry about her concussion. "Your choice, baby. Top or bottom?" he asked. "Whichever will hurt your head less."

She jerked in surprise, but then her eyes softened in appreciation. Every time he did something for her, she seemed taken off guard. She'd had too little caring in her life and he hoped she'd come to realize that she deserved more because he certainly planned to give it to her.

Finally she lay back against the pillows and beckoned him with a crook of her finger.

So she wanted him on top. "This puts me in control and I don't want to hurt you." He had to be sure.

"Actually, this puts my head against soft pillows and you couldn't hurt me if you tried," she said, parting her legs and opening herself to him.

He took one look at her, hair spread wildly over the pillow, her soft body offered to him, and he smiled, easing himself up and over her. He breathed in the luscious scent he'd come to think of as unique to her.

He paused to kiss her, to let her know *she* mattered. Then he nudged his cock at her entrance, finding her slick and wet, eager and ready for him. He shook with the strength it took to hold back, needing to fill her as much as he was afraid to hurt her.

"You won't hurt me," she promised.

Had he spoken out loud? He had no time to find out. She reached between them and cupped his shaft in her hand, causing him to lose all semblance of restraint and control. He thrust inside, filling her, taking her, like she wanted.

Like he needed.

Finding her so damned hot and tight and perfect, he wished he could feel more, take her without barriers between them, but that was something he never did. Had never even considered before.

"Oh, you feel good," she said, her words a whisper in his ear.

"Yes." He slid out and back in, repeating the motion, easing his passage, letting her get used to him, his fullness, their friction.

Had he ever taken such care with a woman before?

"Dare?" she asked.

"Hmm." He met her gaze and brushed a strand of hair off her forehead.

"I changed my mind. I want to be on top," she said, hooking her leg around his.

He laughed, liking her honesty and her enthusiasm. The flip was easy enough to accomplish and soon he had her over him. She met his gaze, an aroused look in her eyes he'd never seen before and damned if it didn't make him harder.

She bent her knees on either side of him and pivoted her hips in a slow circle, groaning each time his pubic bone hit just the right spot. He gritted his teeth as she contracted around him. She'd wanted control and now she had it. He'd given it willingly and found it was even better with her on top, taking her pleasure, grinding herself into him as her breaths came in shallower gasps, her moans became deeper and sexier.

She took him along with her, milking him as her tight inner muscles brought him closer and closer to climax. He was too close too fast and he needed her with him when he fell over. Reaching out, he cupped her breasts in his hands, kneading the plump flesh before he focused on her already hard nipples, pinching them between his thumb and forefingers, rolling the tight buds until she cried out.

Pleasure? Pain? He wasn't sure and immediately released his grip, but she shook her head wildly.

"Don't stop, please don't stop," she urged him, and he grabbed for her breasts once more. She rocked her hips against him harder, her moans turning into cries of pure pleasure and he couldn't hold on another second, was going to explode.

"Come for me, baby," he urged her, tightening his hold on her breasts, thrusting his hips up, his cock higher, deeper, reaching for everything.

Then, as if he'd released the floodgates, she came apart, her soft cries melding with his, her body grinding against him as he pumped into her over and over again, coming along with her, lost to thought and reason. All he could do was feel, everything shattering inside him, then slowly, slowly rebuilding as he became aware of his surroundings again.

Liza had collapsed on top of him, her body pressed tight against his, and he wrapped his arms around her and held her tight. Slick with sweat, they lay together, her breathing harsh in his ears. He could barely catch his own breath. Seconds turned into minutes as neither of them moved.

He threaded his fingers through her hair and rolled them over, keeping her tight against him as he wondered.

What the hell had just happened? Because he'd sure never felt anything like it before.

Liza slept like a baby, she realized as dawn came, beams of sunlight streaming through her bedroom window. She'd slept curled into Dare and she awakened the same way, at peace. Except now she was aware and her mind couldn't stop spinning. Not with regrets.

Never those. Not after the most explosive sex of her life with a man who'd been so aware of her needs she'd had a lump in her throat more than once. And Liza didn't cry during sex. She didn't. The act had never moved her emotions to such an extent, but last night had been different.

Everything about Dare and being with him was different. Unique. And scary.

"You're up," he said, sounding too confident for a man who held her, her back to his stomach.

"How did you know?"

"Your breath is coming in shallow pants. Ready to bolt?" he asked tightly.

Caught, she expelled a long breath. "Would you let me if I tried?"

"Hell, no." His arms squeezed around her more tightly. "Then again, I won't force you to stay." He eased his grip giving her wiggle room if she wanted to roll away.

She stayed put. "I knew what I was doing last night. I'm not going to run away from you now." She'd fight her fears. She could handle a morning after, she told herself.

His tension seemed to ease and he turned her over for a long, leisurely kiss. One she eagerly returned.

"Morning," he murmured when he was through.

She smiled. "It is. Which means I'm going to be late if I don't shower," she said, truly disappointed.

She had to be in Connecticut early or she'd definitely want to spend the morning getting reacquainted with Dare and his amazing body. Once had been all he'd allowed last night. He was insistent on watching out for her head. Which, she realized, didn't hurt all that much this morning.

"I'd join you, but you'd never get out of here on time."

"I know." But visions of them together in her shower, warm water licking over his tanned skin, had her trembling.

"Go." He lightly pushed against her. "I'll make breakfast and shower when you're finished," he said, and headed for the kitchen, leaving her alone and sexually frustrated.

No doubt about it, she'd be thinking of him for the rest of the day, which had her wondering if that had been his intention all along.

Twenty minutes later, Liza had showered and dressed. Her head didn't hurt nearly as much as it had the day before. Dare Barron was more potent than any medication a doctor could prescribe. She'd enjoyed last night and was unwilling to let any stray thoughts get in the way this morning. She met him in the kitchen where he was finishing a bowl of cereal.

He wore his jeans, unbuttoned and slung low on his hips and no shirt, revealing the ripple and pull of muscle. Liza swallowed hard. She was suddenly hungry and it wasn't for food.

She looked him over, her gaze settling on the tattoo on his left arm. She'd been too busy focusing on his other body parts to pay much attention to it last night. Curious, she walked over and placed a hand on his shoulder.

"Hey." She settled in the seat next to him where he'd laid out a similar breakfast for her.

He looked her over, his hot gaze devouring her, and he whistled. "Nice outfit."

She couldn't withhold a smile. She'd chosen her favorite sexy beige suit and killer pumps just for him, not that she'd admit it. The man's ego was big enough.

"I thought you said you were making breakfast," she asked, glancing at the cold cereal on the table.

She did like teasing him.

"This is as good as it gets," he said with an easy shrug. "Might as well get used to it."

She wasn't about to touch the last part of that statement, she thought. "At least you make a mean toast and jelly."

"Glad you think so." He tilted his head in acknowledgment. "How's the head?" he asked.

"Much better, actually."

"Great." He smiled, obviously pleased she was feeling better.

She had no doubt he'd helped her speedy recovery. She glanced at him and once again her gaze found his tattoo. "Dare?"

"Yeah?"

She pulled her chair closer to him and lightly traced the tattooed band around his arm. He stiffened at her touch but didn't stop her from studying or touching the intricate design. At a glance it appeared to be a basic tribal band, but there was also what looked like a symbol woven into it that she couldn't see well, let alone decipher.

The one thing she did know was that she found the inking extremely sexy. "What does the tattoo mean?" she asked, genuinely curious.

"It's nothing," he said in a sharp voice that took her by surprise.

She jerked her hand back, hurt by his cold tone. She narrowed her gaze and studied his suddenly closed expression.

In an instant, the relaxed man she'd come to know over the last couple of days had vanished. The happy, easy-to-laugh, easier-to-smile guy had disappeared.

Shut her out was more like it and that hurt more than it should.

"It was just a question." She rubbed her arms, annoyed with herself for being bothered by the sudden chill.

He didn't reply.

This was why she didn't do relationships. Relationships involved emotion, and emotion led to disappointment. She looked at the cereal in front of her and decided she was no longer hungry.

She reached for the bowl, intending to put it in the sink, when Dare placed a hand on her arm. "Wait," he said.

She paused but remained silent.

"The tattoo has meaning. Deep, dark, personal meaning," he said, his stare on the table and not on her.

"So sorry I pried," she said, not hiding her sarcasm.

It wasn't okay for him to get into her head and her feelings about family, only to decide later that not only were there some things he wouldn't reveal, but that he would freeze her out for asking a simple question.

"Look, it's not something I usually talk about. People don't usually ask."

She hadn't realized she was just anyone. She stiffened, her pride and her hurt getting stronger with every word he spoke. "If that's supposed to help, it doesn't."

He exhaled hard, and though she could see this was difficult for him, she needed more than a surface explanation. But she wouldn't beg for him to let her in.

"Would it help if I said that if I was going to talk to anyone, it would be you?"

She blinked at the unexpected, softer admission. "Whenever you're ready," she heard herself saying.

"How about now?" he asked, surprising her in an equally soft tone.

She curled her fingers into a tight ball, angry at him for drawing out her feelings when she wanted to stay distant, to remain in a place where Dare and his emotions couldn't touch her.

But they did. "I'm listening," she said begrudgingly, because she still wasn't sure that he wanted to share this with her.

He raised his head and met her gaze. "I thought you had to get on the road?"

She had an early appointment in Mystic, Connecticut, to discuss the first phase of renovations with a client. "I was supposed to head over, but I got a text from my accountant. He needs me to stop by this morning before I leave."

Peter Dalton always arrived at the office before everyone else and left promptly at five, his work meticulously completed. If he'd contacted her so early, she knew it was important and probably had to do with her brother. Her stomach churned at the thought of more Brian drama, but that wasn't her concern at the moment. Nor did she want to discuss her brother with Dare.

Liza turned toward him. The pain in his face was unmistakable and she realized she shouldn't have been so sensitive. Whatever the story was behind the tattoo, it was deep and obviously important.

And he was willing to share it with her.

"I'm listening," she said softly, with more of her heart than she'd opened before.

"Remember we talked about the party your brother threw back when we were kids?" Dare asked, the words sounding torn from inside him.

She nodded, her stomach in even more knots now.

Before Dare could continue, the front doorbell rang.

Liza frowned, annoyed at the interruption. "Just ignore it," she said. She wasn't expecting company.

For all she knew it could be a neighbor and she didn't want anyone to interrupt his story. "Go on," she encouraged him.

The doorbell rang again, followed by loud banging.

"Someone's impatient," Dare said, turning in the direction of the sound.

With a groan, Liza rose to her feet. "I'll get rid of whoever it is," she promised. She headed to the door, Dare following behind her.

She peered through the small window that overlooked the porch, took one glance at her visitor, and muttered a very unladylike curse.

"Who is it?" Dare asked.

She shook her head, wishing she'd followed her gut and ignored the bell.

"Brace yourself," she muttered as she

opened the door. "Brian," she said, greeting her sibling who waited impatiently outside.

NINE

Liza stared at her brother while feeling the heat of Dare's body and probable glare behind her. She had to get rid of Brian and do it fast.

She braced her hand on the doorframe. "This isn't a good time."

Brian looked from Liza to Dare, who'd stepped around her, still bare-chested, as he took his place close by her side.

Blatant disbelief, then anger, flooded her brother's features. "What the hell is he doing here?"

She swallowed hard. "That's none of your business. You need to go and I'll call you later." She gripped the doorframe harder, her fingers aching under the strain.

As usual, Brian ignored her request. "I thought I was crazy when I saw an SUV in your driveway. I mean it's eight A.M. and you never have guys over."

"Brian!" She didn't need her brother

broadcasting her lack of a personal life now.

He shook his head. "How could you get involved with a *cop?*" He sneered the word as if Dare's profession disgusted him. Which it did.

A quick glance to her right told Liza Dare's jaw was set, but so far he was remaining silent. A fact that could quickly change given the tense set of his muscles. He was ready to pounce given the right provocation. And Lord knew Brian would have no trouble providing it, especially if her brother was not in control.

So far Liza couldn't tell. Though he was dressed for work, outward appearances didn't mean he wasn't hungover from the night before.

"What are you doing here?" she asked, resigned. It was obvious her brother wasn't leaving as she'd insisted.

"I'm not talking in front of him." Brian tipped his head toward Dare.

Liza blew out a stream of air. "Well, he's not leaving yet."

"Why? Because he's not dressed? Or because you haven't finished yet?"

Now she had her answer, and mortification swept over her. It was bad enough she had Dare witnessing yet another Brian moment, but now he was turning his anger on her. The brother she knew and loved would never talk to her like that before he started drinking.

"That's it," Dare muttered. Before Liza could react, he headed onto the porch. "It's time for you to leave," he informed her brother.

Brian narrowed his gaze. "It's not your house."

"I'm just repeating what your sister already said."

Dare's lazy shrug didn't fool her and she glanced from man to man, trying to figure out the best way to diffuse the situation.

"It's none of your business," Brian said belligerently, still pushing Dare when it was obvious the man was a simmering volcano.

Unable to think of a solution, Liza reached out and grabbed Dare's arm, hoping her touch would calm him before he let Brian provoke him into doing something he'd regret.

Anger pulsed through Dare and he didn't take his gaze off Liza's brother, who stupidly kept pushing Dare, obviously hoping to goad him into a fight.

Liza's nails dug into his forearm, but she didn't have to worry. Dare wouldn't do anything stupid. Still, someone had to shut this asshole up. Dare wouldn't allow him to insult Liza.

And she'd asked him to leave more than once. "It wasn't my business. Until you started insulting your sister. Now I'm making it my business. So you can leave now," Dare said, deceptively calm.

"Or what?" Brian puffed up his shoulders with a sneering sense of bravado.

Dare glared at the man, giving him more time to sweat, which he was already doing. Profusely.

"Brian, *go*," Liza pleaded.

"Like I said, or what?" The pigheaded man glared at Dare, not bothering to look at his sister.

At the station, when Dare was on duty, it was his job to deal with the trouble Brian McKnight caused and do it in a professional way. Nothing he was feeling now was remotely professional.

And Dare wasn't on duty.

Still, he braced his hand on Liza's back in an attempt to reassure her. "Or you'll be looking at more trouble than you can handle," he promised Brian.

The other man raised his hand as if ready to fight.

Dare shook his head at his stupidity. "It's one thing to hit a defenseless woman, McKnight. It's another to come after me."

Brian's eyes opened wide and regret flashed across his face. "Liza knows it was an accident."

Dare raised an eyebrow.

Liza said nothing.

"Liza Lou, I just need to borrow some money," he said in a little-boy voice. "Then I'll go."

Dare frowned, disgusted at the man's gall.

"You just got paid on Friday," Liza said, sounding stunned.

"I can't explain now." He shot another glare at Dare. "But I need your help."

Dare knew he was getting a firsthand look at the brother-sister dynamic and he didn't know how Liza handled the man.

Brian took a step toward his sister.

Dare blocked his way.

"Please, Liza?" Brian all but whined.

"Fine," Liza said, stunning Dare as she turned and hurried back inside.

She returned a second later, giving him no time alone with her brother.

She had her wallet in hand and Dare's eyes opened wide.

"Liza, come on. You know this isn't a solution."

She didn't meet his gaze but instead fumbled with the wallet and pulled out all the bills inside. "Here," she said, thrusting out her hand. "Take it. It's all I've got on me. Now will you go?" she asked, her voice shaking.

Disappointment rippled through Dare at the exchange.

"I need to talk to you later, though," Brian said.

Not a thank-you came from his mouth.

Liza remained silent.

Brian shot a smug and triumphant grin at Dare before heading for his car — a BMW 7 Series no less — and drove away.

Dare blew out a breath, unsure of what to think or say. He wanted to comfort Liza, but she'd just done the unthinkable, and inside he was torn.

Dare hated her brother with a passion born of years of regret, self-blame, and disgust. Brian's behavior in the time since they were kids hadn't allowed for Dare's attitude to soften. Not even now.

Not even for Liza.

The realization knocked the breath out of him and forced him to take a long look inward. When he'd gotten involved with Liza, he'd pushed her relationship to her brother to the back of his mind, to a place where he could pretend they weren't related and the past didn't exist. Even after McKnight had coldcocked his own sister, Dare had merely stepped in to help the woman he wanted, blocking out the reality that just hit him square in the face.

With Liza came this son of a bitch. And Dare didn't know if he had it in him to accept it.

Now or ever.

They headed back inside the house in silence. Dare couldn't bring himself to speak, and even if he could, he didn't know what to say. Last night had been incredible, the best sex of his life with a woman he'd wanted to know better. Today he couldn't see past the chasm between them.

He headed upstairs to get his shirt, and when he returned Liza had finished cleaning up the breakfast she hadn't eaten. She remained silent and he felt the hurt coming off her in waves. He knew he should say something to break the awful tension.

"All you did was enable him, you know." Dare winced at the words that unwittingly spilled from his mouth. Not the best choice at the moment, but at least it was the truth.

She flinched. "It's easy to judge something you can't possibly understand." She gathered her bag and her briefcase and together they walked out to their cars.

His Ford SUV was parked beside her white convertible. Nice but not something he could see her being too willing to repeat. Everything inside him rebelled at the thought of driving away and not seeing what else they could share, but the sight of her handing cash to her drunk alcoholic brother turned his stomach and brought up the past in vivid color.

The party. Brian throwing the punch at Stuart Rossman. His yell to either help clean up the mess before the cops came or to get the hell out, stepping around the injured kid as he went into panic mode. And Dare himself following his friends as they ran for the door.

"He's going to hurt someone — worse than he already hurt you — if he doesn't get the help he needs," Dare said.

"Do you really think I don't know that?" Liza turned to glare at him, her big brown eyes full of pain and betrayal.

He swallowed hard, knowing that, yes, it was easier to give advice than to take it. "Then stop making it so easy for him to keep doing it. He's got to hit rock bottom and if he has you to prop him back up, he never will."

"He's my brother," she said, her voice cracking. "You might not have had a relationship with yours for over a decade, but I have. And Brian was there for me. He saved me when —" She caught herself and clammed up, gripping her briefcase harder in her hand. "He's my brother," she repeated.

As if that was enough of a reason.

But Dare stayed focused on her other words. "How did he save you?" he asked, wondering where, beyond blood ties, her loyalty came from.

Because as sure as he was standing here, Dare knew she didn't condone her brother's drinking or his behavior, no matter how much she enabled it by helping him.

"It's nothing," she said in an icy cold tone that stung.

The same words and tone he'd used when she'd asked about his tattoo. He didn't miss the irony any more than he liked how it felt turned back on him.

His hand came to rest on the dark ink. It wasn't just a tribal band. Inside was the date of the party, the date Dare had done nothing and someone died. It had been a way to honor the kid's memory and to remind Dare of his promise to change how he lived his life. The inking of karma was a symbol for new beginnings without forgetting the sins of his past.

It wasn't "nothing," any more than whatever Liza was hiding from him now was.

Still, he doubted they'd get anywhere this morning. Not with tensions and hurt so high between them.

So when she turned to get into her car, he let her go.

He needed a breather and no doubt so did she. But he couldn't shake the memory of how he'd hurt her this morning. Twice.

He'd promised himself he wouldn't be another person who let her down and damned if he hadn't gone and done just that.

Liza drove up to her office. Every time she approached the old building that she used to visit when her grandparents worked there, she smiled. Her grandfather had renovated an old large Victorian, turning it into office space. Liza usually got a kick of pride that she was now in charge. No such kick hit her this morning. Instead, she was numb. This morning with Dare had been nothing like the night before, and, as much as she hated to admit it, the fault had been hers. Well, her brother's, technically, but in her mind it equaled the same thing. She couldn't change who her family was any more than he could change his. As furious as she was with Dare for judging her, at the same time, she understood why he hated her brother.

The question was, would he grow to hate her too?

She shook off the heavy thoughts and headed straight for Peter's office, wondering what was so urgent that he'd had to see her in person. It couldn't be good.

"Peter?" she said as she knocked on his open office door.

"Come in!" He rose as she stepped inside. Liza ran a business-casual office, but Peter always presented himself in a three-piece suit and today was no different. "Thank you for coming so quickly," he said, fixing his tie as he spoke.

"What's so important?" she asked, not wanting to give him any indication that she assumed the problem had to do with her brother.

He glanced down at his desk where everything was meticulously organized, rifled through a few file folders and pulled out the one he was looking for. "There's something unusual you need to see in Accounts Receivable," he said.

"Brian's department." She kept her tone neutral.

"Yes. You see, we have two checks made out to Annabelle's Antiques." Peter handed her two photographed copies.

Liza recalled the purchase. "We bought antique window frames from them." She'd chosen them herself. "Twenty-five hundred dollars a piece, as I recall."

"So why were *two* five-thousand-dollar checks issued?" Peter asked.

Liza looked at the papers he'd handed to her, confirming his words at a glance. "Did you check with the bank to see if they were both cashed?"

"Of course." Two red spots highlighted the man's cheeks. "I'm always thorough." He clearly bristled at her question.

"I didn't mean to offend you, Peter. I was just asking."

He cleared his throat. "Yes. I inquired. Both checks were cashed. However, the signatures on the back of each are markedly different. Poor bank oversight if you ask me," the man muttered.

Another glance at the next set of documents he handed her proved his assertion right. Both were signed in the name of Annabelle Block, but one had distinctly masculine handwriting on the endorsement. Handwriting similar to her brother's.

She felt the heat of Peter's stare as he waited for her to come to a conclusion. She'd already reached one that churned her already upset stomach. Just this morning

Brian had come begging to borrow money and now . . . What was going on here? He'd issued two checks and cashed one himself?

Or was she jumping to unwarranted conclusions and maybe this was just an innocent mistake. She bit the inside of her cheek. Only her brother or Annabelle Block, the shop owner would know. Liza needed to decide who to talk to first.

She glanced at Peter, who looked at her expectantly. "Thank you for being so thorough," she said to her accountant, careful to feed his need for approval.

She didn't want to alienate the man and put him on Brian's trail. Even if Accounts Receivable was his department, they'd both been careful to skirt the issue and not mention his name. She'd like to keep it that way for now.

"I'm very grateful you called me in to see this," she added.

"What do you want me to do?" Peter asked, obviously eager to help.

Liza gripped the papers tighter in her hand. She needed to look into this herself and if Brian was involved, figure out what he was up to before she involved the office or Peter directly.

She gave Peter a forced smile. "Just your normal work. I'll take it from here." She folded the papers he'd given her and put them in her oversized bag.

Liza glanced at her watch. "I have to get going. I have a meeting I'm going to be late for, but thanks again."

"Well, if you change your mind, I'm happy to call the account in question." Peter inclined his head, as usual, beaming with pride that he'd done his job so well.

Liza strode out of his office and was headed for the exit, preoccupied with thoughts of what Brian was up to and whether she should confront him outright or do a side investigation first. *Dare would know.* The errant thought brought her up short and she stopped in the entry hall.

She'd spent one night with him and she'd dropped defenses she'd spent years building, only to have him withdraw over the tattoo and then judge a situation he knew nothing about. He'd wormed his way in and hurt her in a short span of time. *Lesson learned,* Liza thought. Dare had nothing to do with her business or her problems with her brother. So while the cop might well have answers she needed, Liza was capable of figuring out what to do on her own. She had no intention of relying on Dare Barron again for anything.

She pulled herself together and started for

the door, bumping into Jeff as he entered through the other side.

Liza hadn't seen him since the awkward "this isn't a date" incident at the fair and she really wasn't in the mood to deal with him now.

"Jeff, hi!" Liza said, hoping all she'd be facing was a quick conversation between co-workers.

"It's good to see you," he said, his gaze looking her over. "How's your injury?"

"My head is doing pretty well. It still hurts occasionally and sometimes I have to take painkillers that knock me out. Which is why I didn't get back to you," she said, knowing she owed him an explanation.

She wouldn't tell him she'd been afraid he'd read too much into a return call. "But thank you so much for calling to check on me."

He nodded in understanding. "Frankly I'm surprised your watchdog told you I called."

"Dare told me," she assured him evenly.

"How did you like the flowers? I wanted to make sure you got them."

Liza blinked in surprise. "*You* sent the flowers?"

"You didn't know?"

She shook her head.

"No wonder you didn't call," he said, more to himself than to her.

Embarrassment flooded her. "I'm sorry I didn't acknowledge them, but there was no card and I just thought . . ."

Jeff's eyes widened in sudden understanding. "You thought your cop sent them," he muttered, and shook his head.

Liza gritted her teeth, a mixture of embarrassment and frustration filling her. Could this mess with Jeff get any worse? They'd had a great working relationship until she'd gone and screwed it up in a misguided attempt to be nice and invite him to meet her at the fair. So she could introduce him to people in town, not because she had any romantic interest in the man.

"Jeff, listen. I realize this is awkward and we've had a lot of misunderstandings in a short time —" Liza began.

"It's fine. You already told me where I stand. The flowers were just what the card said — if you'd gotten it. A friendly get-well gesture from a colleague," he assured her, sounding like he meant it. "And I'm sorry for what I said about your cop friend. He just stepped up and took over before I could." He shrugged and his cheeks flushed.

He was embarrassed, she realized. Men and their egos.

"I hope we can get back to where things were before?" Jeff asked.

Liza smiled and nodded, admiring his honesty. "Of course we can. And I appreciate the flowers. They really were beautiful."

"Well, I'm glad you're better. And now I should get upstairs to work."

"You've got a tough boss, so yeah, you probably should."

Jeff laughed and Liza joined him. "I'm heading for Mystic, so I probably won't see you back here until tomorrow."

"Okay. Let me know when you're ready to move forward there."

"I will."

She raised a hand in a wave and walked out to her car, once more.

The sun shone down and Liza put the convertible top down for the ride. Maybe some fresh air and a road trip would help settle her mind and her mood. She ignored the urge to check her phone to see if Dare had called. It wouldn't matter if he had, since her brother would always be an issue between them.

Which shouldn't matter if what she wanted from Dare was a quick fling. That's all she would allow in her life. So why were all these unwanted feelings and emotions rioting around in her head? Why did her heart feel like it was breaking a mere morning after just because Dare had walked away so easily?

She ground her teeth in frustration and pulled out of the parking lot, heading through town. Her brakes felt funny — mushy-like — and she narrowed her gaze.

She'd just had the car inspected last month. At the end of the road, there was a stop sign and she decided to test the brakes before getting onto the highway. At the intersection, she slowed and still didn't like the squishy way the brakes felt. And when she attempted to bring the car to a stop, nothing happened.

The vehicle still rolled and she began to pound on the brakes. Still nothing. Panic filled her and she hit the floor harder with her foot. Still nothing.

Someone was looking out for her because no more cars were coming on either side of the street, but her heart picked up speed, since ahead of her was the main traffic light in town. Cars would be coming from all directions.

Liza glanced around frantically. To her left was a row of shops. To her right was the main lawn and the beautiful flowers lining the street. With no alternative, she cut her wheel right and held on as she deliberately turned her small car onto the lawn.

She shut her eyes and screamed as the car hit the gazebo.

Dare walked into the station, hot and annoyed. His first call of the day was spent arguing with the Delaneys, an older couple, over the fact that, yes, their barking dog was creating a disturbance and either they'd have to agree to take him inside or Dare would be forced to call the pound. As it was, he issued them a citation for animal cruelty for keeping their pets outdoors for so long in ninety-eight-degree heat.

"You look like you've been through the ringer," Cara said from her seat behind her desk.

"Says the woman who drew desk duty," he muttered, wiping the sweat off his forehead.

He shook his head and walked to the water cooler, filling his water bottle with cold water and guzzling it fast.

"A car just slammed into the center median in town," Sally, the dispatcher, called out. "I sent Marsden over."

Cara raised an eyebrow. "That's something you don't see every day. Wonder if it's a drunk and disorderly or an old person who shouldn't be behind a wheel?"

Sally shrugged and put her headset back on.

Dare's cell phone rang and he pulled it out of his pocket. Sam's number showed on the screen and every nerve he possessed screamed in warning.

"Talk to me," Dare said.

"The accident in town? It's Liza."

Dare's family history immediately flashed through his mind; his parents' deaths, Faith being hit by a car while trying to push Tess out of the way, and the ever-present vision of Stuart Rossman as he lay dying on the floor.

"Hey, did you hear me? I said she's okay." Sam's voice intruded on Dare's run down memory lane. "I just thought you'd want to know."

Dare ran for his car before Sam had finished his sentence, Cara yelling at him to wait as she caught up to him in the hall.

"What is it?"

"Liza's car hit the center median."

Cara's eyes opened wide. "If it weren't for bad luck, she'd have none at all. Give me a second to clear it and I'll go with you."

"Move it or I'm leaving without you," Dare said. Sam and Cara were officially partners, and since Dare's partner moved out of state, he'd been solo until the police chief, who just happened to be Sam's father, Simon Marsden, handled reassignments and new hires.

Five minutes later, they pulled up to the scene to find Sam's cruiser parked at an angle, blocking off Main Street, while another officer rerouted traffic around the side streets.

An ambulance pulled up seconds behind Dare.

He strode across the lawn and past the police barrier. By the time he reached the scene of the accident, his heart was permanently lodged in the back of his throat. Then he saw Liza's small convertible wedged into the gazebo. The top was down, the front end had taken a beating, and the air bag had deployed. Liza sat on the ground, Sam by her side, and she looked fine.

As Dare approached, Sam was talking too quietly for Dare to make out what he was saying. Liza, on the other hand, was speaking loud and clear. "I'm fine. I do not need a hospital and I just want to go home."

Dare held back a grin, relieved that she really was okay and clearly feeling well enough to argue with Sam.

"What happened?" he asked, kneeling down beside them.

Liza looked up at him and narrowed her

gaze. "That's who you called when you stepped away from me?" she asked Sam, accusation and anger powering her voice.

"If I didn't call him, he'd kick my ass," Sam explained.

Damned right, Dare thought. And though he understood why she didn't want to see him, he'd be damned if he was going anywhere now.

"Well, I'm going to kick it now," Liza said, and Sam held up his hands as if he needed protection.

"You don't want him to have to arrest you for assaulting an officer," Dare said to her.

"Go away." She refused to look at him.

He muttered a curse under his breath. "Can't do that."

The paramedic strode over before Liza could reply. "What happened?" he asked.

"Ms. McKnight had an accident," Sam explained. "Air bag deployed. No visible injuries and she's been coherent and awake since I arrived on the scene."

Christopher knelt down. "We meet again."

Liza wrinkled her eyebrows in confusion.

"I took you from the fair to the hospital," he explained.

Liza shook her head. "I'm sorry. I don't remember you."

Christopher smiled. "That's pretty normal

215

for a head injury. How are you now?"

"I'm fine. I just want to go home."

"As soon as I check you out, I'm sure you can."

Sam rose to his feet and Dare followed him to a private corner while Christopher examined Liza. "What the hell happened?" Dare asked.

"She said her brakes felt spongy. She planned to pull over after the traffic light and had already slowed down some, but when she tried to brake for red, the car kept going and all she could do was pick a fairly empty spot and brace for impact." Sam shook his head in disbelief.

Dare was nauseous. "What kind of new car loses its brakes? I want that vehicle thoroughly checked out."

Sam nodded. "You know I'm on it."

"Thanks. And I appreciate you calling me."

Sam smirked. "You owe me one. She's pretty pissed at me now."

"You'll live," Dare said wryly.

"Yeah, well, in the meantime, I called Mason's Towing. He'll be here in a few minutes."

"Good. I'm going to go back and see how she's doing."

Sam raised an eyebrow. "Didn't seem like

the lady wanted to see you."

Dare shoved his hands into his pants pockets. "Yeah, well, maybe I gave her good reason."

But the minute he'd heard Liza had been in an accident, all the problems between them hadn't seemed important. It would become apparent soon enough, though, that she didn't feel the same way.

By the time he approached Liza again, Christopher had finished examining her and had given her the all clear. "Your neck will be sore tomorrow," he warned her. "Your ribs and chest too. The air bag does a number on the body, but it definitely protected you."

"What's a few more aches and pains?" she asked, and Dare recognized the forced joke for what it was.

"And you're sure your head is okay?" Christopher asked. "You do have a recent injury."

"Yes. And if anything hurts, I'll call Dr. Collins," she promised. "May I go home now?"

"It's fine with me. Officer?"

Christopher turned to Sam, who nodded. "I need to finish taking witness statements and I'll need you to come by later to sign yours," he said to Liza. "But for now you can go."

"I suggest you get some rest," Christopher said as he gathered his equipment. "You're probably more shaken up than you realize."

Given Liza's pale face, Dare had to agree.

"Do you have a ride home?" Sam asked her.

And Dare braced himself for the inevitable argument as he volunteered his services.

TEN

"I'll take her home," Dare said.

"Here we go again," Liza mumbled. The difference today was that she had her wits about her and she'd also had the opportunity to experience the flip side of Dare's do-gooder persona. It wasn't going to happen again. "I don't think so," Liza said, responding to Dare. "But no," she conceded to Sam, "I don't have a ride home."

Dare growled low in his throat.

"I have to take statements here. Why don't you let Officer Barron take you home?" Sam actually sounded like he felt bad. "Since he's on duty, it's not like he can stick around," he said to Liza.

"Way to help a buddy, Sam."

She couldn't help but laugh. The poor man was caught in the middle. "Fine. I'll take the ride, Officer Barron."

Liza was pleased to see Dare's face had turned red with anger and frustration.

"Remember, I need you to come by and sign a statement," Sam said.

Liza nodded. "I'm going to rent a car, so that won't be a problem," she said before Dare could possibly jump in and say he'd bring her down to the station.

He could drive her home, drop her off, and go back to work. She didn't need another thing from him. But when she rose to her feet, she was horrified to realize her legs were trembling.

Dare grabbed on to her elbow. "Normal reaction," he assured her as he led her through the gathering crowd.

She glanced back, wincing as she saw the damage her car had done to the beautiful center of town. She'd mowed down the impatiens and taken out the gazebo. "So much for getting the Beautification Committee to put the fund-raiser money into the youth center." She shook her head, beyond disappointed she'd undermined her own cause.

"I wouldn't worry about that right now," Dare said.

She ignored him and continued to do so on the walk to his car and the entire drive home.

He pulled into her driveway and cut the engine.

"Thanks for the ride," she said in a polite if frosty tone.

It was his turn to ignore her. He climbed out of the car and walked around to her side, too late to open her door, but he still attempted to help her up the path to the house.

"I can get myself inside." In fact, she already had her keys in her hand, since she'd planned on bolting away from him as soon as possible.

"Liza, you have every right to be angry as hell —" he said, looking too damned handsome in his uniform, his sunglasses covering his eyes until he slipped them to the top of his head.

"Thank you for your permission," she sarcastically answered, holding on to her lingering hurt from earlier by a thread.

She let herself into her house. Unfortunately, she failed at her attempt to leave him on the other side of the door.

He barreled his way inside, following right behind her.

"I thought you had to go back to work," she said, exasperated.

"I do. But not until I make sure you aren't hurt." He stared at her with such concern in those gorgeous brown eyes, he'd melt her heart if she let him.

She shivered and stepped farther away. "The paramedic already said I'm fine, so you have nothing to worry about. Which brings up an interesting point. What is with this sudden show of concern?"

And where had his caring been earlier?

He glanced down, obviously embarrassed. "I shouldn't have taken my feelings for your brother out on you."

"No, you shouldn't have. It's not like you didn't know the situation before you sweet-talked your way into my bed."

"Ouch."

"What can I say? The truth hurts." She let out a sigh, the exhaustion of the last couple of days catching up with her and she leaned against the wall for support.

She still hadn't processed the fact that she'd destroyed the center of town, crushed her beloved car, and nearly killed herself in the process.

The whole morning seemed surreal and made no sense.

"Can you just go?" she didn't care if she had to beg. Her defenses were too low to deal with Dare now.

"Do you promise you're okay?" He reached out to touch her cheek, then obviously thought better and dropped his hand.

She dug her nails into her palms, torn

between disappointment and satisfaction that she'd gotten what she wanted. He was keeping his distance. And it hurt more than this morning's argument had. At least then she'd had her own anger to bolster her emotions.

Now she was drained. "I'm fine."

He inclined his head. "I'll make sure Mason makes your car a priority."

She nodded. "Thank you."

"Take it easy for the rest of the day, okay?" he asked, his gruff voice winding its way through her veins.

She managed a nod.

He started for the door and she walked him out, locking up behind him. Only when she was alone did her legs begin to shake again, and she headed for her family room couch where she curled into a ball and let the trembling take over.

An hour later, Liza's earlier shock had begun to wear off. Knowing she had things to do, she pulled herself together. First she checked in at the office with a quick explanation of what had happened. Then she called the company her firm was dealing with in Mystic to explain her absence and reschedule the meeting. Then she turned to focusing on the accident. She reported the accident to her insurance agent, who assured her the costs of a rental car were fully covered.

She was deep in thought when her doorbell rang. Liza glanced up, surprised by yet another visitor, this one in the middle of the day.

She walked to the door and discovered Kelly Barron on the other side. "Hi," Liza said as she opened the door to let the other woman inside.

"Hi yourself." Kelly looked Liza over thoroughly from her now bare feet up and over her wrinkled suit. "Well, you look like you made it through unscathed. The center of town doesn't look nearly as good."

Liza winced at the reminder. "I'm fine. Just really embarrassed."

"By an accident? Don't be silly. I'm just glad you're okay. Your brakes failed? That's so scary."

"Tell me about it." She shivered involuntarily. "I'd ask what you're doing here, but I have a hunch Dare sent you?" Liza flexed and unflexed her fingers, waiting for an answer.

"Well, I'd have come anyway as soon as I heard what happened, but yes, Dare called."

Liza shook her head. "Don't you need to be at work?" she asked, knowing the other woman was a paralegal.

"It'll wait. Today's a light day, so no worries about me. What about you?"

"What about me?"

"Dare mentioned you might need a ride to a car rental place . . . or to the police station to sign your statement." With a light laugh, Kelly shrugged. "Sorry, but those Barron brothers like to take control."

And it didn't seem like it bothered her all that much.

"I realize that." And though Liza should be angry, she was strangely touched as well. "I just don't get it," she added softly.

"Get what?" Kelly asked.

Liza sighed. "Come on into the kitchen," she said, figuring they could sit down for this conversation. "Soda? Water? Iced tea?"

"Whatever you're having." Kelly settled into the kitchen chair Dare had been in just this morning.

After handing them each a can of diet soda, Liza joined her at the table. "Remember, *you* asked," she warned Dare's sister-in-law before she dove into any conversation. If she dove in. Liza wasn't used to sharing.

"And I'm listening." Kelly, wearing denim shorts and a cropped T-shirt, crossed one long leg over the other one.

Again, Liza reacted against type and

225

decided to confide in her. She didn't understand it. She was usually so self-contained, but there was something about the fact that these strangers kept showing kindness that got to her. Liza genuinely liked Kelly and Faith. More than that, she was embarrassed to admit she was starving for the friendship they seemed to willingly offer.

Liza only hoped that friendship wasn't contingent on her relationship with their brother-in-law because that seemed dead in the water. "Dare and I . . ." She trailed off, not knowing how to explain.

Kelly waited patiently, not pushing her to divulge more than or before she was ready.

"It's just that we have more things that divide us than we have in common."

Kelly popped the top of her cola can and pulled a long sip. "So? Nash and I didn't have an easy go of it either. But it was worth the hassle, even when things got really bad. And believe me they did. And that good relationship you see between the brothers now?" Kelly shook her head. "It wasn't always that way."

Liza should have been surprised at the other woman's candor, but everything about her seemed so warm and open, she'd almost expected it. "Dare mentioned something about their difficult road."

Kelly nodded. "Ethan got his shit together first. Pardon my French," she said, laughing. "And he came home to make amends. He and Dare warmed up to each other next. But Nash? He came to the party kicking and screaming. In fact, he actually decked Ethan."

Liza blinked, startled by that revelation.

"Yep. It took Nash a long time to forgive his older brother. And Dare? We all thought Dare was the most easygoing of the brothers, but it turns out he had secrets nobody knew." Kelly eyed Liza over the rim of the soda can.

What kinds of secrets, Liza wondered, but knew she wouldn't ask any more than Kelly would tell. Whatever secrets Dare kept hidden, Liza would learn or not from Dare himself.

When Kelly continued to stare, Liza grew uncomfortable. "What?"

Kelly shrugged. "It's just that Dare projects this easy persona, but underneath? He's been hurt and abandoned and it's hard for him to trust. Like all the brothers, really. But he's hidden it the deepest."

This revelation, though not specific, came as more of a surprise. Liza had assumed his harsh words about her behavior with her brother came from his being a cop with a judgmental personality. But from what Kelly was telling her, Dare wasn't as judgmental as he was scared of trusting.

Just like she was. Which made them quite a pair, really.

Could he have been looking for an excuse to push her away this morning? Was the tattoo and then Brian's arrival an easy way for him to not deal with his feelings? Or was she reading more into Kelly's simple words because Liza was falling for the man and wanted an excuse to let him back in?

She groaned out loud.

"Are you okay?" Kelly asked.

Liza nodded. "Yeah." Just more confused than she'd been before and even more wary, if such a thing were possible.

"Do you want to go into town and take care of your errands?" Kelly offered, letting her off the hook and ending personal conversation — at least for now.

These Barron women were as pushy as the men. And Liza liked them just as much as she liked one Barron brother in particular.

Dare promised himself he'd give Liza space. She was clearly angry and he understood her reasons. He'd been an ass. And the scary thing was he couldn't say he wouldn't do it again. Brian McKnight flipped every known switch he had inside him and some he didn't know he'd had. The rest of the morning dragged on, and when Nash called to see if he wanted to grab a late lunch at the Family Restaurant, Dare was only too happy for the break.

He pulled up to the family-owned restaurant on the edge of town. The place had been around longer than most in Serendipity, and that was saying something, but each generation had kept the place up and added modern touches.

Dare walked inside and waved to Macy Donovan, the daytime hostess, and found Nash already waiting in a booth in the back.

"What's up, big brother?" Dare asked.

Nash raised an eyebrow. "You're asking me that? I heard you had some excitement this morning."

"You can't go a couple of hours without talking to your wife?" Dare asked, hoping to deflect the subject.

Nash treated him to a smirk. "You're one to talk considering you practically moved into Liza's over the weekend. How's that going for you, by the way?"

Before Nash could answer, Gina, their waitress, strode over. Middle-aged, happily married, and with a heart of gold, the woman knew every customer by name and order. "The usual, boys?" she asked them.

"Thanks, Gina."

Dare nodded, his stomach rumbling. "Tell Tony I'm starving and to add extra fries."

The redhead grinned. "Will do. Be back in a few minutes with your drinks." She walked off, pausing at other tables to check in before disappearing in the back.

"So?" Nash asked.

"How the hell could I fall for the one woman in this town whose baggage is tied up with mine?" Dare asked, giving in and talking to his sibling.

He and Nash had always been close, even when circumstances dictated they shouldn't be. Even when Nash found out why Dare hadn't gone to live with the Rossmans, thereby allowing the brothers to be split up, he'd eventually come around. Because from the beginning, they were a team.

Nash burst out laughing. "I'm the one who married our half sister's sister. And you're asking me about shared baggage?"

Dare shook his head and laughed. "I guess you've got a point. Which means you'd know the answer?"

With a groan, Nash leaned back in his seat, his arm across the back of the booth. "The hell if I know. You learn to accept what you can't change, I guess. If it's not just sex, if she means enough to you . . . time will tell."

"Who the hell knows if I've got time. I manage to piss her off as much as I . . . Never mind," he said with a shake of his head.

He'd been about to say turn her on, but thought better of it and shook his head. Was it just sex with Liza?

"Hey, the wives are having a meeting at Ethan's pool on Saturday to talk about the fund-raiser," Nash said, preventing Dare from answering his own silent question. "Want to join your brothers while we hang out and ogle them in their bikinis?"

Fund-raiser business, which Dare took to mean would include Liza. In a bikini. He broke into a sweat. "Yeah. I'll be there."

Nash grinned. "I thought so."

Dare's cell phone rang and a glance told him it was Sam. "What's up?" he asked, answering on the second ring.

"Someone cut the brake line on Liza's car. She didn't lose control by accident," Sam said.

Gina chose that moment to show up with their meals. "I'm sorry, but I'll take mine to go," he said to the waitress. "I'll be right there," he told Sam.

"Meet me at Mason's."

Dare shut his phone. "Sorry."

Nash waved him away, unconcerned as he dug into his food.

By the time Dare arrived at Mason's, Liza was already there with Sam. She'd changed out of her business suit and now wore a pair of frayed cut-off shorts, a tank top and flip-flops on her feet. She looked sexy as ever, but there was a fragility to her that Dare had never noticed before he'd slept with her.

Gotten close to her.

Come to understand how many different things in her life pulled at her. How many people in her life let her down. And now he'd become one more person who'd done the same.

Dare curled his fingers into tight fists, fighting the urge to walk over and pull her into his arms. He was the last person she wanted right now. He also held back in deference to Sam, who was the cop in charge of the case.

So while Sam spoke to the mechanic and caught Liza up on the situation, Dare hovered nearby, listening.

"What do you mean I had a leak in my brake line? The car was just serviced last week," Liza said to Sam.

Sam glanced at her. "I'll need the name of the place that handled it."

"A BMW service center in Manhattan. I was visiting friends and dropped the car off, since I knew I wouldn't need it in the city." She gave Sam the name and address before turning back to Mason.

"The line was cut," the mechanic explained.

"What kind of cut? Slice? Pinprick?" Sam asked.

Mason rubbed his grease-stained hands on his working coveralls. "Small nick. The fluid leaked out over time, so you wouldn't have noticed it right away."

"I haven't moved the car in a few days," she said. "Not until this morning."

Mason nodded, his long dark hair falling over his forehead. "There's probably a puddle in the driveway where your car was parked then."

Sam made a note, probably to check the driveway, something Dare hadn't thought to do.

"Could I have driven over something that cut the line?" Liza asked.

"No ma'am. This was deliberate."

Liza stiffened. "Wait. You're saying someone cut a hole in my brake line on purpose?"

"Looks that way."

She wrapped her arms around herself, a protective gesture Dare recognized as Liza's means of retreat and defense.

He itched to walk up behind her and pull her into his arms, offer comfort, and promise her he'd make sure no one ever hurt her again. He refrained because his gut told him she needed to handle this on her own. Like she dealt with everything else in her life, Dare thought, disgusted beyond belief with her family but most of all with himself.

He'd already decided to give her the illusion of control for now. There was no way she was alone in this and she'd understand that shortly.

Which meant that this thing between them was more than just sex. For him, anyway. He'd sensed the possibility from the beginning. He'd even warned her he wasn't the type to get involved and walk away. But now Dare knew he'd also been warning himself. Because there was no way he could walk away. The pull he felt toward her was too strong.

Every man had a weakness and apparently she was his. Because being with her meant dealing with garbage he'd hoped to leave in the past. He only hoped he was strong enough to handle it.

"I have to order the part," Mason was saying. "Because it's a foreign vehicle, it might take a couple of days."

Liza nodded, feeling numb. "That's fine. I rented a car. Keep it as long as you need to."

"I'll be right back," Sam said to Liza before following Mason into the smaller office area behind the garage, probably for a more detailed conversation.

Liza didn't care. She'd heard all she needed to. Someone had cut her brake line. Someone wanted her brakes to fail while she was driving. She blinked in shock, unable to come to terms with the undeniable fact that someone wanted her hurt. Or worse.

Shaking, she turned only to find Dare waiting, arms open wide. She'd sensed his presence as soon as he'd walked into the garage, had managed to ignore him while she was listening to Mason and Sam, telling herself she didn't need him. She didn't need anyone. Knowing too that the words were a big fat lie.

So though she'd hate herself for the weakness later, she stepped into his embrace now. He slid his hands around her waist and held her tight. She wasn't sure how long she stood there, his strong arms comforting her, breathing in his comforting and, yeah, arousing scent.

"It's going to be okay," he promised.

"I know." She let out a shaky breath and forced herself to step away.

"Any ideas on who would want to hurt you?" Dare asked, his gorgeous brown eyes filled with a combination of concern and fury.

She shook her head. "I keep pretty much to myself."

"You said you got flowers the other day?" he asked, his jaw tight.

She swallowed hard. "Turns out they were from Jeff Montana."

Dare's eyes darkened. Anger? Jealousy? Liza didn't know nor did she want to deal with his hot-and-cold routine when it came to his feelings for her.

"He said they were just a get-well gesture from a colleague."

"I'll bet. Get flowers from anyone else in the office?" he asked.

She blew out a frustrated breath. "No, but he was there when I got hurt and you wouldn't let him anywhere near me to see how I was. The man works for me. He was just being polite."

"We'll see," Dare muttered, and she knew he'd be questioning the architect soon. "We can't afford to assume anyone's innocent without checking them out," he said, his voice sounding calmer.

"Fine."

"What about . . ." His voice trailed off.

"What?" she asked. "Just say it. Don't beat around the bush, don't play games. If you have someone else in mind, spit it out."

"Your brother. Is there any reason your brother would want to hurt you?" he asked.

Liza narrowed her gaze. "No chance in hell." She folded her arms across her chest and glared, letting Dare know he was dangerously close to crossing a line.

"Look, I'm not saying your sober brother would want to hurt you, but what about your drunk one? Is it possible that during one of his binges, he got angry over something? Hell, he might not even remember doing it the next day."

Liza shook her head. She wasn't sure of many things these days, but she was certain her brother wouldn't hurt her unless it was an accident. Not deliberate sabotage. "Not possible," she said once more.

"Everyone has their limits, Liza. Everyone. And you can't afford to eliminate *anyone* as a suspect when your life is on the line."

"Is that the cop in you speaking? Or the man who hates my brother with a passion?" she asked, her voice sparking with anger.

"I'll give you that one because I earned it."

She sucked in a surprised breath. She didn't know why she'd be so shocked that Dare would admit when he was wrong, but his doing so took the wind out of her righteous anger.

"Look, I can tell you for sure Brian would never knowingly hurt me."

"That's my whole point! I'm not saying he'd do it sober."

"He wouldn't do it drunk either!"

"How do you know? What makes you so damn sure?"

"Because he's the one who was there when —" No. No. No. She wasn't going there. Not now and not with Dare, a man who Liza couldn't be sure would really be there for her the next day let alone the next hour.

"When what?" Dare asked, his voice gentling.

"It's not relevant." She pulled her purse off her shoulders and dug for the keys to the rental car. "I need to go." She turned but didn't get far.

Dare grabbed her shoulders and spun her back around to face him. "You've been through more in the last few days than many people go through in a lifetime. You're exhausted and I respect that. I've been an ass and I know that too."

She blinked, stunned by him once more.

"I want you to go home and rest. Please. No work. Just go unwind," he said, back to the caring man she'd spent so much time with this past weekend. The man who made her think she could trust and maybe even fall hard. "Sam and I will arrange for drive-by protection when you're at home or at work," he promised.

"Thank you for that."

He inclined his head. "That's me doing my job. What I say next isn't. I'm coming over after work around six. I'm bringing dinner and we're going to talk."

"There's nothing to say."

He merely raised an eyebrow. "You can't shoulder all this yourself and you need to know I'm going to be there."

"Don't make promises you can't keep." The lump in her throat nearly undid her, but she wouldn't break down in front of him. "Brian could show up or do something and we'll be back to square one. I have too much going on in my life to deal with you too."

"But you will. Because I can't stay away." A sexy smile tipped his lips. "And you really don't want me to."

She had the sudden urge to step on his feet hard. "Arrogant jerk," she muttered.

"Go home, Liza. Rest. We have a lot to talk about when I get there."

Knowing she was fighting a losing battle, she turned and walked out. But she wasn't giving in. As hard as he planned to push her, she planned to push right back. He had no idea how hard she could fight to protect herself, even from people she cared about. She'd shut out her parents when she realized they couldn't give her what she needed.

And she'd shut him out too. Because this man posed a big risk to her — body, heart, and soul.

ELEVEN

For some reason, Liza couldn't believe someone wanted her hurt. Or worse. Cars failed all the time. Surely when Sam investigated, he'd find out that Mason didn't know what he was talking about and something had happened at the dealership when she'd had her car fixed. Nothing else made sense. Similar to the rest of her life, which had somehow turned into a jumble she didn't understand surrounding Dare Barron.

By the time Liza's doorbell rang at 6:30 P.M., she told herself she was prepared for him. Walls up, guarded, prepared. Then she opened the door and came face-to-face with a man bearing wildflowers in one hand, a box of pizza balanced on the other, and a bottle of wine under his arm, and all her defenses went out the window.

Why did he have to be so handsome? Sexy. And caring. It was the caring that got to her every time. Because, really, when had anyone in her life given her something so basic and simple?

So necessary . . .

"Come on in," she said, gesturing for him to enter. "Can I take something from you?" she asked, struggling not to let him see how his very presence affected her.

"The flowers. I've got the rest."

She accepted the bouquet. "Thank you," she murmured.

"My pleasure." His words warmed her.

He followed her into the kitchen. In silence, she filled a vase with water and put the flowers inside, placing them on a prominent place on the counter. He worked alongside her, unnerving her because he knew exactly where to find the paper plates, the corkscrew, and even her wineglasses. One weekend in her home taking care of her and he knew the place as well as she did.

"Want to eat outside?" He gestured to the patio off the kitchen.

"Sure," she said, surprised by the idea.

A few minutes later, they were settled on a blanket on the ground, eating picnic-style. The air around them was hot and humid, but it was still a beautiful night.

"This was a good idea."

He grinned. "I figured we both needed to

relax and unwind."

"Agreed."

He cocked his head to one side. "So can we eat and save the serious talking for afterward?"

Knowing there'd be no avoiding conversation, she appreciated the delay. "I'd like to enjoy my pizza without indigestion."

He shook his head and laughed. "At least you're not throwing me out."

She raised an eyebrow. "Would you go if I tried?"

"Nope."

He had no idea how happy that made her.

He bit into his pizza and she did the same.

For the next few minutes, they ate in silence. Enjoyable, easy silence. She could almost forget the reasons she had to keep him at a distance. But not quite.

So when they'd both finished and she pushed the pizza box off the blanket, she curled her legs beneath her and turned to face him.

"Why are you really here?" she asked.

Dare blinked, obviously surprised by the question. His brows furrowed in concentration, taking the question seriously. "Because I can't stay away. And because I want to be."

A delicious ribbon of warmth spread

through her limbs. She nodded slowly, acknowledging the pull between them. "Attraction. I get it. I feel it too."

Dare let out a laugh that sounded harsh to her ears. "If that's all it was, I wouldn't be here."

Liza ran her tongue over her lips, tasting the wine she'd been sipping. "That's all it can be."

"And now we come to the crux of things. Why?" he asked.

Liza owed him more than her standard "because that's all I'm willing to give" answer. "For one thing, because I can't take the hot and cold reactions you have to me depending on my brother's behavior or your moods." Liza glanced down, unwilling to let him see how much he'd hurt her. Not wanting him to know why his withdrawal affected her so badly.

"Hey." He reached out and lifted her chin with his hand, forcing her to meet his gaze. "You deserve an explanation for that."

She swallowed hard. "Okay." She hadn't expected that, but she was curious.

"Oh boy." Dare leaned back on his elbows and looked up at the darkening sky.

She studied his chiseled profile, struck again by how handsome he was. Attraction? Oh, yeah, she felt that in spades. She wished it were all she felt.

"Remember when you told me about the night Stuart Rossman died? How you felt responsible?" he asked.

She narrowed her gaze and managed a nod. "Why?"

"Because I feel the same sense of responsibility."

"You? Why?" she asked, surprised.

"I was there that night. At the party."

She stared at him, stunned. "But you were only —"

"Fifteen. Yeah, I know. But I wanted to be like my brothers. I wanted to run with the older kids. And . . ."

He paused and she waited.

"I wanted to see you." An embarrassed grin tugged at the corner of his mouth. "Yep, I knew who you were way back when. I guess you could say I had a crush on you."

She flushed, also embarrassed by the admission. "Wow."

"Yeah. Well, you weren't home that night and I wish to hell I'd never gone."

They both sobered at the memory of what happened next. "You were there when that guy punched Stuart?"

Dare blinked and pushed himself to a sitting position. "When *what guy* punched Stuart?"

An uneasy feeling prickled over Liza's skin. "Brian told us that a guy from another school got into an argument with Stuart Rossman and threw the first punch. Stuart was drunk, stumbled and fell, his head hit the concrete and . . ." She didn't have to continue. He obviously knew the rest first-hand.

"Liza?"

Goose bumps prickled over her skin despite the heat, his deep tone scaring her. "What is it?" she asked.

"There was no guy from another school that hit Rossman." She studied his face, knew from his expression he wasn't lying.

"Then who did?"

He stared at her intently, not saying a word. He didn't have to. His silence spoke for him. If an outsider hadn't struck Stuart Rossman, then . . .

"No." She shook her head back and forth in denial. "Oh, no."

"I'm sorry." Dare's tone was gruff but sincere, and as much as he hated her brother she knew he was sorry for being the one to break the news. News she should have known over a decade before.

"Brian's friends backed up his story to my parents and to the police," she said. As if that made a difference.

She didn't realize she was shaking, rocking back and forth, until Dare moved in, pulling her against him in an effort to stop the trembling. She couldn't tell if the tremors stopped, but she liked the warmth and strength he provided. Needed the comfort.

"This shouldn't be so easy for me to believe," she whispered almost to herself. "I should be arguing with you. Calling you a liar. But it makes so much sense. The whispers, the secrecy, the meetings with my parents' best friend, the old district attorney."

Oh my — her parents. They knew. Brian knew. And they all covered it up. As if a boy's death and how it happened hadn't mattered as long as *their* son's life was spared. And for what? What had Brian done with the future his parents had no doubt bought for him except drink it away? No wonder Dare hated him so much.

She forced herself to turn and face him, pushing out of his arms to look at his tortured face. "What did you do?" she asked him.

He didn't pretend to misunderstand. "Everyone did one of two things. Stayed and cleaned up the mess while preparing a cover story or ran." He splayed his hands in front of him. "Both choices left Stuart Ross-man bleeding out on the ground." He blinked hard. "I ran."

His words were short and clipped, filled with a suppressed rage, pain, and the obvious guilt that had been eating at him ever since.

"You were only fifteen," she reminded him.

"Should age excuse your brother?" Dare asked.

She looked down and shook her head. "It doesn't excuse me either. If I'd been home like I was supposed to be, there would have been no alcohol. No party." She swallowed over the painful lump in her throat. "No death."

"Would have, could have, should have," Dare muttered. "It doesn't change the past. For any of us. What matters is who we are now. And I made sure I would never forget that night."

She looked at him in confusion.

"The tattoo? The reason I snapped when you asked me about it the other day? I had the ink done as a permanent reminder." He turned so she could see his left arm, the detailed etching of the band encircling his bicep. "Look closely."

She ran her fingers over his muscled flesh.

"There's a Sanskrit symbol for karma, which I translate as atonement or getting out of something what you put in," he said gruffly.

She traced the foreign lettering and nodded. "I see it," she murmured.

"And here . . ." He turned his arm to reveal the inner flesh, normally hidden. "There's the date of the party."

"The date Stuart Rossman died," she whispered, understanding and humbled that he'd finally let her in. "Thank you for sharing."

On impulse, she leaned down and pressed her lips to the inside of his arm, directly over the date. His entire body shivered in response, and despite everything, her inner core contracted with yearning. She needed him.

But first they had to finish this. For all she knew he might not even want her when they were done. "That's why you hate Brian, isn't it? Not just for what he did but for who he became?"

Dare shrugged. "I'm not sure myself. It's so complicated and tangled. I just wanted you to know so that you can understand my extreme reactions. And trust me when I tell you they're not about you."

"I know that now." But she also knew that

what stood between them was a whole lot bigger with more gray areas than she'd originally thought.

There might be more than attraction between them, but they could never contemplate a future. And it wasn't just that Dare was a cop and she was enabling her troublemaking sibling. It was because her brother was a living, breathing reminder of Dare Barron's biggest mistake.

And by extension, so was Liza.

Oh, the tattoo was a daily reminder, but Dare had willingly taken that on knowing that he'd work hard to make his life meaningful and worthwhile. But by virtue of his very existence, Brian had done the exact opposite. So no matter how attracted she and Dare were, no matter how much he tugged at something deep and untapped inside her, *sex* was all she could let herself share with him from now on.

Or else her heart would be in serious jeopardy.

Dare glanced her way. "Hey. I didn't tell you so you'd pull away."

He was reading her again and getting it right. Liza didn't respond and suddenly found herself pulled and flipped on top of him, her entire body prone against his.

"Hey! What was that for?" she asked, trying to sound outraged and failing.

He grinned, his face *this* close to hers. "To get you to stop thinking."

Easy enough. He was hot and hard beneath her, all male, and she couldn't help but be aware of his erection, which pulsed against her core.

She wriggled against him and sighed, giving up the fight.

"Mission accomplished," she said, conceding with not just her words but with her body's complete acceptance of his as she molded into him.

"Good girl." His hand slipped beneath her shirt and slid up her back until his palm lay flat over her bare flesh.

She inhaled his scent, musk and man, mixing with the outdoors, and she wanted to crawl into his skin.

She ought to fight this and knew she couldn't. The one thing she could do was take control. Of him, of herself, and mostly of her feelings so she wouldn't be hurt when the inevitable happened. And she couldn't imagine him fighting what she had in mind.

She let her legs settle around either side of his hips, pressing herself intimately against him.

"Oh, baby." His big body shuddered beneath her.

His words triggered an immediate wave of sensation that rushed through her, and she circled her hips once more, deepening the pressure and the connection between them.

He felt *so* good, but more important, she could control this and keep her emotions in check while finding so much pleasure she thought she might die from it. And they weren't even naked yet. She picked up the pace, rocking against him, and he met her thrust for thrust, his hips jerking upward, his hardness rolling against her.

They were out of control and she loved every minute. The fullness between her legs grew heavier and more insistent, wetness saturated her panties, and still it wasn't enough. She gripped his shoulders and bore down with her hips and the contractions inside her built until they exploded behind her eyes, white stars bursting as she soared out of her body.

Distantly she heard a scream and realized it had come from her. And still she came, the orgasm lasting long, shaking her hard, not letting up.

Dare groaned and without warning, he captured her cry with his mouth, pulling her into a long, deep kiss that shattered her soul and stole the control she'd mistakenly believed was hers.

"Clothes off," he said through clenched teeth.

With the contractions still quaking inside her and her body fully aware that she'd been satisfied but not filled, she didn't hesitate to comply. She sat down beside him and worked off her shorts and panties, while he unbuttoned and pulled at his jeans, his hands shaking with need.

No man had ever trembled for her before and the effect was devastating, turning her on and making her want to give him anything he asked for, whatever he needed and do it now.

His jeans had barely hit his ankles when she pushed him back to the ground and straddled him once more. This time, they were flesh to flesh, the heat of the outdoors no match for that of their aroused bodies. She reached down and circled his erection with her hand, feeling every hard ridge of his silken length as she ran her thumb over the already moistened head.

"Yes," he said, on a low groan.

"Oh, yeah." She lifted her hips and placed him where she needed him most. Her body, already wet and ready, accepted him readily and she sank down onto his swollen shaft.

He filled her completely, the sensation of slick bare skin slamming into her consciousness without warning.

"Oh my God, no condom," he muttered, obviously coming to the same conclusion she had.

Why had she ever thought she had control? "I'm on the pill," she said, even as common sense had her attempting to pull off him.

He gripped her hips and held her in place. "I'm safe," he said. "Tested annually and I never have sex without a condom. Ever," he said, his brows furrowing at the notion that he'd damn well violated that rule without thinking.

"So am I," she murmured. Yet she'd been the one to jump him without thinking, and the whys of that didn't bear dwelling on.

Dare saw in her face he was about to lose her. *Not happening,* he thought, and reached out to bring her back into the moment. He pushed her shirt up, found no bra, and let his thumb graze her nipple.

She sighed and rocked her hips back and forth in response. "What you do to me," she whispered, her eyes glazing over.

"Back at ya, baby." She had him tied up in knots, doing things he never did for another woman, taking care of her, wanting to protect her, and now making love to her with nothing between them.

Without warning, she began to rock against him and he went with it, following her cues, shifting his hips in time to the rhythm she set. She moaned and her eyelids fell shut. Dare held on long enough to watch her face as she milked his body inside hers, her obvious ecstasy and pleasure bringing him higher.

"Come here," he said, his voice rough.

She lay down over him, her shirt pushed up to her neck, her bare breasts crushed against his chest. Taking him by surprise, she kissed him, her lips sealing his, her tongue flicking inside his mouth. And suddenly the frenzy between them grew once more. He thrust upward, taking control, plunging into her as her hips ground back into his. It didn't matter that he'd just brought her to the brink and over a few minutes before, all of a sudden she was there again, crying out, the sound echoing in his ears and triggering his own long-held-back release.

He came long and hard, emptying himself inside her, feeling her slick walls wrapping him in snug warmth and heat. She writhed above him, giving in to her climax, her nails clawing his shoulders, her face burrowing deep into his neck as she came.

Beneath her, as reality refocused around

him, Liza sprawled over him, Dare stared up at the night sky and wondered what the hell had just happened between them.

Liza pulled her clothes back on in silence. Dare did the same. She was too shaken up by what happened between them to pretend otherwise. He gathered up some things from the patio and headed inside while she cleaned up the rest. By the time she returned from dumping the trash in the garage, Dare was waiting for her in the kitchen.

He'd splashed cold water on his face and pulled himself together. She needed some time to do the same and hoped he wouldn't ask to stay the night. Space would be a good thing about now and not because she planned on freezing him out or turning her back on him.

She just needed to find her equilibrium because he'd blown it to hell and back.

He held out his hand and she accepted the gesture.

He didn't push for more and she was grateful. Wasn't she? So what was the disappointment winging through her stomach that he wasn't asking for more than she wanted to give.

"We need to talk about the car."

She blinked, startled by the subject he chose. "That's really not necessary. I mean, the more I think about it, the harder time I have believing that anyone deliberately cut the brake line."

He raised an eyebrow. "Mason said —"

"Mason's a small-town mechanic. I'd rather wait and see what Sam turns up before panicking."

He nodded slowly.

She doubted he agreed, but he wasn't arguing. "Besides, I have a police car driving by periodically, right? So in case there is some phantom person, they're looking out for me."

"It's not enough." He hesitated before speaking. "I should stay over." Yet he looked torn about it.

Boy, what had happened on the patio hadn't just shaken her up, it had thrown Mr. Confidence into a tizzy too.

At least she could reassure him on that score. "Hey, I'm not looking to insult your manhood, but let's face it, if someone did cut my brakes, they did it while you were here in the house." She squeezed his hand. "Really. I'll be fine here and we obviously need space."

"But not a break."

She managed to smile, so relieved the

cramping in her stomach eased. "No. Not a break."

"We're still together," he said.

"Yes." By *her* definition of a relationship, not his.

Not that he needed to know that. Liza would find her equilibrium and with it the safe place she'd carved out that let her tuck her feelings away where nobody could hurt her. Not her parents, not her alcoholic brother, and definitely not another man.

"Good." Dare grinned that sexy smile she adored. "Then I'll get going."

She walked him to the door. "Thanks for dinner. And the wine and the flowers."

"You're welcome. I'll call you tomorrow."

She nodded. Before she could open the door, he pulled her into a mind-blowing kiss. And then he was gone.

Dare woke up Saturday to a full weekend off, and man, he needed it. After a normal workday on Wednesday, he'd switched shifts as a favor for a friend, and on Thursday he'd worked an all-nighter, then pulled a late afternoon through early evening shift on Friday. Today and tomorrow were all his own. No sooner had he rolled out of bed and his feet hit the floor than his thoughts turned to Liza.

He hadn't spoken to her since he'd left her house Tuesday night. They'd played phone tag for the better part of the week. Between her busy schedule and his, they'd completely missed each other. Dare could have tried harder to reach her, but he'd needed breathing room.

Even for a man who liked relationships, this thing with Liza had thrown him. The feelings she aroused in him were new to the point where he didn't recognize parts of himself anymore.

There were still things he recognized. The man who'd been atoning for his sins by becoming a cop. Dare got that. And his position in law enforcement made him protective by nature. Dare understood that too. But this desire to take care of Liza ran deeper than some job.

She rattled him to the point where he'd forgotten to question her about things that were important, like why she was so sure no one had sabotaged her car — because Dare knew someone had. For one thing, he trusted Mason. And Sam had checked with the service center that had worked on Liza's vehicle and learned the brake line had been in perfect condition when the car left the shop.

Then there had been Liza's insistence on

the day of the accident that Brian would never intentionally hurt her. What was it she'd said? *He was the one who was there when —*

It wasn't the first time she'd alluded to . . . something.

What didn't she want to tell him? The thought kept him pacing, his curiosity running rampant and not because he was a professional.

He padded across the floor in his small apartment and drew open the blinds. The morning had dawned bright and sunny. Maybe the weatherman had heard Dare's threats about what he'd do if it rained because today was the perfect pool day. And he was off from work so he could enjoy it.

Enjoy Liza.

So much for distance, he thought with a harsh laugh.

An hour later, he was standing with his brothers on the deck of Ethan's pool. This mansion still blew him away. The pool house was bigger than the house he and his brothers had grown up in; the pool was massive with a built-in waterfall, and the heater ensured the perfect water temperature. Who knew his brother's penchant for video games would translate into government contracts and a multimillion-dollar career?

He glanced over at the sparkling water where Kelly and Faith were in bikinis, relaxing on floats and talking quietly. Liza was nowhere to be found, and disappointment didn't begin to cover how Dare was feeling.

"Are you going to ask where she is or are you just going to keep watching the door and sulking?" Nash asked, laughing as he tossed Ethan a bottle of water and then did the same for Dare.

Nash twisted the top and took a long, cool drink. Instead of cursing at his brother, he groaned and said, "Okay, I'll bite. Where's Liza?"

"She called and told Faith she'd be late. She had to stop at an antiques shop first." Ethan took a long swig of water.

"See? That wasn't so hard, was it?" Nash grinned.

Dare flicked him with the end of a wet towel like they'd used to do when they were kids.

"Don't make me throw you into the pool," Nash muttered.

"Do it and the women will drown you." Ethan grinned.

Dare flung himself into a lounge chair that felt more like a plush recliner. "Can't you two shut up for five minutes?"

"Ethan, can you get us some iced tea?"

Faith called from the pool.

Dare raised an eyebrow as Ethan headed inside without a word of complaint. "He's whipped."

Nash took the chair beside him. "And you're not?"

"I'm not married," Dare muttered.

"Maybe you wish you were." Before Dare could respond or haul off and hit his sibling, Nash continued. "Ever been in love, little brother?"

Dare broke into a sweat that had nothing to do with the heat of the summer sun. "What the hell kind of question is that?"

"The kind you ask your brother who's on edge. Who's worried about a woman he barely knew until a few short weeks ago." Nash frowned. "Are you telling me anything about your reaction to Liza is normal? I mean normal for you."

Dare scowled. "I've always been a relationship guy."

Nash nodded. "You have. And in those relationships, you've never hovered."

"I'm not hovering."

"You can't leave her alone."

"I haven't seen or spoken to her in four days," he muttered.

"And I bet you've thought about her for

every hour, minute, and second of that time."

Dare jumped to his feet. "Fuck you."

"If you'd gotten any in the last four days, you might not be in this sucky mood," Ethan said, joining them.

A glance over his shoulder told Dare he'd brought out a big pitcher of iced tea, three large acrylic cups and ice for the women. Dare shook his head, about to storm out and get some air that didn't include his brothers, when the door to the house opened and Liza stepped outside.

Suddenly the stifling air around him eased and Dare began to breathe easier.

He glanced at Nash. His brother grinned. Dare flipped him off and turned to Liza, pretending the word *love* wasn't floating around his brain, put there by his good-for-nothing sibling.

Ignoring his brothers' stares, he headed to greet Liza.

Liza wore a white sheer cover-up beneath which he caught sight of a hot pink bikini and lots and lots of bare skin. It didn't matter that he'd seen and touched every inch, his entire body tightened with need, not to mention the relief he felt at knowing she was here, with his family, and safe from the threat she didn't believe existed.

"Hi," he said, coming up beside her.

She glanced at him, confusion in her gaze. "What are you doing here? I thought this was a fund-raiser meeting."

Could she at least appear happy to see him? "My brother lives here too, remember?"

"I didn't mean . . . Never mind. I just didn't expect you to be here."

"Ethan and Nash said they'd be hanging by the pool and I'm off, so here I am."

Her gaze traveled from his face down his bare chest, over his swim trunks, which now sported a definite bulge, to his bare feet, and back again. "I see that." She grinned. "Actually, I see a lot." Her strained expression relaxed, easing into a smile.

"Funny," he muttered.

"Liza, grab a glass of iced tea and join us in the pool!" Faith called. "We're working here."

"Working hard," Kelly said laughing. It sounded more like a giggle and Dare wondered what Ethan had added to their iced tea.

"You heard them. Work calls." With a shrug, Liza strode around him.

He watched as she headed to the pool, paused by a chair, and proceeded to strip off her top, revealing a barely there two-piece bathing suit. His tongue stuck to the roof of his mouth.

"Easy there." Nash patted him on the back hard enough to cause Dare to choke.

"Would you lay off," he muttered.

"When you admit you're so gone over her." Nash burst out laughing.

Dare gave him the finger. Again. By now, the gesture had lost any import whatsoever. And Dare couldn't say his brother was all wrong.

TWELVE

Liza hadn't expected Dare to be here, though if she really thought about the kind of morning she'd had, she should have anticipated him. She'd spent the last couple of days trying to come to terms with what he'd told her about her brother having killed Stuart Rossman. And the obvious conclusion that her parents among other adults in the community, people in positions of importance, must have covered up the crime.

Liza had lived her life under a delusion they'd created, and as a result she'd done nothing to help Brian deal with what he'd done. The truth must have eaten away at him every waking moment. His escape into alcohol made so much more sense to her now. Though Dare saw Brian as entitled — and he was — Liza knew the boy he'd been and she'd been trying to save him as best she could for as long as she could remember. It wasn't enough. Had never been enough.

Shaking those thoughts off, she arranged her bag, top, and towel on a spare lounge chair. In her bag were the copies of the two checks to Annabelle's Antiques. Nothing about her trip to see Annabelle had gone as planned. Or should she say, nothing had gone as she'd hoped. Everything about the dual checks and her brother's possible involvement was still a puzzle, and to make matters worse Liza had inadvertently upset a very important vendor.

Eager to put the incident and the problems with her brother behind her for now, Liza accepted Faith's wave to come into the pool. Once there, she took a chair float, complete with a cup holder on the side. She settled into the water and leaned back, feeling the hot sun on her skin and the delicious water lapping over her as she relaxed. *Heaven,* she thought.

Her house didn't have a pool like her parents' did and she rarely had the opportunity to lounge and just be.

"This is amazing," she said to Faith.

"You're welcome any time," the other said with her usual friendliness. "And I mean that."

Liza smiled in gratitude. "I may take you

up on that."

"We hope you do," Kelly said. "Since I tend to be here often."

Faith leaned in close. "And so is Dare."

Liza smacked her hands over her ears. "I didn't hear that. Nope, I didn't. I thought I was here for a fund-raiser meeting."

Kelly laughed. "You are. Faith and I just wanted to make sure you knew the lay of the land," she said with an impish grin.

Faith must have caught Liza's look because she said, "Okay, so on to business."

"Why don't I start?" Liza offered. Anything to take her mind off the half-naked Barron brother with his golden, tanned chest, staring at her from across the way.

"Okay, go." Faith hooked an elbow on the side of the pool, lounging comfortably half in and half out of the water.

Liza noticed Ethan hadn't taken his hungry gaze off his wife. Same for Nash, of Kelly. The testosterone in this pool area was off the charts and even Liza was squirming in her seat.

"Well, let's see," she said, forcing her attention back to the business at hand. "I've single-handedly destroyed the center of town, which means any money I hoped would go to the youth center is now gone." *Poof,* she thought, an invisible cloud dissolving over her head.

"Wrong." Faith waved her hand in the air. "An anonymous donor has generously offered to pay for the repairs and replanting in town, so where the fund-raiser money goes is still up for discussion." The other woman treated Liza to a pleased grin.

And Liza didn't trust that smile for an instant. "You didn't. Or should I say, *Ethan* didn't." Liza's stomach twisted uncomfortably at the thought that they had paid for her mistakes.

Kelly raised an eyebrow. "Does the word 'anonymous' mean anything to you?" She wagged her finger in front of Liza's face.

The chastising didn't work and Liza expelled a long breath of air. "You didn't . . . shouldn't have . . . I want to donate too." She had savings of her own and surely she could contribute to the cause even if it did put a dent in her personal funds.

"No, the check's been written. I'm sure the town won't need more," Faith said. "As for the proceeds of the fund-raiser, this month's Beautification Committee meeting is next Wednesday night at Caroline Bretton's house. Six thirty P.M. Don't be late, either of you. It's the three of us against the old guard. I want to present a united front."

Liza merely nodded, overwhelmed. A

permanent state around anyone with the last name of Barron, it seemed.

"Now, on to the party itself," Kelly said. "I have a copy of last year's menu and the chef's recommended suggestions for how to tweak things so this year is different but just as fabulous. That said, I don't know anything about cuts of steak or different kinds of wine. I need you to go with me to the tasting." Kelly, whom Liza never thought of as shy, blushed at the admission.

"I'd be happy to go through it with you," Liza said, grateful she had something positive to offer. "We could meet at the catering hall and go over things?"

Kelly nodded eagerly. "Oh, and another piece of good news. I've recruited a new volunteer."

"Who?" Faith asked.

"Annie Kane."

Faith grinned. "The more the merrier."

"Annie . . . Do I know her?" Liza asked. The name sounded familiar.

"Maybe. She was a year or so behind us in school. And she's Nash's ex-wife," Faith said.

Liza nearly tipped out of her chair. "Whoa." Her gaze darted to the men who were engaged in serious conversation and for once not paying attention to the women.

"It's okay. Kelly and Annie are very good friends," Faith said.

"Huh."

"I can read your mind, but I swear those two are more like brother and sister than exes." Kelly leaned her arms on Liza's float and let herself hang from the end. "Annie's with Joe Lockhart and has been for the last, oh, I don't know, six or eight months? Believe me when I tell you, there's nothing for me to be jealous of."

Liza nodded, and though she believed Kelly, she didn't understand. "You're a better woman than I am," Liza said, and immediately regretted the outburst.

She was admitting too much to these women whom she didn't know well. And yet they made it so easy for her to talk to them. They accepted her in a carefree way she hadn't experienced on an everyday basis. Just like Dare did when he wasn't choking on her brother's very existence. But it was that acceptance that made her feel so . . . proprietary. As a result, she definitely didn't think she could be close friends with any woman Dare had been intimate with let alone married to. The jealousy factor would be off the chart. And Liza had never once been jealous about any of the men she'd been with in her past.

Uh-oh.

She turned toward Dare and found him watching her intently. He met her gaze and she flushed hotter than she was before.

"Is it me or did the temperature just spike?" Kelly asked, laughing. "Come on now, Liza. Business first, then you can find Dare and . . . whatever it is you two want to do."

"Hey!" Liza splashed water at Kelly, who merely laughed.

"I just call 'em like I see 'em."

"And then she wonders where Tess gets it from," Faith muttered.

Speaking of the teenager . . . "Where is Tess?" Liza asked.

"She's at her friend Michelle's." Faith glanced at her watch. "Actually Michelle's mother should be dropping Tess off soon."

"So let's finish up fund-raiser talk. Once my sister gets home, we'll never stay on topic," Kelly said.

"As if we're staying on topic now?" Faith asked, but she didn't seem too concerned. "Okay, so there's four of us to face the committee and push our agenda. Kelly, will you ask Annie to be at the meeting Tuesday night?"

Kelly nodded. "I'm sure she will as long as she's feeling up to it."

Liza tilted her head. "Is she sick?"

Kelly hesitated before answering. "Annie has MS." She paused once more. "But she's very open about her condition, so I don't think she'll mind that I told you."

Liza's head was spinning with all the information she'd learned in such a short time.

"Okay, now as for the smaller but equally important details." Faith held up one hand. "The band is set, the decorator is working with me, you guys are handling the food and drinks. Invitations?" She ticked each item off her fingers.

"Coming back from the printer this week," Kelly said.

"And with that, business is concluded." Faith held up her glass and took a drink. "Meeting adjourned."

Faith and Kelly eased their way out of the pool and Liza followed, grabbing the towel she'd brought with her, wrapping it around her waist and tucking in the end to hold it in place.

Before Dare could waylay her, she walked up to Ethan, wanting to have a word. He was the oldest. With his dark hair and deep brown eyes, he was the most similar to Dare in looks, but Dare's hair was shorter, his build tighter and more defined. And where

Ethan still possessed the badboy persona he'd perfected in high school, Dare, the cop, projected a completely different kind of aura. Competent, strong, in control. Everything about him, from his good looks to his character, drew her in.

Ethan still intimidated her a little, but obviously he'd come a long way and Liza was the last person to judge anyone for their past. "Ethan?"

The man turned to face her. "Liza." He greeted her with what for him passed as a warm smile.

"I just wanted to thank you for your donation to fix the center median in town." Liza had no doubt he was the anonymous donor. If I can contribute or help . . ." Liza trailed off, her point made.

Ethan narrowed his gaze. He paused, then finally shook his head. "Don't be ridiculous," he said. "It's fine."

Dare watched the exchange, recognizing immediately that his brother had no idea what Liza was talking about. Faith had clearly taken the reins on this one. As usual, Ethan wouldn't undermine his wife's plan, whatever it might be.

"Well I just wanted to say thank you." Liza laid a hand on Ethan's forearm. "And thanks for having me over again."

"You're welcome," Ethan said, placing his hand over hers in a friendly gesture.

The sight of her fair hand on his brother's darker skin irritated the hell out of Dare for no good reason. He clenched his hands into fists and drew in a steadying breath. No reason to act like an ass toward his brother just because Dare was feeling irrational and crazy.

But he could talk to Liza and he suddenly had a burning need to get her alone. Overwhelmed by a host of emotions he could barely contain, he stepped between Ethan and Liza, meeting Liza's startled gaze. "Pool house. Now," Dare practically growled at her.

Liza's mouth opened in surprise. "Dare!"

"I need to talk to you."

More like he just needed her, he thought as he grabbed her hand and pulled her toward the pool house. He slammed the door shut behind them.

He glanced at Liza, who stared at him, eyes wide and uncertain. Her lips were lightly glossed, her body glistening from the heat, and thanks to the damned air, her nipples puckered through the bikini's top.

He stepped toward her. It had been too long since he'd seen her last and he'd missed her. Needed to know the distance hadn't changed anything between them, hadn't given her time to shore up those damned defenses of hers.

He raised his hand in the air, wanting to cup her face and bring his lips down on hers, but to his shock she flinched.

He immediately dropped his hand in confusion. "Liza?' he asked softly, having regained complete control. "You know I wouldn't hurt you. I just wanted to touch you."

She blinked and started to shake. "I'm sorry. I can't believe I reacted like that. It's just that you looked so angry, and then you dragged me in here like a caveman and I was surprised, but I wasn't scared."

He remained stock-still, not wanting to move a muscle until she finished. This woman had gone toe-to-toe with him ever since he'd first met her at the police station, and he needed to know what the hell had set her off so badly. Yeah, he hadn't been himself, but she had to know he'd never lay a hand on her in real anger.

"I was actually kind of turned on," she admitted, and her cheeks flushed. "But then you slammed the door and I turned around and you had your hand raised and suddenly I wasn't here . . ."

"Where were you?" He swallowed over the

nausea rising in his throat, certain *this* was tied to why she felt she owed her brother so much. *Because he's the one who was there when . . .* "Where were you?" he asked again. "And this time I'm not letting you get away with not telling me."

She walked over to the oversized sofa, which happened to face a massively over-sized television screen, and sat down.

He wondered if she planned on fighting telling him. He watched her internal struggle and saw in her face when she finally gave in and decided to trust him.

"It was the beginning of my sophomore year of college. My first year I pretty much flew under the radar, but guys started to notice me the following one."

"They'd be blind not to," he said.

She shook her head and shot him an embarrassed smile. "Anyway, Tim was a senior and it was beyond flattering that he'd focused on me. I was too naive to realize that focus would later come back to haunt me."

"What happened?" He eased himself beside her on the sofa, letting his legs touch hers but not pressuring her.

As a cop, Dare knew the signs of abused women, and by now he also knew Liza well enough to know she hadn't been permanently scarred by whatever had occurred. She'd gotten past it on most levels. He'd guess the stress of three traumas in almost as many days had built up her anxiety levels. And he never wanted to see that look on her face aimed his way again. He still hadn't gotten over the notion that for a split second, even her subconscious believed he'd been about to hit her. Jesus.

He placed his hand over hers.

"At first, Tim's possessive behavior was kind of endearing, at least to someone like me who'd never had anyone to look out for her. But things quickly changed. His behavior was classic, really. He was jealous of my friends, men or women, and controlling over the time I spent away from him. And the longer we were together, the worse it got. Honestly, I was always so used to being on my own, he was strangling me by just existing."

Dare wasn't surprised in the least. The woman he knew did and said whatever she wanted.

"One weekend, I went home from school and he insisted on coming with me. Five minutes with him in my space at home and I knew I had to end it. I was planning to wait until we got back to school, but something happened. I can't even remember the trigger." She shook her head. "I do remember we were alone in the house and had an argument. I told him it was over. We argued some more, and he said I was his. I walked to the front door and opened it. I told him to get out."

Dare ran his thumb over her hand, encouraging her to continue while his silence told her to take her time.

"He slammed the door hard, turned around, and slapped me." She blinked, as if still stunned.

Dare clenched his jaw tight, wishing he could wrap his hands around the bastard's neck himself.

"Hey." He waited until she turned to face him. "I may get my inner caveman on, but I will never touch you in anger. Ever."

She smiled. "Believe it or not, I know that. It's just that for a split second, from the door slam to the lift of your hand, I wasn't here anymore. You know?"

He managed a nod. "You've had a lot of stress this past week. I'm sure that didn't help. So what happened next? How did your brother save you?" he asked, wanting the story over and done with.

She tipped her head to the side. "How did you know about Brian?"

"I put together the clues. You said Brian

would never hurt you drunk or sober because he was there *when . . .* This had to be the when."

She nodded. "He'd been home earlier and had met Tim for the first time. Brian told me later he didn't like the vibe he got from the guy and something made him come home to check on me."

For the first time, Dare felt something akin to respect for the other man. His gut had worked correctly and he'd done something for someone other than himself.

"I was fighting Tim off. No way was I going to let him rape me and show me what it meant to be his." She shuddered in complete revulsion. "We'd trashed the entryway — broken an expensive lamp among other things. Then Brian walked in from the garage, took in the scene, and in a split second he had Tim against the wall by the throat." She swallowed hard. "Brian told Tim if he left now and never bothered me again, he might let him live."

"Tim bought that?" Dare asked.

She nodded. "Apparently he was a big man when it came to intimidating and controlling me, but with another man? He crumbled like a cookie. He walked around with Brian's fingerprints on his neck for the next few weeks, but he never came near me again."

Dare rubbed the back of his neck with one hand. "How did your parents take things?"

"Leave it to you to get to the heart of things," she said on a laugh. "Brian sent me up to shower and he cleaned up the mess before they came home. He must have known they'd blame me for everything. It's just what they did. By the time I came back downstairs, he'd guzzled a bottle of my father's best vodka and was claiming he'd stumbled in and caused the mess himself."

"Holy shit," Dare muttered.

"You can say that again." Liza stared at her feet. "I let him do it. I knew they'd shake their heads and say it was Brian being Brian, so I never said a word. I can't say it was my finest moment." She raised her gaze to his. "And that is why I know for sure Brian would never hurt me. That's also why I'd go to the ends of the earth to protect him, even from himself."

Liza had spilled her guts to Dare and then spent the afternoon with his family as they barbecued, laughed, and joked with each other, including her as if she belonged. Tess came home and Liza enjoyed watching the teenager interact with her brothers. She

281

obviously knew each one well, and which buttons to press to drive them crazy, but it was equally obvious that the teen was loved. She might not have parents in the traditional sense, but she had family, people to rely on, and as Liza knew firsthand, that was more important.

Watching Dare with his sister, Liza was struck by how comfortable he was with Tess. While Ethan had clearly stepped into the authoritative parent role and Nash was still finding his way with the teen's sarcastic nature, Dare walked the fine line between friend she trusted and confidant on a different level from Ethan — whom she obviously adored.

"He runs the DARE program at all school levels," Faith said, coming up beside her.

"You caught me watching him, huh?"

Faith bit down on a raw carrot. "You weren't exactly being subtle. He's great with kids."

Liza sighed. Of course the man was great with kids. He'd make a great father some day, but Liza wasn't going to be a mother. She didn't know squat about kids or even doing what was right with them. She hadn't exactly had the best role models. And why was she even thinking about these things? Lord, she was losing her mind.

"I'm so glad you're here," Faith said, squeezing her arm.

Liza forced a smile. "Me too." And she meant it. Each time she was with the Barron family, it became easier to feel a part of their intimate group and harder to want to pull away.

But she had to go.

Each time she was with Dare, one of them opened a vein and poured out their lifeblood. How much more deeply connected could they get before he remembered he couldn't be with her because of her brother? Dare would leave eventually. Everyone in her life did. And when he left, he'd be taking all these wonderful people with him.

"Would you think I was rude if I said I needed to get home? I'm just so tired," Liza said.

Faith smiled. "Not rude at all. I don't know anyone whose been through what you have who wouldn't be wiped out. Go home. I'll see you this week at the Brettons'."

Liza nodded. "Would you do me a favor?"

"Of course!"

"Tell Dare I said good-bye?" He was in the pool with Tess on his shoulders and she couldn't face him while she was feeling so raw and emotional.

Faith frowned. "Are you sure you don't

want to tell him yourself?"

"He's busy." Liza grinned when Tess reached down and pulled at his short hair.

Faith laughed at the antics too. "Okay, I'll tell him. Take care of yourself, okay?"

"Always," Liza said.

She let herself out of the gate that led to the driveway and headed for her car. The side of the house had an extra driveway with a patch of blacktop for guest cars and she'd parked in one.

She reached into her purse and was looking for her keys when someone tapped her on the shoulder. Already antsy from earlier events, she jumped back, letting out a little shriek.

"Ms. McKnight?" A man wearing a black T-shirt with gold chains and denim jeans stood too close for comfort.

Liza narrowed her gaze and clutched her bag tighter in her hand. She hadn't yet found her keys and she stepped closer to her car in search of personal space, but the man wasn't taking the hint.

"Who are you?" she asked the man with dark hair and a short crew cut.

"A friend of your brother's."

"Who somehow found me here?" She shook her head, better than letting the rest of her shake, which would only show her fear. "You followed me."

"You're smarter than your brother."

Only because I'm sober, Liza thought. "I'll ask you again. Who are you?"

He grinned. "I like you, Ms. McKnight. So it would really pain me if you had another accident, only this time you were on the highway with no flower beds to cushion your crash."

Her mouth grew so dry, words failed her. "What do you want with me?" she managed to ask.

"Your brother owes my boss money and he'll get it one way or another. Your accident was a warning. Tell him to pay or next time you won't be so lucky."

Her legs started to shake and she leaned against the car, watching as he ran, not walked down the driveway.

"Liza!"

She whirled toward Dare, torn between sending him after the guy who'd disappeared at the end of the long driveway or jumping into his arms. But when she heard the roar of an engine in the distance, she knew the guy was long gone.

THIRTEEN

Liza had jumped Dare the minute he'd stepped into view. He'd caught her and wrapped her in his arms, but it wasn't enough and she was practically crawling inside his skin, trembling.

"What the hell happened?" Dare asked, holding her tight. He wasn't about to let go. "I came out to see if I could catch you before you left, and thought I heard voices."

"Some guy was waiting for me by my car." She spoke in his ear. If he wanted to see her face, he'd have to peel her off him and she clearly wasn't ready.

"What do you mean? Who was waiting by your car?"

"Some guy. He said that Brian owes his boss money and my accident was a warning. That next time, I'll be on a highway and there'll be no flowers to cushion my crash."

Dare's stomach churned. He slowly lowered her feet to the ground. Bracing his hands on her forearms, he held her out in front of him. Her dark eyes were wide in her pale face. Real fear embraced her and he wanted to take off down the driveway after the guy.

"Liza?" He needed to make sure she was hearing him.

"What?"

"Where did he go?"

"He ran off. Down the driveway. I heard a loud engine at the same time you came outside. He's gone." She wrapped her arms around herself and started shaking once more.

"Hey. Nobody is getting near you," he promised her. He had unused vacation time and he planned to take it. "I'll be with you twenty-four/seven until we figure this out. Okay?"

She nodded. That she wasn't arguing with him told him how flat-out scared she was. At least now she'd take the threat seriously.

"Can you describe the guy?" Dare asked, then remembered something. "Wait. Hang on." He looked up at the house, searching for the security cameras his brother had talked about putting in.

Bingo. Up near the corner of the window above the garage.

"Let's go back inside and talk to Ethan. He's got this place under surveillance. We might be able to get a photo of the guy." He held out his hand and waited for her to take it.

"Umm, there's something else you need to know first," Liza said, obviously coming back to herself.

"What is it?" he asked.

Her eyes grew watery and she drew a deep breath. "I'm also having a problem at work, which involves checks. I think my brother might somehow be involved." She looked away, unable to meet his gaze.

Dare knew what the admission had cost her. He wouldn't let her regret it by going ballistic about her sibling.

He grabbed her hand. "It'll be okay. Let me get Ethan working on the cameras. Then you and I will go back to your place and you'll tell me everything." He grasped both her hands in his. "I'm here," he promised her.

They started back toward the pool when he thought he heard her ask, "But for how long?"

He had no time to answer. They walked into the gated pool area. Ethan took one look at them and strode over, demanding to know what was wrong. From there, Dare gave orders and everyone listened.

Nash and Kelly took Tess inside. Faith sat by Liza while Ethan pulled the tape. Since very little time had passed, they were able to find the footage and make a DVD to bring to the station. At the very least, they could try to identify the man, but Dare already knew they were dealing with someone who'd stop at nothing to get his money.

Liza's cut brake line was proof of that.

Who did that son of a bitch owe money to and for what? Dare wanted to beat her brother senseless for involving Liza in anything, but all that would do was put distance between Dare and Liza. And she needed him by her side now more than ever.

As much as he wanted to question her and see what was going on both at work and with Brian, she was too shaken up for him to grill her tonight. Between her concussion, the accident, and everything with her brother, she was more fragile than he'd ever seen her.

Dare knew a good night's sleep would do wonders, and by morning she'd be ready to handle whatever needed to be done. Liza was strong and she was a fighter.

But for tonight she needed some TLC and Dare had no problem giving it to her.

■ ■ ■ ■

Liza felt as if her brain had short-circuited. For a woman who'd always been in control of her life, her emotions, and her destiny, the last week had shredded any notions she had about being in charge. So when Dare offered to drive her home, she agreed without question. When he parked in her driveway and instructed her to sit tight, she listened too. He came around to the passenger's side of the car and opened her door, helped her out, and walked beside her to the house. He held out his hand and she gave him the keys.

Oh, she knew by tomorrow she'd pull herself together, but for tonight if he wanted to order her around and take complete control, she decided she'd allow it. Her brain had already shut down and it felt good to not fight the person who wanted to pamper her.

He locked the front door and checked the garage exit and windows, and for once she was grateful Dare Barron was a cop. She put all thoughts of Brian, people he owed money to, and men who wanted to hurt her out of her mind. Or tried to. The lingering fear and anxiety hovered just below the surface.

Dare must have sensed her fragile emotions because he was steady and calm. He asked her no questions, demanded no answers. He was just there.

He guided her to the bathroom and turned on the shower. "Long day at the pool means we need to clean up."

She merely nodded.

While waiting for the water to get hot, Dare stepped closer. He lifted the sheer top she'd put over her bathing suit and drew it over her head. The cool air-conditioning blew over her skin and she shivered, her nipples hardening instantly beneath the bathing suit top.

He noticed but said nothing, merely reached around and unhooked the bikini top and let the material fall to the floor. Her breasts grew heavy under his insistent stare.

"Beautiful," he said almost reverently, and brushed the pad of his thumb over one distended peak.

She moaned and realized the sound came from her throat. Realized too that at his touch, her body came alive and so did her mind. Her senses, which had been dead since the incident on the driveway at

Ethan's, fired up at his intimate caress.

He switched to the other breast, swiping his finger over her other nipple. "Just trying to give them equal treatment," he said with a sexy grin.

She laughed for what felt like the first time in hours. She couldn't resist him one bit. And for right now, she didn't want to. She needed this, needed him too badly. The worry and the issues she knew were between them could wait.

She eased one finger inside his bathing suit trunks and his stomach muscles jumped, stiffening beneath her touch. She could imagine other muscles stiffening as well and wanted to find out firsthand.

"Uh-uh." Dare grabbed her wrist. "Tonight is about you."

At his words, moisture pooled between her thighs. "But touching you makes me happy," she murmured.

His eyes glazed over. "I'll make you even happier," he promised. "Now keep your hands to yourself like a good girl." He placed her hands back at her sides before hooking his fingers into the sides of her suit bottom and easing them down her legs.

He lowered himself along with them, slowly revealing her to his hungry gaze. She stepped out of first one side, then the other, and he tossed the bottoms across the floor.

He stood and with one swift yank removed his trunks. Next thing she knew, he'd lifted her up and placed her inside the shower, joining her in the enclosed steamy area. The space wasn't tiny and they both fit just fine with room to move and turn.

Dare settled her, back to the wall. He lathered up his hands with her favorite coconut-scented soap and began to wash her body from her toes on up, massaging with his fingertips, easing his strong hands over her calves, up her knees, her thighs, and slowly inching his way to her feminine folds. All the while, his erection pulsed strong and hard, rigid and upright against his belly.

Her sex clenched with need and she tried to touch him, wanted to slide her hand along the hard, rigid shaft, but he shook his head once more.

"No." He placed her palms against the wall behind her and while he was positioning her, he spread her thighs open wide. "This is about you, remember?"

She nodded, feeling vulnerable because the position exposed her to him in all ways.

"You trust me, right, baby?" he asked.

She melted like butter. "Of course I do." Her legs trembled at the admission, her body contracting and craving him like never before.

"Then let me make you feel good. You need this," he said gruffly.

She did. She needed *him.* She relaxed, let her palms feel the cooler shower tile and allowed sensation to take over.

Dare felt the minute she stopped fighting and gave herself over to him. Her muscles slackened and she leaned against the wall, trusting him to take care of her.

From this woman, the submission was humbling. He slid his slick hands from her thighs, higher, bypassing her dampness. She let out a cry of disappointment.

He laughed and pressed a kiss to her belly. "Soon," he promised. "Soon."

He continued his deliberately sensual assault, lathering the rest of her, taking his time with her breasts, palming the firm flesh in his hands, arousing her by rolling her nipples between his fingers. With every squeeze, she thrust her hips forward in a silent plea.

He set his jaw and ended his cleaning, leaning in for a long kiss, devouring her lips and thrusting his tongue into her eager mouth. To her credit, her hands remained in place and she let him do the work, taking possession of her mouth. He slid his tongue in and out, mimicking the act her lower body desperately sought until his cock was so hard he thought it would break.

Dare leaned his head back and drew a deep breath. He caught sight of the shower handle and unhooked it from the holder. He rinsed her off, watching as the soap slid over her skin, the white foam easing over the slope of her breast, the curve of her hips, and down between the V of her legs.

Once he'd finished his task, he was about to drop the handle and shut off the shower when another idea hit him and he lifted the pulsing water jets. Up, up, over her thighs the water pelted against her skin.

He met her gaze for a brief moment, watched her eyes first widen in surprise and then glaze over in understanding and desire. Knowing he had her permission, he refocused on his task, aiming the water at her center. The streams struck at her sex, gliding over and onto her inner and outer lips, hitting her directly on the small bud he desperately wanted to take into his mouth.

But not yet.

Instead of easing up, he brought the shower head closer, so the power and pressure of the stream did its job. Her legs began to shake and he slipped one hand behind her back to hold her up, all the while never letting the water pressure ease.

She leaned against him, panting in his arms. Head thrown back, hips thrust out, taking the pleasure he delivered, she was the most gorgeous thing he'd ever seen. And suddenly she cried out, her orgasm overtaking her.

Dare dropped to his knees and replaced the water jets with his mouth, suckling her clitoris into his mouth, pulling her deeper into sensation, letting her ride her climax and him to completion.

When she'd finished and nearly collapsed, he slammed the shower off and wrapped her in a towel, then pulled out one for himself. A few minutes later, he'd dried them as best he could and led her to the bed. She was still too malleable, too willing to let him call the shots.

That was okay. He knew it wasn't a permanent state. It just meant she still needed him. Once on the mattress, he pried the towel off her body, baring her to him once more. She shivered and so did he, but he knew they wouldn't be cold for long.

He lay alongside her, letting his body heat fuel hers. Then, reaching out, he slipped his finger between her legs, finding her wet and ready for him.

"Tell me you want this," he said, needing

to hear her voice. Her certainty.

"I want *you*." As if to prove it, she bent her knees and reached for him.

He raised himself up and over her, coming down so his erection poised at her entrance. They'd had the protection talk and he wasn't stopping now.

He leaned over and nipped at her lips at the same time he thrust deep, and if he didn't know better, he'd think he'd found home.

Shit.

Have you ever been in love, little brother?

His brother's words reverberated inside his head to the rhythm of Liza's body contracting around him.

He braced his hands on either side of her and pulled out slowly, feeling her soft, willing flesh grip him as he withdrew, then plunged back in to the hilt and started all over again. The only sounds in the room were their harsh breathing, his groans, and her breathy sighs, urging him on.

Words like *harder, faster,* echoed in his ears as Liza gripped his shoulders and dug her nails into his skin. All thoughts of gentleness and care fled, but she didn't seem to mind. She wanted what he did, everything and anything they each had to give. Over and over, her hips rose to meet his, picking up his rhythm, accepting him as he plunged into her again and again, lost to the needs of their bodies and, Dare feared, his heart.

Liza woke up feeling much more like herself. She just wasn't ready to face the world yet. Why would she want to when Dare's warm body was curled around hers and her limbs were deliciously leaden from last night? Speaking of last night, he'd given to her, but today she wanted to return the favor, and since he seemed in no rush to jump out of bed, she assumed she had time.

She deliberately squirmed to let him know she was awake, and he rolled onto his back, exactly where she wanted him. She turned to face him, well aware of the fact that they were both completely naked. Was it any wonder she'd slept so well despite the uncertainty and problems in her life?

She pushed those thoughts aside for now. A little more time wasn't too much to ask, was it? She braced her hand over his hair-roughened chest and a groan rumbled through him.

"You're up."

"In more ways than one," he said gruffly.

She laughed. "There is definitely something I can do about that," she said, reaching over and cupping his erection in her hand.

He sucked in a deep breath. "You don't —"

"Shh. I want to." Liza needed to taste him, to give back, to do to him what he'd done to her last night.

She didn't know how long they had together before her life ultimately imploded their relationship. And she didn't kid herself any longer. This was a relationship. Probably the first real, genuine one she'd ever had and she planned to savor it, even if it was short-lived.

She snaked her way down his body, taking in his musky, masculine scent until she was inches from his rigid erection. She licked the head, teasing him, taking in his salty taste before pulling him into her mouth completely.

He groaned and jerked his hips upward, pushing himself harder against her throat. She forced herself to relax, to take him deeper than she thought possible. His entire body shook and she reveled in how out of control she made him, that *he* could react this way because of her. It only made her more aware of her feminine power. She wanted to take more of him into her mouth, to bring him higher and send him over that edge. And from the way he was thrusting into her mouth, he wasn't all that far away, and she found it extremely arousing. Moisture pooled between her legs along with a pulsing that beat in time to the thrusts of his hips.

She curled her hand around his balls, running her fingertips over the heavy sacs.

"Liza, baby, that feels good." The words sounded torn from him. "I'm close, sweetheart, come here."

She shook her head and continued to work him, gliding her tongue along the firm ridge and popping her lips over his wet head before going back in for more.

"Gonna come," he warned her.

As if that would make her stop? She picked up her pace and her own body throbbed in time to the rhythm they'd set. Unable to control herself, she reached down and began to rub herself with her fingertip, seeking the same relief she was giving him. Waves began to crest inside her immediately and she circled her tiny nub harder, faster, the pressure building as fast as his.

Dare's hand came up to tangle in her hair and he held on as she brought him to climax. He pumped his hips into her, and when he came with a shout she followed, her orgasm blinding in its intensity, and she worked at swallowing every last drop while at the same time, grinding her pelvis against her own hand.

She released him and collapsed on his thighs, his fingers still tangled in her hair as he held her close.

"Hell of a way to wake up," he said at last.

She managed a laugh. "I thought so."

"I'd offer to take care of you, but I realized you already handled that."

"I've never . . . not in front of anyone before." A warm flush rose to her cheeks. "Does it bother you?"

"I think it's hot."

She rolled her eyes. "You would." She shook her head. "Men," she muttered, and crawled back up to meet his gaze.

He pulled her into his arms and to her surprise, into a long kiss. "Feeling better this morning?" he asked.

"Much. Thanks to you."

He met her gaze, his hot stare lingering. "Can't say I minded."

She settled her hand on his chest and placed her head against his shoulder. He pulled her close and they lay together in silence. Liza enjoyed the sense of peace and rightness surrounding her and realized how foreign both sensations were to her.

"We need to talk," Dare said, breaking the peace.

"I know." She drew a deep breath and prepared to face reality. "Let me take a shower and pull my thoughts together, okay?"

He nodded. "I'll jump in after you. If I join you, we won't get any talking done."

She grinned, visions of him taking such good care of her last night before taking *her.*

And, oh, he'd taken her. Possessed her was more like it. She'd come apart, and when she resurfaced she'd wondered if she'd ever be the same.

Now in the light of day, she knew she wasn't the same woman she'd been before her life had become entangled with his, and she wondered how she'd cope when he was long gone.

Before Liza and Dare settled in to talk, Liza grabbed her cell phone and locked herself in the bathroom to call her brother. She needed to talk to him in person and to do that she had to make sure he'd be around. What she didn't need was an argument about Brian with Dare, so she chose the most private room in the house.

She dialed, but her brother's phone rang and rang and nobody answered. She didn't even get voicemail on the other end. Same for his cell phone. She'd check in with work later, but she had a hunch they hadn't heard from him either. If all else failed, she'd have to call her parents, but she dreaded that almost as much as she dreaded the thought that someone wanted to hurt her brother. Through her.

Her stomach cramped as the memory of the guy with the heavy chains and threats came back to her. What if he'd hurt Brian? Her knees went weak and she lowered herself to a small vanity chair, forcing herself to think. If the guy had given her a message for her brother yesterday, surely that meant Brian had time before whoever he owed money acted or hurt him.

A knock sounded on the door.

"Come on in," she called.

Dare stepped inside. "Are you okay?"

She clasped the phone in her hand. "Yeah. I'm fine."

He leaned against the door frame. "You look upset."

"No more than I should be considering what's going on." She drew a deep breath. "Are you ready to talk?"

"I am. Are you?"

She shook her head and laughed. "Ready? No. Willing? Yes."

He stepped forward and held out his hand. She took it, letting him pull her to her feet.

They sat down in her family room and Liza curled her legs beneath her. "What do you want to know?"

"For starters, why you snuck your cell phone into the bathroom." He stared at her with those perceptive eyes and the determined gaze she remembered from when they were merely acquaintances. A few short weeks, yet it seemed like forever.

"I was trying to reach my brother," she admitted.

"And you think I'd have a problem with that."

She shrugged. "Wouldn't you?"

"I'm going to have to get used to it."

But he wasn't there yet. She ignored the kernel of disappointment in her stomach. "Well, I didn't want to ruin the mood. Anyway, he didn't answer."

"Okay, let's start at the beginning."

She nodded. "Where is that?"

"With your brother. He owes someone money. Forgive me for asking, but doesn't he have plenty?"

She bit the inside of her cheek. "We have trust funds. We have access to the monthly interest if we need it. I don't. I don't know about Brian, but I'd guess he dips into his. His lifestyle is more extravagant than mine."

Dare raised an eyebrow. "He lives in your parents' house. Does he pay rent?"

She shrugged. "I figured the less I knew about the extent to which my parents enabled him, the better. It's enough I do my share."

"Relax. This isn't an interrogation. I'm just trying to get the facts because I'll be damned if someone's going to hurt you again." Dare placed a hand on her bare thigh, just where the denim fringe of her shorts ended.

She didn't pretend his touch didn't affect her. It did. But she knew how important this conversation was, so she ignored the warmth spreading upward.

"Well, Brian makes a more than decent salary. It should cover living well. But as I said, he likes nice things."

When Dare remained silent, Liza felt compelled to add more. "Okay, he thinks he's entitled to them."

"I didn't say that."

She expelled a long breath. To his credit, he hadn't. "But you thought it."

"What does Brian do in his spare time?"

"Other than drink, you mean?"

Dare closed his eyes in frustration. "Look,

we're not going to get anywhere if you keep assuming I'm out to hurt him. All I want to do is protect *you*."

She smiled, appreciating his strength and caring, his very presence more than she could say. "I'm having problems at the office that might have something to do with Brian." She blurted out the truth before she could talk herself out of it again.

She could no longer tell herself she didn't need Dare Barron.

She did.

FOURTEEN

Dare was doing everything he could not to verbally blast Brian's actions in front of Liza. She'd trusted him with what was going on in her life and Dare didn't want to make her regret it.

Even if the information led to the conclusion that Brian was involved in fraud or embezzlement from his own sister's company, something Liza hadn't yet acknowledged out loud.

From what Liza had explained to Dare, two checks had been printed to an antiques store and both had been cashed. One signature on the back looked like her brother's. Without saying a word against Brian, Dare had merely offered to go back to Annabelle's Antiques along with her because no way was he leaving her alone and unprotected.

They arrived at the small shop early the next morning in time to greet the owner when she opened. The parking lot was empty, and with a little luck the woman would be free to talk to them.

Dare walked to the entrance, Liza by his side. She was dressed in an outfit that fell between her business suits and her outside the office shorts. A flirty skirt hit her mid thigh and a ruffled top belted around the waist completed the look, along with a sexy pair of heeled sandals. As usual, the woman made him drool with little effort or intent. He was getting used to being in a constant state of arousal around her, which didn't bother him as long as she seemed happy to indulge him when they were alone, which she did.

Liza paused outside the door and put a hand on his arm.

"Remember, I upset her last time I was here so I wouldn't count on her being too helpful. And I don't think we should mention that you're a cop either."

Dare nodded. "For now, I agree with you." But if it became necessary in order to get information, he had no problem pulling out his badge.

He held open the door and Liza walked through. Inside, the shop was the epitome of an antiques store, a hodgepodge of items and accessories littered around and tagged with handwritten prices.

A tall woman with long dark hair turned at the sound of the ringing bell, which had announced their arrival.

"Hi, Annabelle," Liza said.

"Liza," the other woman said stiffly. "What are you doing here? I thought we covered everything the other day."

"I upset you and I'm sorry. I came to apologize and to try to talk about it again."

Annabelle lifted her chin. "You all but asked me if I deliberately cashed two checks."

Liza shook her head. "No. I told you that two checks had been written and deposited, at least according to the bank. You refused to discuss anything more with me."

"I had customers."

"And you were upset." An apologetic look crossed Liza's face. "I was hoping you'd had time to calm down and understand I need to look into this."

Annabelle wouldn't meet Liza's gaze. She turned to Dare instead. "Who is this?"

"My . . . boyfriend," Liza said, stumbling over the word.

Dare bit back a grin. The woman who didn't do relationships had just confirmed she was in one.

"Dare Barron, this is Annabelle Block.

Annabelle, this is Dare."

He nodded. "We're spending the day together and Liza wanted to stop by and see you before we did anything else. She's been upset all weekend," Dare explained.

The other woman let out a long sigh. "All I know is that I received one check, signed the back, and deposited it. I never saw another one." Liza nodded. "Is there anyone else with access to your mail? Someone who does your banking?"

Dare had prepped her and she was doing a fine job of questioning Annabelle while attempting to convince the shop owner she was deflecting blame away from her.

Annabelle shook her head. "It's just me. You know I'm a small business. I have one part-time employee and that's it. I do all my own banking." She forced out each word.

Liza gave the woman a smile. "Okay. I appreciate your patience and your honesty."

Annabelle immediately turned away. "I told you everything I know," she said over her shoulder.

If that were true, then why was the woman so uptight and unable to look either of them in the eye? Dare wondered.

"Thanks," Liza said. "Come on, Dare." She tugged on his hand and they turned for the door.

"Have you spoken to your brother?" Annabelle asked just as Liza gripped the handle.

Liza pivoted back around. "You know Brian?"

Dare turned as well, wanting to see the woman's face and gauge her reaction.

"He's come in looking at antiques." Annabelle's gaze darted around the store, not focusing on any one of her items in particular. Definitely not making eye contact as she spoke.

"Brian's an accountant," Liza said, her gaze narrowing.

"He . . . ummm . . . he's been here," the other woman said lamely.

Liza started forward, but Dare stopped her with a hand on her arm. If they crowded Annabelle, they wouldn't get any answers. She'd clam up fast.

"Weren't you just telling me this morning that you couldn't reach Brian for the last couple of days?" Dare asked Liza.

She nodded. "He hasn't answered his phone or returned my calls. Do *you* speak to him often?" she asked Annabelle.

The other woman looked distinctly uncomfortable. "Sometimes. We talked yesterday. He was in a rush and said he'd call me back. He hasn't."

Dare wondered if that had been before or after Liza spoke to Annabelle about the two checks.

"And that's unusual?" Dare asked.

She shook her head quickly. "No, he's a customer. I just . . ."

Dare forced a grin. "She's got a thing for him," he said to Liza, deliberately speaking loudly and laughing as if he'd just figured it out.

"No, I . . . well, we used to date," she finally admitted.

Liza's eyes opened wide. "I had no idea," she murmured.

And Dare had a hunch she wasn't supposed to.

"We kept it quiet . . . and then we broke up. But we've kept in touch," Annabelle admitted.

"If you hear from him, will you let me know?" Liza asked.

"I sure will. And . . . I understand why you had to ask about the checks. I'm sorry I got touchy."

"It's okay."

But Dare felt the confusion vibrating through her body as if it were his own.

Annabelle shifted uncomfortably. "And if

you hear from him, will you tell me?" she asked.

"Of course."

They stepped outside into the heated summer air and headed for the car. No sooner had Dare opened the door for her than she turned and wrapped her arms around him tight.

"Thanks for coming with me," she said.

"Anytime."

Liza spent the next day doing normal things, like working. She'd let Jeff handle the Mystic job. As long as someone was threatening Brian through her, Liza wanted to stick close to home. After the trip to Annabelle's, Liza left twice-daily messages on her brother's cell phone, but she hadn't heard from him, which left her on edge and worried. Something she held back from Dare because no matter how good he was being to her, she still thought asking him to feel pity for Brian was taking things too far.

As for Dare, it had taken some doing, but she'd gotten him to return to work as well. They'd compromised, Liza promising that he could drive her to the office and pick her up to take her home after his shift. She wasn't stupid and readily agreed. She had no desire to be accosted or threatened in town or anywhere where she might be found alone. Dare picked her up at six. They went to dinner and returned to her house where neither could keep their hands off each other.

Their sexual chemistry was off the charts and once again, Liza wished that was all that existed between them. But Liza knew sex, and the emotions that swept through her body when he entered her were so much more.

She shut her eyes against the reality, but all the darkness managed to do was bring her right back to Dare. It didn't matter if he was taking her hard and fast or treating her with the utmost care, he made her feel cherished and cared for. Two things that had always been in short supply in her world. Two things she could never trust to remain. Something would happen to ruin things between them. Something always did.

They repeated their routine the next day, except that Liza had the scheduled meeting with Faith and Kelly for the fund-raiser. Since she'd promised Dare she wouldn't go anywhere alone right now, she asked Faith to drive her. Better to rely on one of her new friends than to have Dare sitting outside in his car playing bodyguard. As much as she appreciated his attentiveness, she needed personal space and normalcy. Or as much normalcy as possible, at any rate.

Faith had already picked up Kelly, and the three of them pulled up to Caroline Bretton's home together. Cars already lined the driveway and the street out front.

"Is Annie meeting us here?" Faith asked.

Kelly shook her head. "She's not feeling well."

"That's too bad," Faith murmured.

"I'd have liked to meet her," Liza said. Another ally would have been nice. She glanced up at the house. "Looks packed." And her stomach cramped at the thought of facing all these women who no doubt knew about the fact that she'd plowed into their beloved center median and gazebo.

"I planned a fashionably late arrival," Faith said, treating her to a grim smile. "This way we can gauge their reaction to us and respond accordingly."

"Swell," Liza muttered.

"These women need to be persuaded to listen to the younger generation," Faith insisted.

"Then we'll just let you lead the way." Kelly hooked her arm inside Liza's and nodded for Faith to go on ahead.

With a groan, Faith lifted her chin and they followed her inside.

Caroline Bretton, an attractive woman with bobbed dark hair, met them at the door. "Faith, it's so good to see you!" She spoke with warmth and gave Faith a kiss on the cheek. "We're meeting in the family room. You know, the room you decorated so beautifully."

"Thank you," Faith said. "Caroline, I believe you know my sister-in-law, Kelly Barron, and you know Liza McKnight. She's been invaluable in offering suggestions for the event." Faith winked at Liza.

"I'm so pleased things are going well!" the older woman said, sounding genuine. Liza smiled at her, grateful for her warmth. "Everyone else is here, so come on inside."

Liza felt somewhat better knowing she was flanked on either side by Faith and Kelly as she stepped into the room filled with judgmental eyes.

At least that's how she felt, as the women and their perfectly coiffed hair peered at them as they made their way in.

Caroline performed the introductions among the group. There were about a half dozen women sitting down, some on a floral sofa, others on a love seat, and still another in a Queen Anne armchair. Faith had done a beautiful job in this room; it complemented, Liza noticed, the marble entryway.

It was obvious Caroline liked her colors — bold yellows and royal blues — and yet somehow Faith had pulled things together.

Someone cleared her throat, and Liza forced her attention from the decor to the women. From the corner of her eye, she realized Faith's mother, Lanie Harrington, was also present and Faith had stepped over to give her mother a hug.

"I didn't realize her mother was a member of the Beautification Committee," Liza said quietly to Kelly.

The other woman nodded. "Since she's been venturing out more and more in the last year, Faith and Caroline finally convinced her to join the committee." Kelly lowered her voice before continuing, "Lanie Harrington is still a raving bitch, but since Faith is trying to keep things civil, we all do the same. Still, if she gives you a hard time, you don't have to take it."

Liza grinned, remembering Lanie and her haughty attitude all too well. In fact, Lanie and Liza's own mother had much in common. They'd been in the same social circles when Liza was a child and until they'd moved down south.

"So, why don't we start with an update from the chairwoman on the fund-raiser," Caroline suggested loudly, essentially calling the meeting to order.

Faith stepped toward the center of the room. Though she wore a simple skirt and short-sleeved blouse, she commanded attention just by virtue of her presence. Not all the women in the room seemed pleased to see her there — a few were murmuring behind their hands. Liza wondered if it was Faith's father's Ponzi scheme and the fact that he was in jail that bothered them or her marriage to the town bad boy that did her in. Whatever it was, Faith was undeterred.

"We haven't kicked into high gear yet, since the fund-raiser is still a month away, but the invitations have been ordered and the vendors chosen. The next step is for us to meet with each, settle the music choices, and decide on the food."

"I think Marjorie did a wonderful job last year," a woman said from her seat on the sofa. She held a fine china teacup in one hand and her lips were so tightly pursed that Liza wondered how she was able to drink.

"Well, of course you think that, Lucille. Marjorie's your daughter!" This from Lanie Harrington. "I'm sure Faith can bring new blood and ideas to this year's gala."

Liza raised an eyebrow, surprised Faith's

mother would speak out. Given all Liza had heard about how Mrs. Harrington had taken to her house and hidden after her husband's arrest, she'd have thought Faith's mother wouldn't want to call attention to herself.

"Listen to you, giving advice at your first meeting," Marjorie said to Lanie.

"Are you sure you're not going to be biased because Faith is your daughter?" Lucille asked.

"Ladies, this kind of bickering gets us nowhere. Faith, do go on," Caroline said.

Faith waved a calm hand. "My committee and I expect to offer a whole new way of doing things, especially since the affair itself will be at my home instead of in a banquet hall this year." She smiled as she confirmed the news.

Whispers and murmurs immediately sprung up among the women. "I didn't know about that!" one woman exclaimed.

Caroline waved her hand, dismissing the concern. "I asked Faith if she and her husband would host the gala, since their home *is* the best-known town landmark. Ethan and Faith graciously agreed."

"I wouldn't say Ethan was gracious," Kelly whispered with a snicker in her tone.

It was all Liza could do not to laugh out

loud, and Faith, having heard too, merely grinned.

"Lanie, how do you feel about that? Seeing as how it used to be your home for many years?" a sour-looking woman asked, with a hint of glee in her tone.

Faith stiffened.

All eyes turned to her mother, whose cheeks turned red.

Knowing what it was like to take the brunt of pain and anger for someone else's actions, Liza actually felt sorry for her.

Lanie drew her shoulders back and faced the room. "If the house had to change hands, I'm glad it's with my daughter now," she said, holding her head high.

Beside her, Liza would swear she felt Faith's relief and pride echo through her.

"And you know Ethan signed the house over to his wife, so really it's back in the family after all," Lanie added.

"Mother!" Faith snapped, the tension back in her shoulders.

"I think it's time to move on to another aspect of committee business," Caroline said smoothly before things could degenerate further.

Good idea, Liza thought.

"Let's discuss where the proceeds of this event will go," Caroline continued. "Faith and the members of her committee have a proposal they would like to present. One I feel has merit." Caroline waved at Faith, indicating she should speak.

But the same woman whose daughter ran the event last year rose to her feet. "Well, we clearly have no choice, as the beautiful center of town has been ruined!" She glared at Liza this time.

As if she'd had any control over her car? And as if she didn't feel guilty enough for the results?

"First, accidents happen. Second, we do have a choice," Faith said. "The committee has been given an anonymous donation that has covered the cost of restoring the center of town."

Spontaneous applause erupted at Faith's announcement, but Liza cringed, still feeling guilty over what had to be Ethan's donation at Faith's request.

"So we suggest the money raised by this year's gala go to the youth center downtown."

"Pardon me? You want to waste our money on a glorified babysitting center for unruly kids who can't find a productive way to spend their free time?"

Liza didn't know the name of the woman speaking, which was a good thing. She didn't want to know anyone that closed-minded. "I would think the point of a fund-raiser's money is to help a cause in need." Liza spoke up for the first time.

"I agree," Faith said.

"Well, of course you do."

Liza put a hand on her new friend's wrist to calm her. There was no point in arguing with someone that ignorant.

Faith had clenched her fists, but to everyone's surprise, it was Faith's mother who stood up in the center of the room. "Mary, that's my son-in-law you are talking about."

Faith's wide-open eyes told Liza that she was unaccustomed to being on the receiving end of her mother's support.

"As I recall, you weren't too pleased with the union or with the fact that he owns your old home," Mary said.

Though Lanie Harrington's face was bright red, she remained standing, facing Mary and the women who'd surrounded her in support. "I was wrong about him," Lanie said in a steel-laden voice. "And so are all of you."

"I have to agree." Caroline, her expression grim, stepped toward the woman. "Mary, I don't expect everyone here to agree on anything, but I do require you to object with respect. If you can't manage that, I'm going to have to ask you to leave my home."

"Well, I never. Gone are the days when the right kind of people chaired these committees." Mary picked up her purse and headed for the door.

The women beside her looked at one another, clearly unsure whether or not to follow. Two did. A few remained.

"Now then," Caroline said when the room had settled once more. "I call for a vote on whether or not to spend the fund-raising proceeds on the youth center. All in favor?" she asked, and followed by raising her own hand.

Faith's mother's hand was the next in the air. Maybe Lanie Harrington's fall from grace and her husband's incarceration had taught her something of value after all, Liza thought. She couldn't help but wish her own parents would come around the same way, not that she held out any real hope. They were stubborn in their beliefs and set in their ways.

The vote came down in favor of the idea, and Faith, Liza, and Kelly agreed to celebrate at Joe's once the meeting ended, and things wrapped up quickly afterward.

While Faith said good-bye to her mother and Caroline, Kelly excused herself to call Nash and stepped outside. Liza followed, checking her own messages. There was one from Dare saying he'd meet her at home by ten and reminding her to call if she needed him earlier. She smiled at his thoughtfulness and looked forward to seeing him later.

A few minutes later, Faith joined them and they headed over to Joe's. The women pulled up chairs around a small table and each ordered a glass of wine, except Faith, who favored club soda. They toasted in celebration.

"Faith, your mother is something else." Liza shook her head. "You must be so proud of how she's holding her head up after everything. And the way she stuck up for you . . ."

Faith smiled. "Yes, but don't be deluded. My mother is still . . . my mother. She can be as obnoxious to Ethan as the next person, but she's learned the value of supporting those close to her. Yeah, I'm proud in a twisted way." She shook her head and laughed. "But ten years ago she would have been no better than Mary."

Liza nodded in understanding. "My parents are still just like her," she said quietly. She was happy when talk turned to plans for meeting up at the caterers, meal tastings, and other things for the gala.

When a yawn escaped her lips, Liza

couldn't help but laugh. "I'm exhausted. Would you all mind if we called it a night?"

"It's fine with me. Just coordinate with Dare so you won't be alone," Faith said.

Liza appreciated but didn't need the reminder. The fear never really left her, and she reached for her phone. She dialed his number but the call went to voice mail. She glanced at her watch. "He's not answering, but he should be off from work by now."

"When I spoke to Nash, he mentioned that Dare was going with Cara to check out a condo complex in Easton."

Liza turned to meet the other woman's gaze. "He what?"

Kelly fidgeted in her chair. "Went looking at condo units."

"With Cara?" Liza didn't know what surprised her more, that he hadn't mentioned it or that he took Cara along with him rather than her.

Which immediately set off alarm bells in Liza's head. Since when did she expect Dare to report his every movement to her? And why should it bother her if he was out with one of his closest friends and co-workers? Even if she was an attractive female.

Liza didn't know, didn't understand it. She just knew the idea of the whole thing had her stomach in an uncomfortable knot.

"Liza, are you okay?" Kelly asked, placing a hand on top of hers.

"Yeah," she mumbled. But was she?

"Maybe he just forgot to mention it," Faith said, shooting Kelly a glare.

Kelly narrowed her gaze. "Hey, nobody told me it was a secret."

"It's fine. He left me a message saying he'd meet me at home by ten. I don't know why it threw me. Silly, really. They work together. It makes sense that they'd —"

"What? Look at condos together?" Kelly asked, being blunter than Faith would have been.

"Kelly!" Faith yelled at her, but something in Kelly's face told Liza she understood her reaction.

"It's not like they're moving in together. They're just both looking to buy something and they went to check it out," Faith said. "Together." She added the last somewhat lamely.

"There's nothing wrong with friends doing that," Liza said.

"Nope, not at all. As long as the current girlfriend is told up front so she isn't shocked by the news. Right?" Kelly asked, looking at Liza.

"Right." She nodded.

Faith did as well, seeming to agree and understand.

But Liza was still thrown by the idea of Dare and Cara condo hunting together. Or Dare condo shopping at all, she realized. Which was stupid. Liza owned her own place. Why wouldn't Dare want to do the same?

And really, since she all but anticipated their relationship to end sooner rather than later, wasn't it better that he obviously expected the same thing as well?

FIFTEEN

"I am in love with these condos," Cara said for the fifteenth time since they'd left Easton.

Dare nodded, not feeling the same pull that his friend did. "It's a nice area." But his heart wasn't in apartment hunting. In fact, he'd been uncomfortable all evening.

The pristine condominiums with their new appliances and empty spaces left him feeling equally empty. Cara, on the other hand, was contemplating buying.

"Come on. Let's go get a drink," she said, pulling into a spot behind Joe's instead of dropping him off at his car so he could drive back to Liza's.

He glanced at his watch. He still had an hour before he was due to meet Liza at her home, and since he hadn't heard from her that she'd be early, he figured he had time for a quick drink.

"Yeah, fine." He walked into Joe's and

within seconds he heard the feminine laughter and distinctive voices.

Surprised, he headed over to the table of women. At the sight of Liza, the constricting feeling that had been banding in his chest all evening, the one that made the condo units seem cold and empty, suddenly eased.

"Hey," he said, unable to stop the smile that took hold.

"Hey yourself." Liza looked from him to Cara. "Hi, Cara," she murmured.

"Hi." Cara nodded.

"Well, this is a surprise!" Faith rose from her seat and kissed Dare's cheek.

"And good timing too, I might add," Kelly said. "Liza was just saying she was ready to leave, which would have ended our party early since we're her ride."

A quick glance at Kelly told Dare she had a full drink in front of her and wasn't ready to go home. Since Dare knew Nash was working on a big case and wasn't waiting for her, he figured that explained that.

"I'll be happy to take Liza home." He glanced at Cara. "Do you mind hanging with them?" he asked.

"Of course not," she said with a genuine smile.

Liza shook her head. "You don't have to

change your plans for me," she said, looking from him to Cara. "I can call a cab."

"Whoa. You're not going anywhere alone."

"It's fine. I don't want you to feel like you have to baby-sit me," she said, not meeting his gaze.

He studied her, confused by her reactions. They'd agreed she needed protection until Brian was located or at least paid back the money he owed. And since when was Dare's spending time with her about babysitting?

"Umm, Cara, why don't you take Liza's seat?" Kelly gestured to the empty chair at the table.

Dare, meanwhile, clasped Liza's elbow and led her away. "What's going on?" he asked, leading her to the door.

Silence reigned until they'd reached his car behind his apartment and settled inside.

"Well? Are you going to answer me?" he asked, turning on the engine. He didn't plan on going anywhere until he had a reply. "Last time we were together everything was fine. We had an understanding about how things were going to be." They had more than that, Dare knew, but he sensed now wasn't the time to bring up feelings she wouldn't admit to.

Liza fidgeted in her seat. "It's nothing. I just didn't want to mess up your night with

330

Cara," she finally said, ducking her head as she spoke.

So that was it. Liza was jealous of Cara. Huh. Dare wasn't sure if he was more relieved or pleased he could affect her emotions so strongly.

"Since you had the meeting, I agreed to go with Cara to check out condos in Easton."

"I know. Kelly told me." She bit down on her lower lip. "It's just that you never mentioned it."

In all the time he'd known her, this was the first time Dare had been privy to her insecurities, and his gut told him to tread lightly. "It was a last-minute decision after our shift ended, and I knew you wouldn't be home yet. I did let Faith know."

"Not that," Liza murmured. "Well, not that *exactly*. I didn't even know you were looking to buy a place."

She spoke as if she cared about his future plans, and Dare's heart began a steady gallop in his chest. "I guess it just never came up."

She nodded. "Because we're always so wrapped up in my problems and my life. I never bothered to find out more about yours."

He'd never felt slighted or neglected. "I

331

would have told you tonight. Now that I saw the place."

"But Cara knew you wanted to buy."

Despite knowing better, he couldn't stop the grin edging the corner of his mouth. Yeah, he took pleasure in Liza's jealousy. So sue him and call him male. "Because I'm around her at work. We have lots of time to talk."

"You're around me the other half of the time," Liza said in a sulky voice. She knew how petty and insecure she sounded. She hated it. She'd never been either of those things in her life. Never felt possessive or jealous over a man before. More alarming was that she was responding to these unfamiliar feelings by acting like a bitch, and she felt helpless to improve her mood or soften her attitude.

"Yeah, but I'm too busy kissing you or wanting to get inside you to remember all the stupid details I tell my friends," Dare said in a husky voice that soothed all her ruffled feathers.

"Really?" she asked, still not meeting his gaze, this time because she was mortified at her typically female behavior.

Dare slid his hand into the back of her hair, turned her head, and forced her to face him. "Do you doubt me?" he asked before closing his mouth over hers, proving his words.

His silken tongue swept inside her mouth and removed all doubts. She sighed and kissed him back, pushing back her fears about how fast this thing between them was moving. She'd already lost all control, so why not accept what he offered.

He broke the kiss and leaned his forehead against hers.

"Sorry I was a bitch," she said, still horrified by her behavior.

He shrugged and leaned back in his seat. "I kinda liked it."

"Have you lost your mind?" she asked, laughing.

"Hey, it shows me you care." Without waiting for her to reply, he put the car in drive and pulled out.

Liza opted to dodge his declaration. "So, did you like the condo?" she asked.

"It's definitely a step up from my place above Joe's."

"That's not exactly a resounding endorsement."

He set his jaw. "I know. The place was okay."

They settled into silence, not as comfortable as what she was used to, and she was afraid to look too deeply into why, knowing in her heart it had to do with him looking at buying a place to live and knowing how permanent that felt. How separate from her.

Liza shivered and wrapped her arms around herself just as her cell phone rang. She opened her handbag and began to search for it, finally finding the iPhone in time to see Brian's face on the screen.

She touched the green button to connect them. "Hello? Brian?" She didn't hear his voice right away, but she felt the heat of Dare's stare. "Brian?"

"Liza?" His voice was low and gravelly, and he sounded far away and scared.

"Bri? Where are you?" She gripped the receiver tighter in her hand.

"I can't tell you that. But I'm sorry I got you involved in my mess. I'm sorry I involved the business. And I'm sorry they threatened you."

Liza swallowed over the lump of fear that wedged in her throat. "Who do you owe money to? Tell me so I can pay them and make the threat go away. Then you can come home and get help."

"You can't keep making things better for me, Liza Lou." His voice cracked on her name.

"Then make them better for yourself," she whispered.

"I'm not sure I know how." She had to strain to hear him.

"We'll figure it out together," she promised him. "Just come home."

"Can't," he said. Then he was gone.

"Brian?" When she didn't hear his voice again, she looked at the phone, but she didn't need confirmation that he'd disconnected the call.

With shaking hands, Liza placed the phone in her lap and stared out the window into the dark night. Then she waited for Dare to yell at her for offering to bail out her brother once more. She prayed he'd trust her judgment and understand the reasons she'd offered to pay off her brother's loans without even knowing how much he owed, to whom, or for what reason he'd borrowed in the first place.

But in her heart and soul, she knew Dare couldn't possibly let that go. Even as she'd spoken, Liza knew she'd crossed a line. Dare and his unyielding sense of right and wrong wouldn't understand. He had uprooted himself and his life to take care of her and keep her safe, and she'd once again sided with Brian. She fully expected him to wash his hands of her for good, and her chest hurt at the thought.

And his continued silence long after she'd

disconnected the call, confirmed her fear.

Dare knew Liza was waiting for him to speak, but he'd be damned if he'd run off at the mouth and start a fight without thinking things through. And as much as he'd hated listening to her part of the conversation, his gut told him she'd been right to make the offer. This wasn't about Brian's drinking. This was about life. *Her life.* The loan sharks needed to be paid off so Liza could be safe.

Her guaranteed safety was the key.

He waited until they'd pulled into her driveway and exited the car. He turned and grasped her hand before she could walk inside.

"Don't." She pulled back.

"Don't what? Tell you I understand why you made the offer? Because I do."

Her eyes opened wide. "Then why the silent treatment?"

"Because I wanted to take my time and think things through. Yes, you have to pay off his debts to be safe. But . . ."

Her hopeful expression drooped at his qualification. "But what?"

"Who's to say it'll be the last time? What happens next time he gets into trouble? Or the next? It's your long-term welfare that matters."

336

"There are no guarantees in this life. Trust me, I know."

She started to turn away, but he grasped her face. "Hey. Don't be angry because I care. I'm telling you I agree with what you have to do."

"You just don't approve." She raised a hand before he could interrupt. "Don't worry. I get it. Look, I'm tired. Can we just go inside and get some sleep? Tomorrow we'll deal with the logistics of how to make this thing with Brian happen."

He let her go, following her to the door. What more could he say? There was no point in beating the dead horse that was her brother, his alcoholism, and the years of enabling him that had led to this moment.

Dare might be *this* close to falling in love with her. Hell, he was probably already there. But his speech about the cyclical nature of her brother's disease and the inevitability of her bailing him out again wouldn't be changing any time soon.

Once and for all, he had to decide whether he could deal with it . . . or not.

Liza couldn't say which of them withdrew first. She only knew that she lay on one side of her bed and he on the other. She pretended to sleep, but she wasn't even close.

Her heart was close to breaking, and if this was how she felt now, imagine the agony she'd feel once she really invested her heart.

Nope, withdrawal was the smart thing. The right thing. The only thing she could do.

Because Dare would be here now while she was in danger. He'd help her get through this situation and maybe even stick around for the honeymoon period after, when Brian did whatever he could to stay out of trouble. And then, after she fell for him completely, Brian would do something, Liza would have to help him, and Dare wouldn't be able to understand.

He agreed with her decision, but he didn't approve. Liza considered those words fair warning and decided to act accordingly.

Dare met Ethan and Nash for lunch at the Family Restaurant on Thursday afternoon. The restaurant had been Dare's meeting place with Nash for years. He'd never imagined Ethan would be included in these impromptu luncheons, but he had to admit he was grateful they'd put the past behind them.

The meal consisted of the usual barrage of insults and jokes, serious questions about other things, and of course eating burgers and guzzling soda.

"So Tess wants to go to a party Friday night," Ethan said, leaning back in the booth.

Dare narrowed his gaze. "What kind of party?"

"House party. She's been good lately. Grades are excellent, hanging out with Michelle, who's been a good influence . . ."

"Kelly mentioned it to me. Is Michelle going to the party?" Nash asked.

Ethan nodded. "Faith's leaning toward saying yes, rewarding her for good behavior and all that. Kelly agreed with her."

Dare listened to the conversation and processed the arguments in favor, but his mind had already been made up. "Are you all crazy?"

Ethan met his gaze. "We can't keep her locked in her room. That'll just encourage her to sneak around when she starts to feel like we'll never trust her."

"And meanwhile she's just gotten her previous record expunged. Why would you want to risk something like this?" Dare asked, fists clenched hard.

"Is this her brother talking or is it the cop in you?" Nash asked.

"Or is it the kid who went to a party and never forgot it?" Ethan asked somberly.

Damn, but his oldest brother was perceptive. Dare glared at him. "Maybe it's a mixture of all three. All I know is that nothing but trouble can happen at one of these high school parties." He cocked his head to one side.

"Is it supervised, or is that a stupid question?" Nash asked.

"Not stupid and surprisingly yes. The parents will be home."

"Doesn't matter. If they're dumb enough to host a party with all the liability these days, I'm not sure that means squat." Dare leaned his elbows on the cleared-off tabletop.

Ethan exhaled a long breath. "I still say I don't think we have a choice. I'd rather she know she's earned our trust. She'll understand she can call us no matter what happens and we'll be there. Better than sneaking out like we used to do."

Nash stretched his arms over his head and groaned. "Sorry, man," he said to Dare. "I'm with Ethan. We have to let the kid spread her wings."

Dare remained silent. Legally, he had no say. Ethan was her guardian, sharing decisions with Kelly. They'd all agreed to it. Dare was just lucky Ethan asked their opinion on big decisions for their new sister.

And maybe, given his background and what he saw on the job, he was ultrasensitive on the subject. "I don't like it," he muttered under his breath. "But I appreciate you asking our opinion anyway."

"I'm not an idiot. I know what can happen at these things. I also know how Tess reacts when she's feeling trapped and unhappy. I just want to give her a little freedom in exchange for how much she's come around," Ethan said.

Dare nodded. "I get it." He did. But as he'd told Liza the other day, even though he understood, that didn't mean he approved.

"So, any luck tracking down Brian McKnight?" Nash asked, knowing when to change the subject.

Not that this topic was any better, Dare thought. "No. Not yet."

"So you're still staying with Liza then?" Ethan asked.

"Yeah." And wasn't that a treat? Ever since their terse talk in the car about her brother, he hadn't had the time to back away so he could consider his options. Liza had done enough pulling back for both of them.

It was as if admitting his inability to truly accept the realities of her life had marked the end in her mind. He fucking hated the distance between them, both in bed and out. But he also knew how unfair it would be for him to push his way past her barriers only to end up back in the same argument later down the road.

"Hey, where'd you go?" Nash asked. "Everything okay with her?"

"No."

"Want to talk about it?" Ethan asked.

"Nope." Dare reached into his pocket for money to pay his share of the bill and tossed the cash onto the table. "I've got to get back to work."

"Not dealing with it won't make it go away," Nash reminded him.

Dare rolled his eyes. "Talking won't change it either." He raised a hand and headed out, unwilling to bare his soul when it wouldn't make one damned bit of difference.

With Dare at work, Liza spent Thursday evening with Kelly at the caterers. Liza had to admit she appreciated the chance to get out with a woman she'd come to consider a friend, away from the stifling time she'd been spending with Dare. When she was home, she had too much free time to think about everything they'd shared before the reality of her life had intruded. What she'd lost was enough to make her crazy.

Which told her she was smart not to let things between them go any further. Not that he seemed to be pushing either. They were two polite strangers who just happened to share a bed until the danger to her had passed.

Kelly drove them to the large catering hall where the head chef prepared choices and dishes for them to taste. To Liza's surprise, she and Kelly agreed easily on most courses and talked through what they didn't. Faith, who'd delegated the task, would approve on paper. Then the menus would go out to the printers.

After they'd chosen desserts and the catering manager who would run the event from Ethan and Faith's left them alone, Kelly turned to Liza. "Spill."

"What?" She met the other woman's serious brown-eyed gaze.

"You aren't yourself and I want to know why. What did Dare do?"

Liza managed a laugh. "What makes you think it's Dare? My life is crazy enough to make me *not myself.*"

"Oh, yeah? Do tell." Kelly nudged her elbow as she leaned in close.

Liza sighed. "Okay, fine. It's Dare." Nuts as it seemed, Liza's mood had nothing to

343

do with her brother, his drinking, debts, or even the loan sharks lying in wait for her.

"Need me to slap him for you?" One corner of Kelly's mouth turned up in a grin.

Liza grinned. "Not quite yet." She thought long and hard before speaking, and when she was ready she'd sobered. "It's not Dare's fault we're having problems."

"Then whose is it? Yours?"

If Kelly minded prying, Liza couldn't tell. She just barged in, and to Liza's never-ending surprise, she didn't mind. In fact, she needed the ear. Needed a friend.

"It's life. Circumstance." She drew a deep breath and dove in. "I'm sure you know about Stuart Rossman's death, right?"

Kelly nodded. "And I'm guessing you know Dare was there."

This time Liza nodded. "Dare's holding so much guilt from that night. So am I. If I'd stayed home like I was supposed to, my brother wouldn't have had the party and that boy would still be alive."

Kelly blew out a long breath. "Well, if you ask me, that's common ground you two share. Not that misplaced guilt is such a great thing, mind you, but how can it keep you apart?"

"He blames my brother and rightly so. Brian's done nothing to fix his life, has made no effort to make some good come of the past tragedy. Not like Dare has, becoming a cop and a good person." Liza bit her bottom lip. "And he blames me for enabling Brian's behavior."

"Now that's unfair."

"But not entirely wrong. But my brother was there for me when I really needed him. He may well have saved my life and shielded me from my parents at the same time. I owe him. And . . . he's my brother."

"I get that. I'd kill for Tess, believe me. But doesn't there reach a point when they have to sink or swim on their own?"

"Maybe . . . yes . . . *of course.* And I've reached that point with Brian — except whatever he's done now has put me in danger." She glanced at Kelly. "You know the rest, right?"

The other woman nodded.

"So once I hear from my brother, I have no choice but to tell him I'll bail him out and pay off whatever he owes. I have to get the loan sharks taken care of — for his safety as well as mine."

"Dare can't object to that?"

She shook her head. "But that will only solve this one problem, and Dare and I both know that there'll be many more in the future. Brian's drinking and irresponsible behavior reminds Dare of a past he'd rather forget. And by extension, *I'm* a living, breathing reminder." She shook her head, unsuccessfully blinking back the tears. "Dammit." She wiped her eyes with her arm.

Laughing gently, Kelly handed her a napkin from the table.

"It's linen," Liza muttered.

"I won't tell if you won't."

Liza smiled. "Thanks." She blotted her eyes, grimacing at the black smears her makeup left behind. She rolled the napkin inside out and placed it back onto the table. "Look, I appreciate you listening, but I don't want to put you in the middle or cause trouble with your family."

Kelly shook her head. "Every person in that family speaks their mind, so forget worrying. And since you told me everything, I'm going to give you my opinion."

"I'm all ears." Another woman's point-of-view would be welcome at this point.

"Dare's being a jerk."

Liza jerked her head up. "Say that again?"

"You heard me. He needs to get over himself. Every family comes with its share of dysfunction and his is no different. How dare he judge yours?" She giggled and Liza couldn't help but find it infectious.

"Thank you for that. But it really is too much to ask anyone to put up with Brian." And Liza wasn't worth the hassle.

She knew that firsthand. Knew it from the cradle, when her parents put her brother's wants and needs before her own.

"Hey. You have to know how wrong you are."

Liza didn't want to continue this conversation anymore, but she didn't want to be rude either. Kelly meant well and Liza valued her friendship.

The only way to get her to understand was to tell her the gut-honest truth. "What I know is that nobody has ever stuck around in my life. Not friends, not family . . . no one. Dare has pretty much made it clear that he can't be any different, and I'm not willing to risk my heart on the off chance he comes around."

Kelly opened her mouth, then closed it again. "I don't know about Dare, but I can tell you something about me. I don't make close friends easily either, but when I do? It's for keeps." Then, to Liza's surprise, Kelly opened her arms and pulled Liza into a warm, friendly hug.

Even if it wasn't everything Liza wanted, it was exactly what she needed. Kelly had cemented a place in Liza's heart that she didn't give away easily either. Still, she couldn't help but realize that not even Dare's sister-in-law could promise the impossible on behalf of her brother-in-law. Which left Liza exactly where she'd started.

Alone.

Which she hadn't been since this nightmare with her brother had started. In the beginning she hadn't minded the twenty-four-hour bodyguard when it was Dare. But since they'd unofficially ended the relationship he was so insistent they shared, she was no longer comfortable knowing his family had to babysit her when he wasn't around. Despite Kelly's warmth and friendship, old feelings died hard.

Though she appreciated their efforts to make sure she was never alone and couldn't be approached by anyone, she couldn't stop feeling like she'd become a burden they hadn't asked for. Just like her parents — who hadn't picked up the phone since Brian had accidentally given her a concussion.

Alone was easier.

She massaged her temples and groaned. Clearly she needed rest.

"I don't know about you, but all that tasting did was make me hungry for ice cream," Kelly said, interrupting her thoughts.

Liza shook her head and laughed, happy

to be distracted from thoughts of Dare. "Ice cream sounds great." Anything to take her mind off her problems.

But when they entered the small shop off Main, Liza was reminded of the first time she and Dare had had a civil conversation — and kiss.

She sighed, not wanting to go that route. "So, how are you holding up?" she asked Kelly as they walked into the store. "You mentioned earlier that Tess wanted to go to a party tomorrow night and Dare wasn't pleased." The conversation had been interrupted by the arrival of the caterer.

In fact, he was beyond pissed and concerned. Telling her about Tess had broken the ice between them for the first time all week. She'd seen his concern and fear for his sister and she'd comforted him the best she could, though words were inadequate. Raising a teenager wasn't easy. He'd run through his brothers' and sisters'-in-law reasons for letting her go and she both understood and respected them. So did Dare.

But he didn't agree or approve of their decision. And Liza knew what it was like when Dare didn't approve.

"Yeah. I'm trying my best not to worry," Kelly admitted. "But I agree with Ethan and

Faith. She's earned our trust and she has to start somewhere." Kelly looked out the glass window onto the streets of Serendipity before speaking. "When we lived in the city, Tess got herself into serious trouble."

"How serious?" Liza asked.

They got their ice cream and picked a table in the corner to sit down and eat.

Once they were alone, Kelly spoke. "Smoking, drinking, and hanging out with the wrong kids were the least of her problems. She got caught breaking and entering with a group of guys and one other girl. She was arrested and had a juvenile probation officer and everything. And no matter what I did, I couldn't reach her." Kelly's vanilla ice cream dripped over her cone while she talked. "I finally turned to Richard Kane, who had handled Tess's father's estate."

"I had no idea," Liza murmured.

"What happened?"

"Honestly? He told me about Tess's brothers and I did the cowardly thing. I dropped Tess off on Ethan's doorstep and told him to man up. Or parent up. Anyway, she needed a firm hand and a man in her life to look up to."

"I don't think you were cowardly. It had to be hard and it took a lot of guts to do what you did."

"If you say so. Nash didn't approve."

"But he got over it."

"Because he eventually saw it was the right thing for Tess. Ethan, Nash, and Dare turned her around. Mostly Ethan."

"And Tess brought the brothers together," Liza said. That much she'd learned from Dare.

Kelly nodded. "Don't give up on him, okay? Dare has always done the right thing. The self-sacrificing thing."

Liza didn't ask what she meant. It was Dare's story to tell and he'd chosen not to tell her all the details.

She ran her hands up and down her arms. "It's getting cold in here."

"And my ice cream's melted," Kelly muttered, and threw her half-eaten cone away. "Ready to go home?"

"Yeah." The vibration on her phone a few minutes ago told her Dare was home.

But her house no longer felt welcoming and she found herself wishing that she could go back to the solitary life she'd had before. Before she knew how good sharing a home could be. The life that waited for her when Brian's current mess was cleaned up and Dare was long gone.

Sixteen

Work used to be Liza's refuge, but lately being in the office was as stressful as being home. Brian's empty office mocked her every time she walked by. Office staff asked where he was. Finally, unable to ignore the obvious, she called Peter and asked him to come to her office.

Almost immediately there was a knock on her door. "You asked to see me?" He stepped inside her office and closed the door.

Liza nodded. "I wanted to see how things in accounting were going . . . in light of my brother's absence."

"I assure you I'm handling everything," he said, beaming with pride.

"That's good to hear since I'm not sure when Brian will be back," she admitted.

Peter cocked his head to one side. "Is he ill?" he asked, sounding concerned.

More like MIA, but Liza wasn't about to

admit such a thing. "He's under the weather."

"I'm sorry to hear that." He tipped his head to the side and paused. "Whatever happened with the duplicate checks?" he asked.

Liza swallowed hard. "I'm handling it."

He hesitated, then walked farther into her office, closer to her desk. "I'm sorry to tell you this. Actually, I probably should have said something sooner, but your brother begged me not to." Peter's pasty skin flushed red.

Unease skittered up her spine and Liza shivered. "What is it?"

"This isn't the first time there have been issues with checks. I hesitated to tell you this time, but I was afraid I'd be the one you blamed if you discovered the problem." He wrung his hands in front of him, clearly upset.

Nauseous, Liza swallowed. "Peter, please start from the beginning and explain."

"The duplicate checks? It's happened before. Your brother periodically *borrows* money by printing two checks, forging signatures, and cashing the second one. He always promises to replace the money, and occasionally he does, but this time he seemed more desperate."

Liza set her jaw. "Why is this the first time I'm hearing about this?"

"I promised Brian."

"Yet you told me about the duplicate checks to Annabelle's Antiques and held back the rest?" Liza rose from her seat until she was eye level with the man.

He bobbed his head up and down. "I . . . I felt guilty knowing. I thought you'd look into it and figure things out on your own. And now your brother's been out of the office and he isn't answering calls . . ."

"What do you know about why Brian *borrows* money?" She said the word with distaste. Her brother was stealing from the firm, plain and simple.

Peter shrugged, his suit jacket bunching around his shoulders. He didn't meet her gaze.

"Peter?" she pressed.

"Gambling?" he squeaked.

Liza shut her eyes. "Are you asking me or telling me?"

"I promised your brother I'd keep his secrets, but I need my job and I'm sorry." Suddenly shaking, Liza lowered herself into her chair. She needed to think. "That's okay, Peter. I understand you were caught in the middle. Please just go. I'll let you know if I need you."

"Thank you. Thank you," he said, backing out of the room.

Gambling. No wonder Brian had borrowed money from a loan shark. Could this situation get any worse? How many addictions could one man deal with before succumbing completely?

She opened her eyes and her gaze fell on a small photo on the side of her desk. Liza and Brian as children, dressed in snowsuits outside the house. Although Liza remembered her grandparents had taken the picture — her parents had been in Europe at the time, one of their many vacations — it had been a good time in her life. A fun day.

There hadn't been many of those.

A dull throbbing pain began in the base of her head. She rose and took two ibuprofen pills and settled back in to work. She even ate lunch in the office, opting not to go out, which would have necessitated taking someone with her. Jeff stopped in to say hi and see how she was doing, and Liza was grateful for the normalcy that surrounded their working relationship. No awkward moments between them.

At five o'clock, she was still digging through outstanding work from the week of her injury but making steady progress. She decided to stay late and keep at it. She had nowhere else to be anyway, and it wouldn't be the first time she stayed late.

Knowing it was Nash Barron's day to be her designated driver, she called and explained. Then she texted Dare and asked him to pick her up when his shift ended at ten. He, of course, asked if someone else would be in the office, which prompted her to make the rounds to see if anyone else would be torturing themselves on a Friday night. Jeff was waiting for changes on the Mystic job and said he'd be there at least as long as she was.

Liza texted Dare back to let him know she had someone to look out for her. And since he'd asked, she took pleasure in letting him know who. If she could be jealous of Cara, he could stew a bit over Jeff. Even if her relationship with Dare was over. With that thought, a pulsing in her head reminded her the pain hadn't gone away.

She and Jeff ordered in take-out Chinese, which they ate together while discussing various jobs. When they finished, Jeff went to check the fax machine and Liza headed back to her office.

She was busy looking over specs when she heard a knock on her door. She glanced up to see a dark-haired man looking at her.

"Sorry to disturb you, but —"

"Do I know you?" she asked warily.

He shook his head. "No, but you come highly recommended. You see, my parents know your parents. They met in Florida. My aunt left me her house in her will. It's an old Tudor and there's a possibility it has historical significance. I want to renovate, but the town has been holding me up. Your father said you'd be happy to help."

"And you decided to come here on a Friday night?" She tightened her hands around her desk.

"I came up to check out the house, and when I passed by here, I saw the lights on. Thought I'd see if I could get lucky and find someone in."

Since the firm was located in a free-standing building that looked more like an old home than an office, his excuse sounded plausible. "It's late, Mr. . . . ?"

"Barton. James Barton. And I promise I won't take much of your time. Can we just talk for a minute and then set up an appointment?" he asked.

He'd come in person and if she sent him away, there was a chance she'd not only lose potential business, she might also ruin any goodwill seeing him now might create.

"Of course. Come in."

He stepped into the office and immediately shut the door behind him, so quietly she barely heard the click.

Liza narrowed her gaze and remained standing, her nerves suddenly screaming. But she wasn't alone. Jeff was next door and so was his assistant, she reminded herself, forcing air into her lungs. Besides, this man didn't look anything like the thug who'd stopped her on Ethan's driveway.

She stepped out from behind her desk. "Can I get you something to drink because I could use some water." And some breathing room. Whether or not she was overreacting to a closed door, she didn't care.

She planned to ease closer to the exit, but he stopped her with a hand firmly on her wrist.

Her mouth went dry. "Excuse me." She stared at his large hand wrapped around her much smaller wrist.

"I just wanted to give you a message for your brother. Or for you. At this point it doesn't matter," he said, his friendly tone gone.

Dizziness swamped her.

Liza dealt with many things in her life, but real threats and confrontation weren't among them and she was scared. "Say what you have to and leave," she said, trying to sound brave.

And probably failing.

His grip tightened. "The fifty grand your brother owes?"

Fifty thousand? "What about it?"

His expression turned menacing. "My boss isn't happy. Seeing as today's Friday, you or your brother have until Monday night to come up with the cash." The "or else" was implied. "Understand?"

Liza thought she nodded. Her ears had begun to ring, a loud sound reverberating inside her head. Not good, she realized when little black dots swirled in front of her eyes.

"Say it," the man said. "You understand?"

She swallowed. "Yes. I understand."

"Good."

"Where does he . . . where do I bring the money?" she asked, knowing she'd have to take it from her savings. Nausea swamped her.

"You'll hear from someone. We're never far away. It'd be smart for you to remember that." Without warning, he released his grip and she realized he'd not only been squeezing tight, but he'd been pressing on her pulse until she grew light-headed.

Suddenly she realized he'd swung open the door and disappeared. She hadn't seen or heard him go. Her heart slammed against her chest so loud she was surprised Jeff couldn't hear next door. Jeff.

She wasn't alone . . . but she hadn't been safe, either. At the thought, Liza reached for her desk before she could collapse and dragged in deep, calming breaths.

"Liza?" Another male voice called her name and she jumped when a large shadow appeared in her doorway.

"Liza? It's me, Nash." Dare's brother stepped into the office, filling the space where the other man had been.

He took one look at her and knelt beside her. "What happened?"

"What are you doing here?"

"Dare called. He didn't like your company and sent me over to check on you." He narrowed his gaze. "Where is your co-worker, anyway?"

"In his office, working."

Nash set his jaw. "So I'll ask again. What happened?"

"Did you see anyone leave?" Liza asked, not answering his question.

"No. Was it the same guy from the house?" Nash asked.

She shook her head. "I didn't recognize him. But you had to be coming in at the same time he left. How did you miss him?"

she asked.

"Is there another exit?"

"A back one." Liza met his gaze. "We only thought to make sure I wasn't alone. I didn't think anyone would bother me with people around. I guess Dare didn't either."

Nash exhaled hard. "He's going to be pissed." Nash looked down and saw her massaging her wrist. "Son of a —" He grabbed for his phone.

"What are you doing?" she asked, stopping him.

"Calling Dare. What else?"

Liza shut her eyes. "Don't. I'll tell him, I promise. Just . . . let it be for now." The man had relayed his message. She wasn't in any danger. Not until Monday night, anyway. "He's working and he's missed enough time."

Nash scowled at her.

"Oh, come on. I will tell him tonight. I swear."

"Fine." He wrapped an arm around her waist and helped her stand.

"I'm better now. I was just shaken up."

Nash led her to the car, his hand on her back, muttering about stubborn women and how his brother was going to kill him. Like Dare, he was a gentleman, helping her into the car, making sure she had her seat belt on, checking to see her wrist wasn't worse than she let on.

Her skin had begun to turn purple and she covered the bruising with her good hand.

Nash buckled himself in when his cell rang. He answered on the first ring. "I've got her," he said before the caller could speak first.

It had to be Dare.

"What? How? When? Is she okay?" Panic tinged Nash's voice, causing sheer panic to settle in Liza's chest.

"What's wrong?" she asked, touching him lightly on the arm.

Nash held up a hand and Liza held her breath until he finally disconnected the call. "Tess is in the hospital."

Oh, no. Liza's stomach lurched. "What happened?"

Nash shook his head and shoved the key into the ignition. "Something about alcohol or drugs." Nash cursed as he pulled out of the parking lot.

Without asking, she knew he was going straight to the hospital.

"She'll be fine," Liza said, praying to God she was right.

Sam and Dare had partnered for the night.

A slow night that consisted of too much time cruising the area, too much time to think, and definitely too much of his best friend's yammering. Dare was glad he was driving. At least focusing on the road gave him some sort of distraction.

"So how's bodyguard duty going?" Sam asked.

"Fine." And it was.

The problem wasn't the so-called job; the problem was them. So what else was new, Dare thought, holding in the rumble of anger that threatened to escape.

"She's behaving?" Sam asked.

"She's perfect," he muttered.

Unlike many people who didn't want to deal with a cop or someone either tailing them or keeping them company, Liza had been smart by accepting it and she hadn't complained. She'd even made sure she wasn't alone in the office. No, Jeff was there, Dare thought irritably. Now he knew how Liza had felt when he'd gone off condo hunting with Cara, and there was nothing fun about it. He didn't even feel guilty sending Nash to check up on her. He believed in Liza. It was the flower-sending Jeff he didn't trust.

"Then what's with the mood?" Sam asked, not taking the hint with Dare's one-word answers.

Dare raised an eyebrow. He wasn't going to discuss Liza tonight. He'd had enough of that with his brothers the other day.

"How's your love life?" Dare asked instead.

"Nonexistent," his friend muttered, and shut up instead of asking more questions.

Dare grinned for the first time all night.

Suddenly a crackling sounded and the dispatcher's voice broke into the silence. "Headquarters to Car Five."

Sam answered. "Car Five on Main."

"Ten-four. Car Five respond to Three Seasons Avenue."

"Car Five en route," Sam said.

Dare's stomach clenched at the mention of the address where Tess had gone tonight.

Static again and then, "Car Five, be advised the caller stated there is an underage female passed out on a bed inside house. Serendipity EMS is en route as a precaution. Advise if any other services are required once on scene."

"Ten-four," Sam said, then muttered to Dare, "Damned kids and alcohol."

Even as Dare swung the car around, he'd broken into a sweat. "Tess is at that party."

"Shit."

Dare hit the siren and floored the gas.

By the time he pulled up to the house, any cars that had been parked out front had disappeared and his stomach dropped, memories of his friends doing the same ten years ago coming back in vivid color.

They sprinted across the lawn and burst through the front door.

"Where?" Sam asked.

A shaking girl pointed to a doorway off the living room, and when Dare beat Sam inside his worst fears were confirmed. Tess lay passed out on a bed, with only her friend Michelle beside her.

Dare ran to her side and checked for a pulse. Thready but there.

"Parents or adults around?" Dare heard Sam ask.

"They went out after we got here," a trembling Michelle said.

Dare kept his hand on Tess's cheek, telling himself she knew he was there with her now. Sam sent Michelle out with instructions to wait in the other room just as paramedics burst in, for which Dare said a silent thanks. Though he and Sam had basic CPR training, for all Dare's cool, he couldn't handle this.

Sam must've known it too.

Suddenly his friend pulled him out of the way. "I called in for backup. You're off duty.

Go with her."

Dare managed a nod, watching in horror as the paramedics slipped an oxygen mask over Tess's nose and mouth and talked to each other, words Dare had heard before but couldn't manage to process.

"Let's get her into the bus and run an IV." Dare recognized Christopher's voice. "The more we hydrate her, the better off she'll be."

They shifted her small body onto a stretcher and began to move.

"Dare," Sam said before he could follow. "I just spoke to Michelle. Tess wasn't drinking to get drunk. She was just nursing a beer to look like she was going along. She went to the bathroom and came back, picked up her drink, and a little while later, she passed out. Sounds like maybe someone slipped something into her drink. Got it?"

Dare nodded. He knew what to tell the doctors. "Thanks."

"Alexa is on call. She'll meet you at the hospital. Now go!" Sam slapped him on the back.

Next thing Dare knew, he'd taken an endless ambulance ride to the ER, where Tess was taken away. Dare paced the corridor and waited for the rest of the family to arrive.

■ ■ ■ ■

Over an hour had passed since Liza arrived
with Nash, joining the rest of the Barrons
while they waited for news. Cara arrived a
short time later. Dressed in jeans and a
T-shirt, she was obviously off duty and had
come for moral support. She spoke to each
of the brothers, then settled into chairs in a
corner to wait along with the rest of them.
Occasionally she stepped into the hall to
call Sam and check in, but she had no solid
news either.

Meanwhile, Nash and Kelly huddled
together, Ethan's arm around his wife as
they comforted each other. Nash held
Kelly's hand at the other end of the couch
while Dare sat on a chair staring straight
ahead. Liza had a seat beside him. He knew
she was there, had lifted his gaze to meet
hers, but he wasn't speaking. Not touching
her, holding her, or turning to her for comfort.

Though this vigil was for Tess, and Liza
was sick with worry for the teen, standing
among this tight-knit family, Liza felt very
much alone.

She propped her shoulder against the wall
and waited, watching the clock on the wall

367

instead of Dare. She'd tried to get through to him, to put her hand on his shoulder and call his attention, but it was as if he weren't here.

Finally, Alexa stepped into the room and everyone came alive, surrounding her and asking questions.

Dressed in hospital green, she held up a hand. "Here's what I know. Tess will be okay. That's the most important thing."

Liza released the breath she'd been holding.

"Will be?" Ethan asked.

Faith placed a hand on his shoulder.

Alexa nodded. "She's okay now, just weak. The labs and urine showed she wasn't legally drunk, which is probably what saved her. We suspect she was drugged with Rohypnol —"

"The date rape drug?" Dare asked, stunned, his brown eyes large and so dark they were almost black.

Liza discreetly slid her hand into his for support. To her relief, he didn't push her away, merely curled his fingers around hers and held on tight.

Alexa shot him a sympathetic glance. "I need you to stay calm and let me finish. Yes, based on her symptoms, we think she was slipped the date rape drug. The turnaround on the test takes time. But she wasn't raped."

"Oh, thank God," Kelly said, and Nash wrapped an arm around her waist before she could collapse.

Dare squeezed her hand so hard Liza nearly lost the circulation in her fingers, but she didn't care. Dare was leaning on her and that's all that mattered.

Alexa spoke with the clinical detachment required of a doctor, but her eyes were kind. "If Tess had been drunk when she'd been slipped the drug, it would have hit her system harder. Rohypnol is a benzodiazepine. In other words, it's a central nervous system depressant like Valium, only ten times more potent. Overused or mixed with alcohol, it can also suppress the respiratory system. Since Tess had had some of the drink, her breathing became shallow and she probably fainted."

"How do you know . . . I mean, are you sure she wasn't raped?" Faith asked in a shaking voice.

"We did an exam while she was still out of it and ran tests," the doctor explained. "There's no evidence of sexual intercourse. And from what the police on the scene discovered by talking to the few kids who stuck around, Tess's friend never left her side."

"Good girl, Michelle," Kelly whispered.

"Is she awake?" Dare asked, clearly needing to see her.

Alexa shook her head. "She's in and out. We didn't have to pump her stomach because the paramedics were smart enough to hook her up to an IV before they brought her in. Flushing her system saved her from that. When she comes to, she's going to feel awful, hung over with a headache, among other things, thanks to the effects of the drug. She may or may not remember much either. But she's alive and that's what matters." She smiled at them. "I'll let you know when you can see her, okay?"

"Thanks," Dare said, his gaze meeting hers.

"I'd say it's my job, but in this case it's much more. I'll get you in soon," she promised, before heading back inside.

Nash pulled Kelly into a hug. Ethan did the same with Faith. Which left Dare staring at Liza.

"Good news," she said softly. "As good as you could hope for given the circumstances."

He nodded.

"Thanks for being here," he said gruffly.

"You'd do the same for me." She shook her head. "What am I talking about? You already have." There wasn't anywhere she'd rather be, but he didn't need to know that.

"Excuse me."

They turned toward the door where Alexa stood. "You can see her now. Family only. Two at a time and for just a few minutes. She needs rest."

"I want to sleep in her room," Kelly said.

Alexa nodded. "She's still in the ER, but once they get her settled, if she's in a private room, we can arrange that."

"I'll take care of the room," Ethan said.

"Okay, then. Who's first?" Alexa asked.

"Since I'm staying over, Nash and I can go last," Kelly said.

"And I want to make sure that if a private room's available, Tess gets it, so Faith and I will handle that now." Ethan inclined his head at Dare. "You go on in first."

Liza marveled at how this family, who'd been estranged not one short year ago, pulled together for one teenage girl. The lump that had been in her throat since Nash took the call grew larger. "I hope Tess knows how lucky she is to have all of you," Liza said, her voice catching.

"If she doesn't, I'll make sure she does." Nash slipped his hand into Kelly's.

Ethan walked up to Dare and met his gaze. "You were right about her not going to the party. We should have listened."

"You weren't all wrong about trusting her, either. She didn't do anything wrong. She was a victim here."

Liza studied Dare's strong profile, amazed at his generosity given the circumstances. Amazed at Ethan's ability to admit he was wrong too. These Barron men were strong and complex. She never knew what one of them would do or say next, but she admired them as much as she envied this family's closeness. She didn't know what it was like to be a part of such a strong unit, but with everything in her, Liza was grateful Tess did.

The brothers clapped each other on the shoulder and Ethan turned, leaving with Faith to go over to the administration offices and arrange payment for Tess's room.

Dare started toward the door leading inside the ER and paused. "Are you coming?" he asked Liza.

"Alexa said family only." And Liza wasn't family.

Dare stared at her for a few seconds. Liza held her breath, wondering what he was thinking, knowing she'd go with him if he asked.

He didn't.

She wasn't surprised, but she was oddly deflated as she settled into a seat to wait for his return. Nobody bothered her as she stared at the bare walls, twisting her hands together, sick to her stomach. Her thoughts ran the gamut from gratitude that Tess would be okay to the reality of owing some loan shark fifty thousand dollars, to her missing brother who'd caused it all.

"How's the wrist?" Nash asked, surprising her by walking over and joining her.

Liza turned her hand over and glanced down. "It's sore and it's bruising. But I'll be fine. I appreciate the concern, but you should focus on Tess."

Nash placed a comforting hand on her shoulder. The sweet gesture took her by surprise and she laughed.

"What's so funny?"

She glanced up at him.

The lighter brother in coloring, he didn't resemble Dare or Ethan, but he was definitely good-looking. He just wasn't Dare. "I was thinking before that you Barron brothers constantly take me by surprise. Then you walk over here, concerned about *me* when your sister's lying in a hospital bed."

Nash lowered himself into the seat beside her. "Just because Tess had a rough night doesn't mean you didn't. It also doesn't

373

mean you don't matter."

Liza shook her head hard. She didn't want to break down and sob because his caring voice was crowding her, the events of the day overwhelming her.

"I'm fine," she said, knowing he was just being nice. Decent to her because she'd had a scare too.

"You need to tell Dare what happened today," Nash said, staring into her eyes, as if he could see straight through to her innermost thoughts.

The Barron siblings had that in common too, the ability to make a person spill their soul. She blinked, not wanting him to know how hard her heart beat for his brother.

She swallowed hard. "I will. When he's not so upset about Tess."

"That's not going to happen anytime soon. We're all upset about Tess. But like I said, that doesn't make what's happening with you less important."

He was wrong, but it was nice of him to try and convince her otherwise. "Don't you have a wife who needs you?" she asked lightly, hoping to distract him.

"She's the one who sent me over to check on you." Nash smiled at that.

"She's special," Liza said of Kelly. She rubbed her hands against her slacks. She was feeling edgy and uncomfortable and just wanted this long, awful day to be over.

"I happen to agree." Nash paused. "I also think you should have gone in with Dare. He would have liked the support."

"Then he should have asked." Instead of letting her get away with the "I'm not family" excuse. Liza bit the inside of her cheek, knowing she should have kept the words inside but unable to hold them back.

"Yeah, well, we Barron brothers don't fall easily, but when we do, we fall hard. Cut him some slack. He'll come around." Nash rose to his feet.

Liza smiled. "Thanks, Nash."

"Anytime." He winked and walked away.

Drained, Liza laid her head back and shut her eyes, closing out the fluorescent lights and ugly beige walls and the pain surrounding her.

Seventeen

Dare walked down the hall to Tess's cubicle, his heart in his throat. He passed rows of closed curtains, whispering families, and beeping machines. As a cop he'd been here before, had brought victims in, dealt with the doctors. Having family here was different.

Tess being here was different.

He came to the last closed curtain and knew it had to be hers. A nurse was just stepping out as he reached for the drape.

"Is this Tess Moss?" he asked.

The kind-looking older woman nodded. "She's sleeping."

"I'm her brother. I won't wake her. I just need to see she's okay."

The nurse nodded. "Go on in."

Dare stepped inside. Tess lay propped up, her light brown hair spread over the white pillow. The makeup she'd probably painstakingly applied ran down her face, giving her black-looking eyes, her face streaked from tears.

She wouldn't be a happy camper when she woke up and took a long look. But at least she'd wake up.

He didn't know how he'd come to love this kid so much in such a short time, but she was as much a part of him as his brothers. He felt as responsible for her as he did for his siblings and even their wives. Even Ethan, as much as Dare wouldn't have believed that a year ago.

He pulled up a chair and eased over to the edge of the bed, taking her hand. She didn't stir.

"Hey, squirt." He knew she was sleeping, but he needed to talk to her, and he kept his voice low. "What were you doing drinking beer? Even nursing one?" he asked, not expecting an answer. "You're too good for parties like that. And heaven knows you don't need to be anything like Ethan or me at your age."

Dare's throat felt dry and raw. "I know you heard a lot about what happened when I was younger. How I was there when Stuart Rossman died and didn't call the police. How I ran away instead." His head pounded with the memory.

Eyes closed, he leaned his head against

their joined hands. "Tonight, when we got the call to respond to the house, I knew you were there. And when I saw you on that bed" — pain and nausea swept through him — "suddenly I was back there again . . ." Seeing Rossman on the floor, the guy lying in his own blood, an eerie parallel to Tess unconscious on a stranger's mattress. Helplessness had flooded him again, along with stark fear.

He kissed the top of her hand. It still chilled him, knowing how close she'd come to dying. "I didn't help Rossman and I was paralyzed thinking I was too late to help you." Even though the paramedics ran in and took over, in Dare's mind, all he'd heard was Brian McKnight yelling at everyone to clean up the evidence or get the hell out.

Brian, who'd punched another drunk kid and watched him fall down, then went into self-protection mode instead of calling 911. And Dare hadn't been any better.

"Just be okay," he whispered to his sister, damn near close to shattered and completely numb.

"Hey." Faith placed a hand on his shoulder.

Dare glanced up into his sister-in-law's worried gaze. "Here, sit down."

Faith shook her head. "No, I don't want to interrupt. I just wanted to let you know that Ethan was able to get her a private room, so she won't be alone tonight. Kelly can stay with her."

Dare exhaled hard. "That's good." He rose to his feet. "You should sit with her for a while. I need some air."

Faith nodded, squeezing his shoulder before switching places with him.

Dare stepped out of the small cubicle, claustrophobic and feeling a startling sense of anger at the entire situation. At his inability to control anything that happened to the people he loved. But most of his anger centered on the fact that once again, alcohol, irresponsibility, and complete stupidity had almost caused an irreparable harm.

Anger and frustration swirled around him, filling his lungs, rising to his throat. Damn Tess and her need to fit in so badly she had to go to one of those stupid parties. The same kind of party he'd cut school to attend.

He wanted to scream, to yell, to punch someone and alleviate the building furnace inside him he couldn't control.

A couple walked by him, the woman bumping into him as she passed. "Sorry," she whispered, bringing him into the present.

He needed to get back to the rest of his family. Somehow, he pulled himself together enough to return to the waiting room, but his head pounded and everything inside him continued to bubble, as if waiting to explode.

He tried to focus on Tess and the fact that she'd be fine, but somewhere in his mind, he was back in time and he couldn't manage to close off the memories as he thought he'd trained himself to do. He'd gotten pretty damned good at it too. Until tonight.

He walked into the room and his gaze immediately fell on Liza. She'd tipped her head back against the wall, eyes closed.

He headed over and touched her arm. When she didn't immediately awake, he shook her lightly.

To his shock, she jumped, startled, and let out a frightened cry.

"Hey, it's me," he said, hoping his voice would calm her.

She blinked and slowly her dark eyes focused on his face. "Dare." She sounded relieved.

"Who else would it be?"

She crossed her arms, hugging herself tight. "No one. How's Tess?" She pushed herself to a standing position.

Dare exhaled long and hard, wondering how to reply. "That's not an easy question to answer."

"Take your time."

She placed a hand on his arm, but Dare barely felt her touch. Not even her soothing voice eased the ongoing turmoil inside him.

"Tess is okay, right?" she asked.

He inclined his head. "Yeah. She's okay."

"That's good. Very good." Liza smiled. "At least she didn't have to have her stomach pumped. I remember that being the worst," she said with a distinct shudder.

"What?" He realized he'd barely heard her. Something about being glad Tess hadn't had to have her stomach pumped, he thought, and forced himself to pay attention.

"In a bad situation, Tess got lucky. I just remember when . . . never mind." Liza shook her head, cutting off her thought.

But he'd focused, damnit, and now that she'd brought it up, Dare knew what she meant. She'd obviously been about to say she remembered when Brian had had his stomach pumped.

And with that thought, all the simmering anger he'd fought to control rose, ready to explode.

Unaware, Liza stroked his cheek and he

recoiled.

"Brian?" Dare asked incredulously. "You're comparing Brian to Tess?" Dare bit out a harsh laugh. "Oh, yeah, now that's rich."

"No. I mean yes. I was just trying to find a silver lining or say how I understood. I didn't mean to imply —"

"I don't want to hear your explanations," he bit out.

Her eyes opened wide and she took one step away from him and then another.

But her distance didn't stop him. "You think you understand what I'm going through because your good-for-nothing alcoholic brother has been brought in here too?" he asked, knowing his voice was rising but unable to shut up.

"Dare." Ethan barked out his name. A warning to stop while he could. Before it was too late.

And though Dare knew he wasn't being rational, the anger since seeing Tess had been building and Liza's words served as a release valve. He was caught somewhere between the past and that room where his fifteen-year-old sister had nearly died. He remembered her birthday party back in January. A heavy weight pressed down on his chest. Guilt for the kid who'd died when

Dare had been there and done nothing filling him with anger along with the stark fear for Tess.

"Dare, I . . ." Liza opened her mouth, then closed it again.

"I know. You *understand,*" he spat, mimicking her words. "But the thing is, you don't. You can't. Because your *brother* willingly guzzles alcohol like it's water and then destroys everyone and everything around him while you not only watch but help. Tess, on the other hand, is a victim. An underage innocent victim. Something your bastard of a brother will never be."

"You're the bastard," she said, her eyes wide, her face drawn and pale, as words he could barely believe he was saying spewed out of him.

"Dare, shut the hell up now." Ethan grabbed his shoulder and shook him hard.

Dare closed his eyes and drew in a steadying breath. By the time he opened them, Liza had grabbed her bag from the floor.

He glanced around and saw his entire family staring at him in disbelief, like they didn't know him at all.

Hell, he barely knew himself.

He jerked his gaze back to Liza, who'd completely withdrawn into herself. He hadn't seen that lost, pained look in her eyes before and it scared him.

Jesus, what had he just done? "Liza —" He reached for her hand, grasping her wrist.

She flinched and pulled away. "Don't touch me." Shaking, she glanced at the door. "I need to go."

"Not alone." The protective words came automatically.

She narrowed her gaze. "Well, you sure as hell don't think I'm going anywhere with you."

Dare winced, the damage he'd caused just now settling over him.

Nash strode over to Cara and whispered something in her ear. She nodded and stepped forward, pushing herself off the wall. "I'll go with you and stay the night." Cara's blue eyes flashed as she shot a scathing glare Dare's way.

Liza swallowed hard. "Thank you. After today, I'm not going to deny myself protection," she muttered.

Dare shook his head, wondering what she meant by that. And stunned at how he'd just sent his life crashing down around him. Why the hell had he just blasted the one person he knew damned well would never hurt him?

Liza bolted through the exit doors, Cara right behind her, leaving Dare in a room full of silent family members who stared at him in disbelief.

Shaking, he lowered himself into a chair, needing a minute.

Nash stalked over and yanked a chair up and settled in beside him. "Care to explain?"

Dare rubbed a hand over his face. "It wasn't . . . I didn't mean . . ."

"Try again," Nash said. "Because what you just did made her brother look like a saint." Disgust echoed in his tone.

Not that Dare blamed him. "Fuck. I don't know. I found Tess on the bed and all I could see was Stuart Rossman lying on the ground." He lowered his head. "Then Liza said how at least she didn't have her stomach pumped because she remembers that part being the worst. The only way she could know that was her damned brother, and something inside me snapped."

"It sure as hell did," Ethan muttered.

Dare looked up.

Kelly and Faith stared at him, disappointment radiating from them in cold waves.

"I need to go see her." Dare stood.

Kelly stepped into his personal space before he could move. "You're not going anywhere near her tonight."

Dare raised an eyebrow. "Excuse me?"

"Even before that display, she knew how

you felt about her. She knew you didn't plan on sticking around any longer than she needed your protection. She has Cara now, so do Liza a favor and leave her alone." Kelly folded her arms across her chest, her face hard and unforgiving.

"I never told her that." Hell, he'd never thought that. He'd needed space, but . . .

"You didn't have to say a word. She told me that Brian was a living, breathing reminder of your past — and, by extension, so was she. And since *nobody in her life ever stuck around* — her words — she didn't expect you to be any different." Kelly's tone told Dare exactly what she thought of him at the moment.

"God," he muttered, remembering everything Liza had confided to him about her parents. How lonely she'd been. How alone. His shoulders sagged.

"Exactly," Kelly snapped. "So I suggest for the moment that you don't go over there with excuses and apologies. Take some time to get your head on straight. Don't approach her again unless you're in it for good. She doesn't deserve to be jerked around."

Dare stared at his sister-in-law in stunned silence.

Kelly drew a deep breath. "I'll be with

Tess," she said, glancing at Nash. Then, without waiting for Dare's reaction to her speech, Kelly turned and walked out.

"She's right," Ethan said, cutting Dare no slack.

Nash nodded in agreement. "No argument here. But there is something else you should know. And I'm not telling you this to add more guilt or to send you running over there. Cara will handle it."

From the tone in his brother's voice, everything in Dare stilled. "What is it?"

"When I got to Liza's office earlier, she was pretty shaken up. She'd had a visitor. Different guy from the one at Ethan's, but someone showed up and obviously made some threats. He'd grabbed her and bruised her arm pretty badly."

Dare remembered her wince when he'd encircled her smaller wrist and closed his eyes, hating himself with everything inside him.

He started forward, but Nash stopped him with a firm hand on his shoulder. "No. Cara can handle it."

Dare forced himself to breathe. He exercised more restraint than he'd have thought he possessed in not going off half-cocked. He wanted to kill someone. To bash down Liza's door and demand she listen and accept his apology.

"For tonight we focus on Tess," Nash said. "Then you figure out how you feel about Liza and what the hell happened here tonight. Then and only then do you go after her."

Knowing his brother was right, Dare nodded.

But the sick feeling in his gut remained — and would stay there he knew — until he made things right with the woman he loved.

Liza and Cara left the hospital. Thankfully the dark-haired officer didn't push or force Liza to talk about the scene in the waiting room. Liza could barely process it herself.

"Mind if I stop home and pick up a few things?" Cara asked.

"Of course not. I'm sorry to put you out."

Cara smiled. "I don't mind. But when we get back to your place, I am going to need you to tell me everything about your brother and the situation. I can't keep an eye out if I'm in the dark."

Liza nodded. What was one more humiliation in a night full of them? "Sure. No problem."

A little while later, Liza curled up on her couch. Both she and Cara had dressed in sweats and T-shirts and had opened a bottle of wine.

"Man, I needed this drink after the day I had," Liza said, taking a long sip of the dry wine.

Cara raised an eyebrow over her glass. "And this nice Pinot Grigio was the best you can do?"

Liza laughed. "It was this or beer. I bought it for Dare," she muttered, sobering. "And I'd much prefer not to be reminded of him. But good point. I ought to keep something harder in the house for just this kind of occasion." Liza lifted her glass and drained the rest, hoping the buzz would kick in soon.

Cara eyed her with understanding. "Seeing as I'm your protection for the night, I'll stay sober. So tell me what's happening. I only know what was in the police report after the accident. And Dare was staying with you because someone deliberately sabotaged your car. Something to do with your brother?"

Liza nodded. Starting at the very beginning, she filled Cara in on her brother's history with Dare, Stuart Rossman's party, and the current situation, including Brian's embezzling money from the firm and borrowing from a loan shark.

She ended her recitation with tonight's threat and the deadline she'd received. "So that's the story." To her surprise, Liza felt more unburdened afterward.

Cara whistled. "Okay, then. I guess that explains an awful lot." The dark-haired woman paused, going over everything Liza had said. "Your brother's in deep."

Liza nodded, appreciating how Cara had skipped over mentioning Dare or the scene at the hospital. Liza knew she'd have to deal with her emotions eventually, but she'd stuffed everything deep, waiting until she was alone in her bed tonight.

"I know. I can't make excuses and I don't want to. He's going to have to take responsibility for his life, but I can't walk around with a target on my back. If that means paying off his debts, so be it."

"Fifty grand?"

Liza briefly closed her eyes, then nodded. "I have it in savings. My grandfather left us both some money. I never touched mine."

Neither of them mentioned the obvious, that Brian had probably gone through his already.

"And his stealing from your firm? What do you want to do about it?" Cara treated her to a grim smile.

"I don't know. What can I say? He's committed a crime. If he isn't forced to own up, he'll keep on doing it and I'll always be in potential danger because of him." Liza swallowed over the lump in her throat, realizing the truth of what she'd just said.

Cara remained silent, obviously recognizing Liza needed time to think.

Her throat hurt from the effort it took not to cry, more over Dare's awful treatment of her than from anything her parents might do or say.

Liza poured herself some more wine and was about to take a sip when her brother's face flashed before her eyes. Alcohol had been the vice that destroyed him, she thought, and she placed the long-stemmed glass down on the table. She no longer had the stomach for the wine or the idea of getting drunk.

"Does Dare know about what happened at your office today?" Cara asked.

"I suppose you had to mention him eventually," Liza muttered. "No, he doesn't know."

Cara sighed, her exasperation clear. "We both know he was a major asshole tonight. And I'm not excusing him for one second. But I know him and he must be kicking himself up and down the hospital corridors right now, regretting everything he said." She leveled her eyes on Liza.

Liza spread her hands in front of her. "It

doesn't matter. What he said? The way he said it? The fact that those things were bubbling below the surface? It all just proves that he can't look at me and separate me from my brother. Or from his own past. I had no idea he was that deeply scarred by it." She'd thought he'd pull away from her eventually. She'd never have believed he'd turn on her so cruelly.

Cara curled her legs beneath her. "You know Nash and Dare went to separate foster homes, right?"

"Dare said it worked out that way."

Cara let out a harsh laugh. "Not really. Stuart Rossman's parents took Nash. They offered to take Dare too, but he refused to go. He couldn't live with them knowing he'd done nothing to save their son. The state could have forced the situation, but a lawyer, Richard Kane, knew the truth and stepped in. Nash went to the Garcias on the low-rent side of town. Nash lived in wealth. And nobody knew it was Dare's choice until last year."

Liza opened her mouth, then closed it again. "Oh my God." Scarred didn't begin to cover what that party had done to him. "He never told me."

"He told Sam and me last year during a really low time. I just want you to understand that what he said to you today? It wasn't about *you*." Cara shook her head for emphasis. "I've never seen him look at anyone the way he looks at you. Honestly."

Liza didn't know whether to laugh or cry. The man could very well love her and it wouldn't matter. Because his past and her brother's role in it stood between them. She was a reminder and that would never change. Dare might be sorry, but they'd find themselves in this position over and over again. So no, it didn't matter what his rant was about.

They were finished.

She met Cara's gaze. "Thank you for explaining. It can't change anything, but maybe it'll help me forgive what he said. How he said it. Who he said it in front of." Her voice broke over the last word and she shook her head. "I'm a mess. I need to get some sleep."

Cara yawned and covered her mouth with her hand. "Me too. But tomorrow we need to discuss the money, the meeting, and how you're going to handle it." She drew a deep breath. "And I need to tell Dare."

Liza stiffened. "I have *you*. He doesn't need to be part of this anymore."

Cara eyed her like she was crazy. "Somehow I think he'd argue the point." Bracing both hands on her chair, she pushed herself up. "I'm telling him. I have to."

Liza inclined her head. "Fine. Tell him. Just make sure he stays far away from me from now on."

Because her heart couldn't take another beating.

EIGHTEEN

At 6:00 A.M. the next morning, Dare's cell rang. He rolled over, feeling like he'd just gone to sleep, and grabbed the phone. "Better be good," he muttered.

"It's Cara." She spoke softly.

Dare forced himself awake. "What's wrong with Liza?"

"Oh, you care?" she asked sarcastically.

He didn't need this now. "You know damn well I do or you wouldn't be calling me at the crack of dawn."

Cara sighed. "Fine. She had a visitor yesterday," she said, still talking low.

Dare figured Liza was asleep. "Nash told me." His gut cramped again at the reminder. "Is she okay?"

"She's a strong woman. She didn't even fall apart after you lit into her in front of your entire family," Cara said, knowing she was torturing him. "Her visitor gave her a deadline. She has until five P.M. Monday to

395

get them the fifty grand her brother owes them."

"Fifty thousand dollars?" Dare shouted. He pulled himself to a sitting position, ignoring the headache pounding at his temples.

"You got it. And, thank God, so does she. She said her grandfather left her money she's put into savings."

"When I get my hands on her brother . . ."

Cara snorted. "I'd say your attitude about her brother is what put you in the doghouse in the first place. But that's not what's important now. We need a plan."

"I'll come over and we'll nail something down." He swung his legs over the side of the bed.

"Not so fast, Romeo. She doesn't want you anywhere near her."

Dare shut his eyes against the pain that knowledge caused. "Thanks for breaking it to me gently."

"Want some advice?" his friend asked.

"Would it matter if I said no?"

"Get your shit together before you lose her because you're close. Now. About that plan?" Cara asked.

Dare glanced around his small apartment, small being an understatement. He hadn't realized how spoiled he'd gotten staying at

Liza's. Not just the large rooms, which were nice, but the company.

Why had he thought he needed space away from her?

Because you hate her brother, he thought. But after his explosion last night, Dare had to wonder if the answer was all that simple.

"Dare? Plan?" Cara asked impatiently.

He shook his head, forcing himself to think. "Right. I need to locate Brian," he said, not relishing the task.

"What good will that do? If he had the money, he wouldn't be in hiding."

Dare needed to find the man for more reasons than just the cash he owed. A confrontation between Dare and his nemesis was long overdue. Dare didn't know if there was such a thing as closure, but he wasn't finding peace by ignoring his past. Not that he'd share that with Cara.

"Take Liza to the bank to get the money on Monday," Dare said, resigned. "Did they give her instructions?" Because like it or not, Dare wasn't letting her meet with loan sharks without him by her side.

Personal problems be damned.

"He told her they'd be in touch. He also said they're always close by."

Dare slammed his hand uselessly against

the mattress. "Don't let her out of your sight."

"Are you telling me how to do my job?"

He caught the teasing tone in her voice. Cara wasn't happy with how he'd treated Liza, but she wasn't abandoning him either.

"Yep. You got a problem with that?"

Cara laughed. "Nah. I'll let you know if she hears from them. You spend the weekend doing some soul searching, you hear me?"

Dare groaned. "I'm on it."

"Good. And kiss that sister of yours and tell her I'll be watching out for her."

Dare smiled. "Will do. Thanks, Cara. You're a good friend."

"I know. Don't let me down, Dare Barron. Better yet, don't let Liza down." She'd lowered her voice again. "I'll be in touch," she said, and disconnected the call.

Dare didn't know what he'd done to deserve friends and family like he had. He sure as hell hadn't earned them.

But he intended to. He just couldn't do it alone.

Tess came home from the hospital early the next morning. For Dare, visiting his sister was easy. Figuring out the rest of his life was hard.

Faith let him into the house and directed him upstairs to Tess's room. Dare figured she'd had her share of talking and lectures, so he saved his for another time. Like Faith had told him, she was embarrassed and upset but physically fine except for the hangover symptoms Alexa had warned about.

Dare reached the top of the stairs and paused outside her door, taking a breath before knocking.

"Come in."

He opened the door and stepped into her room, a vibrant purple and black haven decorated by Faith. Tess sat up in bed and smiled shyly when she saw him.

"Hey," he said, walking over. "You look a lot better today than last night." She'd washed up and her face was clean of makeup and tears.

He winked at her and she scooted back so he could sit down on the end of the bed. "You okay?"

"Yeah." She glanced down, staring at the mattress. "Ethan said you found me."

"I did." And that familiar anger swirled inside him once more.

But he refused to be drawn back to that dark, angry place today, reminding himself that Tess needed him to be strong. So had

Liza and he'd failed her. He wasn't about to repeat his mistake.

"Sam and I got the call. You scared the crap out of me," he said honestly.

She met his gaze. "I didn't do anything on purpose. I didn't even get drunk. I barely took a sip of the beer and anything I drank before that was soda. Someone put something in my cup."

"Which is why you never put your drink down, whether it's soda or alcohol. And if you do, you get a fresh one yourself, and you make sure you see that it's come from a closed bottle."

She nodded.

"Lesson learned the hard way, huh?"

She nodded again. "Are you mad at me?" she asked in a small voice. " 'Cause I'm sorry. I've been so good and now this happened and I don't want you guys to think I'm too much of a pain to have around anymore." Her voice cracked.

Dare reminded himself that the drug was a depressant and she had to be feeling the aftereffects, but he hated to think she'd ever believe they'd abandon her. Nothing could be further from the truth.

"We happen to like pain-in-the-ass kids." He held out his arms and to his surprise, his normally strong, smart-mouthed sister crawled right in and gave him a hug. "You're stuck with us," he told her. "You know that, right?"

She sniffed. "Yeah."

"You mean it? Because if Ethan or Faith knew you were feeling this way —"

She shook her head and pushed back, already pulling herself together. "No, I know. I just feel so awful. Guilty, though I didn't really do anything, sad, mortified . . ."

"You're feeling the aftereffects of the drug. It can make you depressed and sad or like you want to cry. Hopefully it'll be out of your system soon. Try and sleep as much as you can, okay?"

She nodded. "That's what Faith and Kelly said."

"They're smart."

"You're not working today?" she asked.

"I'm off this weekend."

Tess grinned. "Spending it with Liza?" she asked, teasing him, her eyes bright and alert again.

He groaned. "You are so nosy."

"It's one of my better qualities," she said, and he was happy to hear her laugh. "Well? Are you?"

He shook his head. "We're taking a break," he heard himself say. Was he really confiding in a fifteen-year-old?

"Uh-oh. What dumb thing did you do?" Tess asked, arms folded over her chest.

He lifted his eyebrows. "What makes you think it's because of me?"

"Duh? Because you're a guy!"

"Smart mouth," he muttered. "It shouldn't last long."

"I hope not," Tess said over a yawn.

Obviously she was getting sleepy, which was good. She needed her rest. "Why? Do you like Liza?"

Tess studied him through perceptive blue eyes just like Nash's. And their late father's. "*You* like Liza, so yeah. I do too."

Smart kid, he thought, with relief. If she relied on that common sense and steered clear of trouble, she'd be okay. Good thing she had three older brothers and a sister and two sisters-in-law to make sure of it. Dare wanted to add one more female to the mix.

But he still had a long way to go.

"Get some sleep," he told Tess. "I'll come back to visit later."

"Okay." She snuggled back under the covers and he let himself out of her room.

He walked downstairs to find Ethan waiting. "Got a minute?" his brother asked.

Dare nodded and followed Ethan into his office.

"You okay?" Ethan asked.

"Yeah." The word came out automatically, but the truth was more complicated. "Not really."

"I didn't think so." Ethan lowered himself into a chair and motioned for Dare to sit too.

"A year ago we wouldn't be sitting, about to have a serious talk," Dare said.

Ethan shook his head. "A year ago Nash would have blamed me for what happened to Tess. He'd probably have hit me again too." He rubbed his jaw, obviously remembering the brothers' long-overdue confrontation. "But you always held back. You gave me a chance first."

Dare nodded. He had.

"Maybe that was because you understood what it was like to make mistakes."

Despite himself, Dare grinned. "When did you get so smart?"

"I had many years of beating myself up," Ethan admitted, taking Dare by surprise.

He studied the brother he'd barely known and now felt a special kinship with. "How'd you get past it?" he asked.

Because like Dare, Ethan lived with regrets. He'd gotten arrested when he was almost eighteen and their parents were killed in a car accident on their way to bail him out of jail. Then, instead of sticking around for his brothers, he'd taken off for ten long years. So if anyone knew regret and mistakes, it was Ethan.

He leaned back in his seat, folded his arms over his chest, and met Dare's gaze. "Not easily. The army helped. I did a little therapy with the shrinks there. I'm not sure if that helped or not. I do know the discipline and the regulation taught me what it meant to be a man and take responsibility."

Dare got that. "Being a cop did the same for me." He paused in thought. "But I realize now that was more of an external shift."

"Because you still haven't forgiven yourself. All the good deeds in the world won't make up for what happened to Stuart Rossman. But the blame doesn't lie solely on your shoulders either."

Dare looked down, studying his hands, thinking about his brother's words. No, he hadn't forgiven himself. Instead, he'd indulged in enough self-hatred and flagellation for ten lifetimes, but nothing had changed. He was here. A young kid had died. Dare had done what he could with his life to atone while Brian McKnight wasted air and hurt everyone in spitting distance. Meanwhile, Dare nursed his anger and hatred toward the man, and when it exploded he'd hurt the one person in his life who truly mattered.

The hard truth remained. Nothing about the way he lived his life had or would change the past. It never would. But one thing was certain. If he held on to that anger and hatred, the only thing it would accomplish was to ruin his future.

"I need to let the shit go somehow." Dare ran a hand through his hair in frustration.

"Seems to me admitting it is taking the first step."

Dare let out a laugh. "Yeah? What's the second?"

Ethan shrugged. "You'll figure it out."

Yeah, he probably would. And Liza might forgive him. Whether she'd believe in him again, though? That remained to be seen.

Liza passed the weekend by keeping busy drafting sketches and doing work. She'd checked on Tess by calling Faith, and thank goodness, the teenager had come through her ordeal and was getting better. Faith hadn't mentioned Dare or the scene Friday night and neither had Liza. And though it was now Monday morning, she hadn't heard a word from Dare.

Pushing aside the hurt that thought

caused, she called her brother yet again. This time his voice mail was full. Of course he hadn't been in touch either. No big shock there, but a part of her had been hoping Brian would somehow come through. Man up. Bring her the money. Worry about her safety. Something.

Instead, nothing.

As usual, she was on her own.

Though the men who expected her to pay up hadn't called, she headed to the bank anyway, Cara by her side. The teller explained they needed a full business day to get that kind of cash together, and Liza's nerves were jangling as she waited to tell the man who'd be calling.

When she finally heard from him, a phone call at 3:00 P.M., her hands shook as she explained she needed twenty-four hours for the small bank branch in Serendipity to get that amount of money in. To Liza's shock, the guy on the phone understood and didn't threaten her at all.

On Cara's advice, Liza firmly told him she wanted to meet in a public place. As civilized as possible, she thought wryly.

Again to her surprise, he readily agreed. On Wednesday at 5:00 P.M. someone would meet her in her office to take the *package* off her hands.

"No cop boyfriend," the man on the phone warned her.

Liza wanted to laugh out loud and inform him he had nothing to worry about on that score.

Instead, she merely said, "No problem."

"And no cop friends either." He obviously referred to Cara. Which meant Liza was definitely being watched.

She shivered. "Fine. There'll be people around the office, though," she warned him.

"Office staff and employees won't be a problem," he said in a gruff voice before disconnecting the call.

Liza glanced at Cara who'd been sitting by her side. "Well, that was too easy."

Cara shook her dark ponytail. "These guys just want their money. That's all that matters, so honestly this should be a simple handoff." Cara smiled. "You're doing great."

Liza glanced down at her shaking hands and wondered how Cara performed her duties on a daily basis. "I don't feel great." She was worn out from lack of sleep and frazzled from fear.

"It'll be over soon," Cara assured her.

"I know."

Cara's compassionate tone and the fact that she was here helping without complaint reminded her of Dare.

Liza wanted to ask her if she'd spoken to him and whether she'd told him about the threat and the money, but she refrained. He couldn't have made himself any clearer about how he felt, and though she understood his past better thanks to Cara, that didn't change his inability to accept *her.*

Besides, it wasn't as if he'd tried to get in touch with Liza over the weekend either. Her instinct on Friday had been correct. She needed to cut him out of her life, and going cold turkey was the simplest way. No matter how painful the withdrawal might be.

Finding Brian McKnight had been simpler than Dare thought. So simple it boggled the mind. On a hunch, Dare called on Annabelle at her antiques shop. He wanted to look the storekeeper in the eye when he asked her if she'd heard from Brian McKnight. The man had to reach out to someone and Annabelle had seemed to care about him. One glance into her eyes and he hit pay dirt.

The woman wasn't trained in the fine art of lying. Her eyes darted everywhere but at Dare when she answered his question, hemming and hawing while attempting to reply.

He'd finally laid it on the line, telling her

that Liza was in danger because of her brother's actions and that if she knew where Brian was, she'd be helping them both by admitting it.

Now Dare stood at a seedy hotel in a neighboring town to Serendipity. From the looks of the place, guests probably paid by the night and most checked out sooner rather than later.

Dare strode up to the room number Annabelle had given him and knocked once.

"Who is it?" a muffled male voice asked.

"Management," he muttered back.

The door yanked open. "I told you I'd get you your money soon."

Dare slammed his foot in the entry before Brian could react and pushed the door open with his hand. "How are you going to do that when you can't even pay your gambling debts?" Dare shoved his way inside, ignoring McKnight's grumbling and cursing under his breath.

Dare didn't know what smelled worse, the man or the room. Empty liquor bottles, food wrappers, and an empty pizza box littered the floor and night tables.

"What do you want?" Brian asked.

To get the hell out of here, Dare thought. "We need to talk."

Dare took in McKnight's bloodshot eyes,

his overgrown beard, messy hair, and wrinkled clothes. With a shake of his head, he made a decision. "First we're going to sober you up."

Brian scowled. "I'm not drunk. I haven't been in days. I've just got a low-level buzz going."

Dare raised an eyebrow.

"Because I'm nearly out of alcohol," Brian said before Dare could even ask why. "I have no money to buy more and I need to ration what I have left. If I keep a buzz on, I won't go out looking to gamble with what little I might still own."

Dare blinked, surprised at the other man's honesty. He glanced around the disgusting room once more. "Go shower. We'll talk after." He pointed to the bathroom and waited for the argument.

Instead, Brian passively walked into the bathroom and shut the door. A few seconds later, he heard the water turn on.

Dare took advantage of the time alone, grabbing the plastic garbage pail and going around the room, tossing the trash and wrappers. When he found a half-eaten fish sandwich, he figured it was the source of the worst of the odor and deposited the pail outside the room. Back inside, he opened a window, then pulled out a chair and settled in to wait.

Brian emerged fifteen minutes later, a towel wrapped around his waist.

Dare cocked an eyebrow.

"I don't have a change of clothes," he muttered.

Dare shook his head and groaned. "I have a pair of sweatpants and a shirt in my truck for after softball. Hang on."

When he returned, Brian dressed and sat down on the bed, looking marginally better but at least smelling clean. "Why are you here?" he asked.

"I've been asking that myself. The easy answer is because I love your sister."

But that wouldn't be the whole truth and damned if Dare wasn't all about honesty at the moment. He wanted peace from his past and that meant dealing with this bastard.

"The harder answer is I'm here for me. We have unfinished business." Dare stared at Brian from his seat across the small room.

Brian hadn't looked him in the eye since he'd arrived. Hadn't reacted to his pronouncement about being in love with Liza. Obviously he was wrapped up in his own misery.

"You here to give me more shit like you do at the station?" Brian asked.

"Oddly, no. I want to talk about the party."

Brian wrinkled his forehead. "What party? I know I have blackouts but —"

Dare stared at the man in shock. For over a decade, the word *party* had only meant one thing in Dare's mind. The night he couldn't forget. "The one you threw when you were in high school? When Stuart Rossman died?"

Brian winced. "I don't like to remember that night," he muttered. "What's it to you?"

He didn't know, Dare thought. Brian had no idea Dare had been there that day. "I was there." The admission almost stuck in his throat. "I saw everything . . . and I did nothing."

Pain and humiliation rushed through him with the force of a hurricane. "And I've been living with the guilt of that day ever since."

"And you think I haven't?" Brian rose and began to pace like a cornered animal, back and forth between the bed and the wall. "I've spent every day since running from what I did. What my parents covered up."

"You let them," Dare reminded him, unsure where all the anger he'd expected to feel had gone. Instead, he looked at this broken shell of a man and felt something closer to . . . pity.

Brian didn't reply.

"That escape you've been looking for? Did you find it in the bottle?" Dare couldn't help but ask.

Brian looked up, his eyes bleak, as he shook his head.

"How about the gambling? Or stealing from the firm your sister works so hard for?"

Stunned. That was the only word Dare could find for the expression on Brian's face. "Liza *knows?*" he asked, horrified.

Dare nodded. "And she loves you anyway. Go figure."

Brian lowered himself onto the bed, his entire body shaking. "It's bad enough she knows I owe Mikey Biggs that money and he went to her for it —"

Something inside Dare snapped and the anger he'd been searching for came rushing forward. He strode over and grabbed Brian by the front of his shirt — Dare's shirt — and jerked him forward. "He didn't just go to her for the money, you bastard. He put a hand on her. Grabbed her by the wrist and —"

The wailing sound interrupted Dare, catching him off guard. He stopped shaking Brian long enough to realize the man was crying. Not crying.

Bawling like a baby.

"Son of a bitch." Dare released him and

Brian collapsed on the bed.

He hadn't expected this. He'd anticipated a confrontation. A part of him had even been looking forward to it. But this sobbing, defeated man needed help, not a fight.

Watching him, for the first time Dare understood why Liza helped him. Enabled him. Cared about him. Because Brian McKnight was incapable of caring for himself.

"Hey." Dare shook his shoulder. "Your sister's emptying her savings to pay off your debt. She's meeting with this Mikey character at her office today." And with everything in him, Dare wanted to be there, but Cara threatened to castrate him if he went near the building.

Liza needed to do this for herself, she'd said. And he needed to find another way to prove he wasn't the asshole he'd shown himself to be. So here he was, working on the one thing he knew would show Liza he accepted her, family and all. Brother and all. She needed to know he could put the past behind him once and for all.

Hell, he needed to know the same thing. And Dare finally did. He knew now he could let it go. Because all the anger he had been holding on to and directing at this man had been Dare's way of not turning it on

414

himself, but in the end anger was just as lousy a coping mechanism as Brian's alcohol crutch. Nothing could change what had happened and Dare had done the best he could with his life. He saw that clearly now.

"She's always been there for me," Brian said, bleary-eyed.

Though it galled him, Dare nodded and replied. "Well, she said you were there for her too. You took the rap for a broken vase after her boyfriend hit her."

"It wasn't all that hard to guzzle a bottle and say it was my fault. My folks were never as hard on me as they were on Liza."

And look at the spectacular results of that brand of parenting, Dare thought, studying the other man.

"I'd do anything for her," Brian said.

Bingo. "Really? Then let's go."

"Where?" Brian asked warily.

"To rehab. You're going to call your parents and tell them they're paying for your inpatient stay." Dare had gotten a list of places from Alexa, who'd also made a few calls and secured a bed. "And after you check in, you're going to call your sister."

"But —"

"Unless you didn't mean what you said? That you'd do anything for her?"

"The best thing I could do for her would

be to disappear."

Dare let out a laugh. "No, that's the best thing you could do for me. Liza wouldn't survive that." And Dare wouldn't survive losing Liza.

If there was one thing he'd learned in the last few days, it was that. She was his heart and he didn't want to go forward without her. He just hoped she felt the same way about him.

He started for the door.

"Hey, where are you going?" Brian asked, sounding panicked.

"To my SUV. You've got five minutes to decide whether we're taking that trip or not. But if you show up? Don't do it for your sister. Do it for yourself. Otherwise you'll end up right back where you started, and if you ask me, that's a shit place to be."

Without looking over his shoulder, Dare walked out, slamming the door behind him.

NINETEEN

Liza drummed her fingers against her desk. She tapped her foot against the floor. She played basketball with balled-up paper. And she waited for a loan shark to walk into her office and take the money she and Cara had painstakingly stuffed into two cardboard tubes that usually held architectural plans.

Fifty thousand dollars, she thought in disbelief.

A knock sounded on her door.

Her stomach jumped and she rose to her feet. "Come in."

A third man she hadn't seen before strode into her office. He wore a suit and tie and looked like any other client. "May I help you?"

"I'm here for the package, Ms. McKnight."

Hands shaking, Liza pointed to the two tubes.

The man opened the white cap on the end

of each, saw the money inside, and nodded. "This all of it?"

"Do you think I ever want to see you again? Of course that's all of it." *I like my kneecaps, thank you very much,* Liza thought.

The man turned and treated her to what looked like a genuine smile. "Then it's been a pleasure doing business with you. More so than with your brother." He popped the covers back onto the tubes and gathered them in his arms.

"Umm . . . would you be insulted if I asked for a receipt?"

The man tipped his head back and laughed. "Tell you what? I'll go home and count it, and if it's all there, I'll send it in the mail," he said, still chuckling.

"You trust me and I trust you. Fine." She nodded, wondering when she'd lost her mind.

The man lifted his hand in a wave and walked out the door.

Liza's knees shook and she shut the door behind her, grabbed the garbage pail, and threw up.

Liza had been home for all of an hour. Her nerves were still shot, her legs still shaking, but it was over. She'd handled the payment by herself. She'd alerted Jeff that something serious was going on and he knew to listen in case she called for help. In that way she wasn't alone. But the knowledge hadn't lessened her nerves. She couldn't remember the last time she'd gotten sick. She'd called Cara, who'd been sitting in her car around the corner, and assured her all was well. Then Liza had insisted on going home by herself.

Once there, she showered and washed her hair and came out feeling clean, fresh, and completely alone. Her life had officially returned to the status quo she'd known so well before Dare Barron had taken over.

She hated it and she hated him for teasing her with a glimpse at what could have been. Being part of a family, being cared for and maybe even loved.

"Suck it up," she muttered to herself. This was her life.

Her phone rang and she picked it up on the first ring. "Hello?"

"Hi, Liza Lou."

"Brian!" Her heart flipped over in her chest. "Where are you?"

"Will you meet me?" he asked.

"Where?" She grabbed a pen and paper and scribbled down the address he'd given her. "How far from here is it?" She didn't recognize the street name.

"It's an hour away."

She was exhausted, but she wouldn't say no. "I'll see you soon," she promised him.

Needing caffeine, she stopped at Cuppa Café and picked up an extra-large coffee to take with her on the drive. She programmed the address Brian had given her into her GPS and started on her way. It was dark by the time she pulled up to a heavily wooded area on the street Brian had named.

There was only one driveway on the street beside a discreet sign: MEADOW TREATMENT CENTER. Liza pulled to a stop and stared at the sign, not comprehending what she saw.

Her cell phone rang again. "It's me," Brian said. "Are you close?"

"I . . . I'm here. I'm also confused."

"This is the last call they'll let me make for a while. Pull in, park, and go to the entrance. Ask for me. They're expecting you at the desk," Brian said.

"Treatment center?" She still couldn't believe it.

A few minutes later, she'd reached the main desk and asked to see Brian McKnight.

A young woman led Liza down a maze of corridors and into a large waiting room, with a television and a set of matching couches. "Just wait here," the dark-haired woman instructed.

Liza knew she was trembling, but she couldn't stop. She wouldn't until she saw her brother. The minutes dragged by until finally she heard his voice.

"Liza?"

"Brian!" She turned and he stood in the doorway, looking nothing like her brother.

His normally well-combed hair was a mess, he wore a beard that hadn't seen a razor in way too long, his eyes were bloodshot, and his skin was sallow. He was dressed in gray sweats and a faded youth league baseball T-shirt, clothing he'd never normally wear. But none of that mattered compared to the fact that he stood in front of her safe and sound — and in a treatment center of all places.

Liza ran to him and pulled him into a tight hug. "I was so worried about you."

"I don't know why you haven't given up on me yet," her brother said.

She stepped back, meeting his gaze. "I don't want to, but I can't go through this again. I won't. The loan shark, the threats, people following me . . ." Her voice trailed off. She didn't want to relive the day.

"I'm sorry."

She pressed her lips together in a grim smile. "I know." But she also knew apologies weren't enough, not anymore. "But you're here, in this place. I'm so proud of you." She hugged him once more.

"Umm, I can't take complete credit."

She stepped back. Taking his hand, she led him to one of the sofas. "What do you mean?"

"Your boyfriend found me in a dump hotel."

"My what?"

"Your cop boyfriend. He showed up and started giving me orders. He made me shower. He cleaned up the mess I made of the room, tossed the bottles . . . He even gave me clean clothes." Brian ducked his head, obviously embarrassed.

Liza was too stunned to speak. Instead, she fingered the worn shirt her brother wore. Dare had done this? For Brian? A man he despised?

"He read me the riot act and then gave me five minutes to decide whether or not to let him drive me here."

Liza blinked back tears. "You came."

"He pretty emphatically told me not to do it for you but for myself. But I have to say, the man loves you, Liza Lou."

She shook her head hard, not wanting to

hear those words, refusing to believe in fantasies ever again. "Dare's got a lot of his own guilt over Stuart Rossman. He lives to do the right thing now. Helping you was his way of making sure he did right by me to the end. That's all."

"Hey. I'm the one in denial in this family, not you." Brian lifted her chin with his hand. "It's no secret I hate cops, right?"

She managed a smile. "Right."

"But this is me telling you the guy's okay. And he loves you. He told me so."

"But —"

"No buts. You're going to need someone to lean on while I'm in here."

She touched his cheek. "I've been on my own for a long time. I'll be fine." But her mind was reeling from the fact that Dare had not only found Brian but taken care of him.

For himself? Or did his feelings for her play a role, as her brother believed. And even if she allowed herself to trust what her brother said, just because Dare loved her — and her heart sped up at the possibility — didn't mean he could accept who and what her brother was.

When Liza closed her eyes at night, she remembered his harsh words, heard the anger and hatred in his voice. Love? *Not*

423

hardly, she thought. But she *knew* him, and by now he was, as Cara said, probably kicking himself for turning on her. She could forgive him for that night, but she didn't expect anything more from him.

"How long are you here for?" she asked Brian.

"I don't know. There's an evaluation period and treatment plans. I put your name down on my forms. You can call and they'll give you whatever information you want or need." He drew a deep breath. "I'm going to try my best, Liza Lou."

She smiled. "That's all anyone can do." And it was so much more than she'd had to hold on to a few short hours ago.

It was what she needed to do. When she left here, she'd gather the same strength her brother had shown, and go on with her life.

"How will you pay for this?" she asked, knowing from the look of the place that it was a high-end facility. "I can —"

"No." He barked out the word. "I'm sorry. No. Thank you. You've done enough for me. Because of me. I called Mom and Dad. They're footing the bill for this."

Liza exhaled hard. "Wow. Okay, then."

"And they're sending you a check for the money you laid out. If the police recover the money from the loan shark, you can repay them. If not . . . Don't worry about it."

She had to be hearing things. "Brian . . ."

"I told them everything. What I've done, how I stole from the business, put you in danger, and hurt you. And before you ask, it doesn't matter what they think or feel. They are who they are."

She nodded at that.

Brian touched her hand. "In other words, they suck as your parents, but they're doing what I asked. And you'll cash that check. For me."

Liza blinked, but the tears fell anyway. "I love you, Brian."

"Me too."

"Then get better, okay?" She wrapped her arms around him tight.

"You won't be able to visit me for a while," he whispered in her ear.

Throat clogged, she nodded. "But I can call for updates? They'll talk to me?"

"I promise."

It wasn't easy, but she let him go and watched him walk away. Someone, a nurse maybe, met him outside the door to take him back to his room.

Her chest hurt, her eyes burned, and she prayed he possessed the strength to get through this and make it on the outside.

Time would tell, but this was an unexpected yet unbelievably good first step.

And for that she owed Dare her thanks.

Alone in the dark, Liza walked to her car, leaving the rehab center and her brother behind. Summer heat and humidity surrounded her as did a mixture of relief for her brother and a sense of purpose for herself.

She might be as alone as she was before, but she wasn't the same person as a few short weeks ago. She looked at her life, taking stock. She'd miss her brother. Even when Brian had been drinking and out of control, he'd still been in her world, the one person with whom she felt truly connected. And as for friends? She'd claimed to have them in the city, but she hadn't spoken to the girls in a while. They had no idea what was going on in her life. How could she call them friends and claim it was enough anymore?

She couldn't. Since Dare had introduced her to his friends and family, she'd seen the possibilities inherent in intimate human connection, in letting people in. And even though Faith and Kelly were part of Dare's world, Liza had no reason to believe they'd abandon her just because she and Dare were no longer together.

The insecure girl inside Liza rose up, wondering if they'd all just babysat her and put up with her for Dare's sake, but the adult she'd become refused to believe it. They weren't her parents, who made her feel worthless and inadequate. They'd been good to her and she refused to succumb to more self-doubt or pity.

Still, tears stung and she decided she'd definitely done enough crying lately. She opened her bag and looked for her keys, pausing to use a tissue and wipe her eyes. Grabbing the remote, she hit the unlock button.

Her car made the usual beeping sound and the outside lights flashed. Liza looked up — and right into Dare's eyes.

He waited, leaning against the side of her car, and of course, he looked good. Steady, sexy . . .

"Hey." He raised a hand in greeting.

"Hi," she said, startled to see him.

He looked good enough to eat in his faded jeans and light blue T-shirt that showed off the muscles in his arms. She swallowed hard, trying not to stare even when all she wanted to do was crawl into his embrace and never leave.

Instead, she waited, as he did, awkwardness settling around them. Not the awkwardness of the days after Brian's last phone call. Those had been filled with a sense of sadness and despair. And there was no lingering anger from their last meeting. But there was discomfort stemming from not knowing what to say or do. And that was something they'd never had between them.

So Liza stepped up and took control. "I don't know how to begin to thank you for what you did for Brian. For bringing him here." She shook her head, still amazed, a lump in her throat.

He'd pushed himself off the car but still stood out of reach, watching her intently. But she couldn't read his expression.

"Brian had to be willing to come with me. And he was."

She nodded in agreement. "But he wouldn't have done it on his own. So thank you."

Dare inclined his head. "You're welcome."

She bit the inside of her cheek, debating how far to take this conversation and then decided what the hell. She might as well find out everything she wanted to know. At least she'd have answers to satisfy her in the long lonely days and nights ahead.

She clenched her hands into fists at her side. "Why did you do it?" she asked, meeting his gaze.

Dare smiled grimly. "Your brother asked me the same thing."

"And? What did you tell him?"

Dare let out a harsh breath. "Short, easy answer? I did it for you. Seeing if I could talk some sense into your brother was the least I could do after the awful things I said to you."

A muscle ticked in his jaw, the only evidence of emotion she'd seen. So Cara was right. He'd been kicking himself for how he'd treated her.

Liza swallowed hard, knowing his reasons didn't satisfy the longing inside her. "Don't get me wrong. I'm grateful. Eternally so. But you don't owe me anything." Obligation was the last thing she wanted him to feel. If she couldn't have his love — the one thing, the only thing, she wanted from him — then she didn't want anything at all. "People say awful things in time of crisis. I understand that."

His lips quirked upward a tiny bit. "Thanks, but you need to know how sorry I am. Hurting you like that, humiliating you in front of friends and family . . ." He ran a hand through his hair and looked away, obviously ashamed.

"It's okay," she said, giving him the forgiveness he needed. "Your stress level was through the roof and you took it out on the nearest person. Me. It's over and done."

"No," he said, practically cutting her off to correct her. "I took it out on the person *closest* to me and I don't mean in proximity."

Liza narrowed her gaze, unsure of what he meant. "I don't understand."

"Because I'm not saying this right." He shook his head and groaned. "Bear with me, okay?"

This was new. Dare Barron, off balance and unsure. Touched and curious, she nodded. And waited.

Finally, he met her gaze. "I didn't find Brian just to make it up to you. I did it for me, because I needed closure."

She nodded. "I can understand that."

"And I expected us to have an argument, which, in my mind, was years and years in the making."

"Did you and Brian fight?" Liza asked, horrified by the possibility.

Dare laughed at that. "He was in no condition for it, and once I really looked at him, saw him . . . I didn't want to. For years, I hated him. But when I got to the hotel room I realized I couldn't hate him anymore."

He sounded as stunned as she felt and hope sprung up inside her for the first time. If he didn't hate Brian, did that mean *they* had a chance?

"Why not?" she asked.

Dare met her gaze, his eyes clear and focused. "Because Brian already hated himself enough for both of us. He's been punishing himself for years, trying to drown his pain in alcohol and other addictions."

"It hasn't been easy to watch," she whispered.

"But I can see now why you felt so compelled to help him."

"You can?" Her voice rose in disbelief.

But Dare also saw the hope shining in her eyes, and as he stared into the face he loved he hoped and prayed she understood what his breakthrough meant. That the damage he'd done wasn't permanent and that he hadn't come around too late.

He stepped closer. Reaching out, he stroked one finger down her soft cheek. "You, Liza McKnight, have a huge heart and I was wrong for finding fault with that."

Her eyes dilated at his touch, giving him hope that if her body hadn't written him off completely, maybe he could still win over her mind.

"Thanks," she said softly.

"For what? Realizing something I knew from day one?" He shook his head. "Don't thank me for being a jerk."

To his surprise, Liza laughed. "You took care of me when I had no one. The last thing I'd call you is a jerk."

"*That* was a pleasure." He smiled at her and she smiled back.

More hope, he thought, and plowed ahead. "I realized something else when I was with your brother." He drew a steadying breath. "All that anger I was holding on to and directing at him? That was just my way of not turning it on myself."

"Because you still blamed yourself for not helping Stuart Rossman," she said. "That's normal. Human. And so is the fact that you can't look at me without being reminded of Brian and of that night. I get it. I do." She drew a shuddering breath. "So let's part ways now, with all this goodwill between us." Her hands shook as she tried to pull her purse off her shoulders, obviously ready to bolt.

Dare didn't panic. He had no intention of letting her go. "Sorry. Not parting ways. Never again."

"What?" She raised her gaze to meet his.

Dare had done so much talking, he was sick of his own voice. He grabbed her forearms and pulled her forward, sealing his lips over hers. She stiffened in surprise, so he licked her lips to ease her tension. It worked. She moaned. Her lips parted and she let him inside.

So much better, he thought, as she relaxed into him with her body, then gave of herself with her mouth and her tongue, meeting him sweep for sweep, thrust for thrust.

Until she suddenly pulled away, pain back in her darkened eyes. "I can't do this anymore. The push and pull, the confusion, the sex for the moment —"

"Whoa. Slow down," he said, staring into her dark gaze, and in that moment he saw everything he needed.

She was trying to save herself more pain, because she was afraid he'd pull away again. She wanted more than she thought they could have. She was wrong.

He wanted it all and so did she. "I love you, baby. Now and forever."

"Don't say that." She shook her head and tried to pull away. "Don't promise forever when you can't mean it." She started to shake and he wrapped her in his arms, the place where she'd be safe and wanted from now on.

"Didn't I tell you I only do relationships?" He brushed her hair off her cheek. "While you were exchanging money with a loan shark — and don't for a minute think I didn't want to be there — I settled things with your brother, right?"

She nodded.

"And while you were driving here and seeing Brian, I went to the cemetery and made my peace with Stuart Rossman and my past."

"You did?"

"Yeah," he said gruffly. He'd never forget what happened, but it was time he let go of that anger. "I might see the department shrink if I ever feel that dark place threatening. But I won't blame you ever again. I won't leave you ever again."

She hiccupped in his arms and he grinned, then tipped her chin upward and brushed his lips over hers. "I know you don't trust people. And I realize you don't believe anyone in your life will stick around, but I'm asking you to trust me."

Liza's heart beat hard against his chest. While he waited for an answer, he inhaled and took in her intoxicating scent, drawing strength from the fact that she hadn't pulled away.

"You're right. I don't trust. Experience has taught me otherwise. And I realize now part of the reason I began the relationship with Timothy back in college was because his possessiveness made me think he loved me. And when that went bad, I cut off any and all relationships except the casual ones." She lifted her hand and cupped his cheek in her palm. "Until you."

"I can be pretty charming when I want to be."

He winked at her and she groaned. "You're a bulldozer," she said on a light laugh. "But that charm of yours was hiding as much pain as I had inside."

"You're the only person who's figured that out about me." Another reason they were a perfect fit. But she hadn't accepted his declaration.

And he wasn't having it. "So? Where do we stand? Are you going to make me buy a condo and live alone, wishing I hadn't made all those mistakes? Or are you going to —"

"I love you too, Dare Barron." She kissed him then, hard, fast, and all too briefly. "When I walked out of my brother's room, I promised myself if he could find the strength to go forward, then so could I. But I couldn't let myself believe in us. I thought you helped Brian because that's what you do. Help people."

He shook his head. "The only person I want to think or worry about right now is you. I love you, baby, and I will never hurt you that way again."

She grinned and wrapped her arms around his neck. "I'm going to hold you to that, you know."

"I should hope so."

"Know what I want to do now?" she asked.

"Tell me." He'd give her anything she wanted and more.

Her smile lit up everything inside him.

"I want to drive home, crawl into bed, and sleep for a good long while."

He chuckled at the simple request. "Sounds good to me. As long as I'm in that bed with you."

"Come home with me," she murmured. "Move into my house and forget about looking for a place to live." She stared at him with wide, hopeful eyes.

"Only because you asked so nicely . . ."

She laughed and kissed him, clinging to him for so long, he wondered if they'd ever make it to their cars for the trip back to Serendipity.

Not that he cared. As long as he was with Liza, Dare would be happy anywhere.

EPILOGUE

Labor Day Weekend

The house on the hill provided the setting for the biggest fund-raiser Serendipity had ever seen. Faith's wishes prevailed and once the town got wind of the fact that the youth center would be the recipient of the money raised, everyone from every class turned out for the event. It helped that the fund-raising committee insisted on lowering the price for attending, since they had saved money up front by not having to rent space for the event.

God, Ethan adored his wife and her brilliant ideas. And the rest of his family wasn't too bad either, he thought with not the smallest amount of pride.

The house that just one year ago left him empty and cold was now filled with people. And though he didn't want to host this event, Faith was beaming — and that made it all worthwhile.

As if he sensed her, Ethan turned to see his wife gliding down the circular stairs. She wore a royal blue Grecian-styled gown held over one shoulder with a silver clip. The cut of the gown draped over her softly rounded belly, not hiding yet not showing off her pregnancy. Just a little over three months, they'd told family a few days ago, and no one else.

Tonight they'd decided to make it public.

He was going to be a father. Who the hell would have thought it? Certainly not the Ethan who'd hightailed it out of town on his motorcycle a little over ten years ago. And definitely not the Ethan from last year when he'd returned.

Damn, he was grateful.

Faith strode up to him and slipped her hand inside his. "Have I said thank you?"

He looked into her beautiful blue eyes. "For this?" He swept his hand around, indicating the party.

Her lips quirked into a smile. "Well, okay, yes, this. But for everything else, too. You make my life complete."

He grinned. "I feel exactly the same way about you, princess." Before he could kiss her the way he wanted to, a teenage voice interrupted them.

"Don't even think about it," Tess muttered. "You're in public."

Ethan glanced at his sister, taking in her purple dress. He wondered if she'd change her favorite color anytime soon. This particular purple was jewel-toned, she'd informed him haughtily. Apparently Tess had begun reading fashion magazines. Who'd have thought the punk kid dumped on his doorstep had it in her?

"You look gorgeous," he told her.

She beamed at him. "Thanks." She glanced at Faith and crooked her finger.

Faith bent closer and Tess whispered something in her ear.

"Not yet." Faith's eyes sparkled as they talked in conspiratorial whispers.

"I'm going to keep a lookout," Tess declared.

"He won't know what hit him." Faith nodded in certainty.

"You can say that again." Tess ducked away but not before adding a parting shot. "You two behave. PDA is not appropriate."

Faith tipped her head back and her delicious laugh rippled through him. But he hadn't forgotten Tess's earlier side of their conversation.

"He who? What was she talking about?" Ethan asked his wife.

Faith squeezed his hand in warning. "Tess

thinks she's in love with Todd Morgan."

"He's eighteen!" Ethan bellowed.

"Not quite yet. Seventeen and he's just going to be a senior this year."

Ethan scowled, not liking seventeen any better than eighteen. "She's a kid."

"I was sixteen when you lured me onto your bike," she reminded him.

Ethan winced. "*That's* what I'm afraid of."

"Evening, everyone." Nash interrupted, walking up to them, Kelly by his side.

"Ahh, the man who hates formal affairs made it. And I'm so grateful." Faith hugged them both, then pulled Kelly away to discuss details of the evening.

Ethan talked with Nash, the brother who once couldn't stand the sight of him. For fifteen minutes, they discussed things personal, professional, and later, sports-related. It was so normal, Ethan couldn't believe the new normal they shared.

"Hey, brothers." Dare strode up to them.

"How's it going?" Ethan asked.

"Pretty damned good, actually." Dare shook his brothers' hands.

"For a cop, you dress up nicely," Nash said.

Dare shrugged. "Faith insisted on tuxedos, right? Besides, how can I propose to Liza if I'm not in my formal best?" he asked with an excited grin.

In that smile, Ethan saw shades of the kid brother he remembered. Lately, the sparkle in Dare's gaze had been genuine, no longer a cover for old pain and guilt. Yep, he'd come a long way too. Liza was damned good for him, just as Kelly was for Nash.

"Congratulations," Ethan said, slapping Dare on the back.

Nash did the same. "I just hope she's still deluded enough to say yes."

Dare glared at him, but Nash followed up the comment by pulling his baby brother into a hug.

"I have news too," Nash said after a few minutes.

"Well?" Dare asked. "You going to share?"

"Kelly's pregnant. Looks like we'll be having kids close together," Nash said to Ethan, beaming with pride. "It's so early we're only telling you guys for a while."

The congratulations and slaps on the back began all over again. Then they talked some more, before dispersing to find their better halves.

Ethan glanced around, more settled than he'd ever been, and he remembered the day he'd pulled up on this long driveway, thinking he couldn't outrun his past. He'd been right. But all three of the Barron brothers had done something better. They'd made peace with it and with each other, enabling them to open themselves up to the future and all Serendipity had to offer.

And that was the greatest gift of all.

The employees of Thorndike Press hope you have enjoyed this Large Print book. All our Thorndike, Wheeler, and Kennebec Large Print titles are designed for easy reading, and all our books are made to last. Other Thorndike Press Large Print books are available at your library, through selected bookstores, or directly from us.

For information about titles, please call:
(800) 223-1244

or visit our Web site at:
http://gale.cengage.com/thorndike

To share your comments, please write:
Publisher
Thorndike Press
10 Water St., Suite 310
Waterville, ME 04901